UNTIL I KISSED YOU

A MORGAN BROTHERS NOVEL

NICOLE VIDAL

COPYRIGHT

TABLE OF CONTENTS

KEEP IN TOUCH WITH NV

Visit me on social media or online to learn about my newest releases:

Facebook (http://fb.me/NicoleVidalAuthor)

Instagram (http://instragram.com/nicolevidal_author)

My website (www.nicolevidal.com)

Goodreads (https://bit.ly/NVGoodreads)

Amazon (https://amzn.to/2XCLSlR)

Pinterest (http://pinterest.com/NicoleVidal_Author)

SAMSON

Exhausted, I'm exhausted. I need to cut down on my international travel. New York City to Paris to London then back home to New York City in three days. I need as many days to catch up. Thankfully, Savannah can handle the office if I come in late today. It's the main reason I hired her. She's brilliant. *Savannah*.

There was a moment with her during the gala and after when I almost broke. I almost kissed her with every ounce of desire I've bottled up since I hired her. She's decidedly off-limits—or she should be anyway. Yet, I invited her to the gala as my date. Savannah is striking in a pencil skirt and jacket. In a royal blue silk dress with an open back, she's breathtaking. The color brings out the hue of her eyes offset by her midnight hair. Every seemingly professional touch sent unmistakable heat through me. I've never felt this level of heat before, not even with Meghan, and she was my fiancée.

Rather than wallow in my tiredness, I drag myself out of bed to dress for work. Aside from Savannah's capabilities, my name is on the door. Coming in at ten instead of before eight after whirlwind travel across an ocean and back is a legitimate reason to arrive late after a few extra hours sleep.

I pad across my inlaid hardwood floors to my dressing room. My home is absolutely too large for only me, but it offers privacy. The Morgan family is well-known in New York City. My parents, Warren and Margaux Morgan, are members of the rich elite. By birth, so are my siblings and I. Working his way up from the mail room, my father amassed a fortune. When he married Mother, new money and old money combined. Margaux dutifully planned and attended events at Father's request. Caring for my siblings and me wasn't a true priority for her. We had a nanny, Maria-Luisa, most of our childhood.

Cassius, my first younger brother, recently flipped his whole life, trading in venture capitalism for owning an airline. His shift is due to his wife, Noelle. Having lost her parents as a teen, she subscribes to the notion that every choice should lead to happiness. When they met, Margaux impersonated someone else to learn more about Noelle to thwart their relationship and Cash's career change. She failed.

At the same time, she further strained her marriage with my father. Noelle has been nothing short of a game changer for my brother, professionally and, more notably, personally. He's the happiest he has ever been—partly because they left this city for York Beach, Maine, near our younger sister.

After a tragic accident requiring significant repair to her face, Wilhelmina, who prefers Billie now, left New York. Not only has she achieved her dream of couture dress design and owning a storefront, she found love as well. Around the time Peter and Billie met, my parents attempted to force Billie into an arranged marriage with one of our father's competitor's sons. At first the notion seemed off the wall until we learned that the competitor was holding Billie's true parentage over my father's head. Billie was successful in ending their bid to marry her off with Peter's support. Their wedding is in the spring. I'm intrigued to see if Margaux and Warren show up without a fuss. I expect my father. Our mother, she isn't welcome, but I'm not confident she'll stay away.

Finally, my youngest brother, Auggie, recently finished culinary school. He is working as a head chef locally while preparing to establish his own farm-to-table restaurant. Obstacles have slowed his progress. Ideally, he wants to grow the food himself. However, building his dream is astronomical in cost and zoning issues. There simply isn't an area in New York City to pull that off. Luckily, his best friend, Caroline, keeps him from losing his mind.

After donning a custom suit and Oxford, I ride to the ground floor.

"Good morning, Mr. Morgan. Getting a late start?" Jimmy is a middle-aged man who serves as the building concierge and doorman. He controls access to our building with an iron fist. My approved list is concise. It only includes my siblings, their significant others, and Savannah—although, she has never been here.

"Morning, Jimmy. I have a serious case of jet lag this time."

Jimmy nods. "Have a wonderful day."

"You as well."

The air is brisk this morning. New York has some wonderful events, like the Christmas tree lighting at Rockefeller Center or a multitude of Broadway shows. Said events pale in comparison to the foliage and foods of fall, at least in my opinion. After a short walk, I arrive at the office. Stopping by the kitchen, I prepare a cup of coffee before walking to my office. I hear

Savannah talking about the policy from my trip. As I pass, I notice she's wearing a red sheath dress and tall heels—heels with sexy bows on them that drive me to distraction. There's nothing professional about me noting her attire, not even in the slightest.

Once my laptop wakes, I scan my inbox with mild disinterest. I'm always connected, and nothing new has developed since late last night.

"Morning, Sam."

It took almost three months for Savannah to stop calling me Mr. Morgan. Aside from the fact that she's about my age, I'm not that formal.

"Morning, Savannah. Everything set on the Mancini policy?"

"Yes, they're pleased with the policy and your insistence upon viewing the piece personally."

Travelling overseas for one policy is rare for me. Even more rare is the chance to see *Le Givre* by Claude Monet in person. As far as I'm aware, it's only one of twelve privately owned originals.

"Is it as magnificent as I imagine?"

I can hear her jealous inner-art connoisseur just a smidge. "It is. You should travel with me next time." As the words slip from my lips, I consider the danger of that statement. I suppose it isn't any more dangerous than asking her to join me at that gala.

"I may take you up on that." A small smile brightens her gorgeous face. As she walks away, I can't help but admire her sexy legs and the sway of her hips.

Admonishing myself, I tackle my inbox. Near two, my cell phone rings. "Hey, Cash. How are you and Noelle?"

"We're well. How was your trip?"

"Tiring but good. How is the airline industry?"

"I love it. I can't believe it took me so long to take the leap."

"Happy to hear that. I think you needed Noelle for the huge push."

"True, very true."

Cash never would've left investing if it weren't for Noelle. Like me, Cash was waiting for the right woman. Until he met Noelle, he hadn't dated anyone seriously for years before that. I understand his concerns, most of which I share. It's difficult to know whether a woman wants to date a Morgan for the status alone. My intention isn't to sound cocky, but since Cash got married, I rose to New York's most eligible bachelor. He and I have been alternating in the top two spots for the last five years or so. Until I met Savannah, I hadn't seriously considered dating anyone. Now, I want to date someone who should be off-limits. Nonetheless, I'm planning to throw my concerns out the window.

"I need to get back to these flight plans. Any word on when you'll be here next?" Cash states.

"I can probably visit in the next two weeks."

"Good, we'll see you then. I'll make sure Billie and Peter can join us."

After ending the call, I swivel my chair and gaze at the city. After a short break, I sort through the stack of files, reviewing and signing where necessary. When Savannah knocks on my door, I assume it's to get some lunch.

"I'm heading out unless you need something."

I note its after six already. "I'll escort you home if you can give me fifteen minutes."

"You don't need to do that."

"I want too." More than I should.

If she's surprised or completely against it, she doesn't show it.

SAVANNAH

Almost a year ago, when I applied to work at Morgan Insurance, I didn't realize it was *that* Morgan Insurance. I suppose that means I should have done more research, but the starting salary was more than other commensurate positions. Right now stability is key. Scarlett needs to finish college.

I wasn't expecting him when I arrived for the interview. Surprisingly, I held myself together enough to land the job. Now, if I could stop the butterflies when he's near me, that would be fantastic. Honestly, the only reason stopping me from pursing him is he's my boss.

Samson Morgan commands attention when he's in a room. His chiseled jaw, cleft chin, and sexy smile make women swoon, myself included. His broad shoulders carry custom suits with ease. Yet from everything I see, he doesn't date. I'm not suggesting he's a player; I haven't seen evidence of that either. When he invited me to the gala, I was shocked, but I also knew it was more a business event than a date. Until we danced. Swaying to a ballad with Sam was something straight out of a classic romance. The longer we danced, the tighter he held me. His fingers grazing the exposed skin of my back. I may not have seen him shirtless, but I would bet my salary that he spends hours in a gym considering how his arms felt around me. Now, he wants to escort me home. I don't think he realizes how far it is. I suppose it doesn't matter, I take the subway to work. Yet why does he want to give me a ride home today?

"All set?"

His question pulls me out of my reminiscing. "Yes. I'm sure you have better things to do than ride home with me." I'm not sure how to characterize his facial expression right now. Confusion, nervous even?

"Did I do something to offend you?" he asks shyly. I've never known Sam to be shy about anything.

"No, I... never mind." Attempting to squash the fluttering in my belly, I take a step forward.

He sets his hand on my forearm, causing me to stop. Sparks run through me, making the butterflies harder to control.

"Savannah."

Dear God, my name sounds sinful coming from his mouth. It has since we met.

"No, you haven't offended me. I'm simply surprised you want to ride home with me."

"Why?"

"You never have before. What's changed?"

His posture softens a bit. The look on his face, pensive. His hand still heating my arm causes the fluttering to intensify.

"Let's get going. We can talk more on the way."

Moving to the elevator, I push the button. Due to the hour, the doors open almost immediately. With his hand on the small of my back, he guides me inside. The tension in the small space is unmistakable.

Once at the car, he opens the door for me before rounding the rear of the car to the other side. Sam gives the driver my address and immediately puts up the privacy screen.

"How do you know my address?"

"Aside from your application, we rode there together after leaving Cash's the night of the gala."

We went to check on Cash and his now wife, Noelle, that night. Sam's mother, Margaux didn't approve of Noelle and attempted to break them up by questioning Noelle's motives and pretending to be a disinterested neighbor of her young client.

"You're right. Sam—"

"Savannah." Turning to face me, he takes my hand in his. Will every touch feel like that? If I feel this from his hand, what will his lips on mine feel like? I turn toward him, our knees touching.

"Go ahead."

He draws in a breath and slowly lets it out before speaking. How is it possible this charismatic, charming, and devastatingly handsome man is nervous to talk to me?

"Savannah, I'm taken with you. I have been wrestling with asking you on a date since the gala. Will you have dinner with me on Friday?"

A million reasons not to date my boss run though my head in two seconds flat. Only one pushes me to say yes, the flutter in my belly whenever he's nearby. He intrigues me.

"I would love to."

The moment the words leave my mouth, he relaxes significantly more. His status in this city is impossible to ignore, but he seems to handle the attention well. It's probably something we should address. Not right now. The feel of my hand in his is enough for me to grapple with.

The driver pulls along the curb. Sam releases me and hops out to open my door. He offers me his hand. As I slide my fingers into his palm, the same tingles run up my arm. He instructs the driver to wait. Sam drops my hand only to open the outer door of my apartment building. He threads our fingers together after allowing me through before him. While I realize this may seem small to some people, his manners are off the charts as far as I'm concerned. I noticed it at the gala as well. Along with his brothers, he stood when any one of the women left the table. I'm fully capable of taking care of myself, but acting like a gentleman is significant for me.

Sam is walking ever so slowly to my door, and I'm not offended in the slightest. I don't want him to rush away either, but I know Scarlett should be home.

"This is me."

"I know," he whispers near the shell of my ear, sending chills cascading through me.

I slide my key into the door before turning to face him. I tip my head up to look at him. With these heels on, his lips are a few inches above mine.

"I'll see you in the morning. Good night, Savannah."

The air around us is charged as he leans down ever so slightly. His lips a mere inch above mine now. The notion that Sam intends to kiss me puts my nerves on high alert. I inhale to prepare myself as my door swings open.

"I thought I heard you. Hi, Savi."

I lower my head lightly, resting it on Sam's chest.

"Hi, Scar. I'll be right in."

She closes the door most of the way and retreats into our apartment.

I lift my gaze again. "Good night, Sam. I'll see you in the morning."

"Good night, Savannah."

He waits until I completely close my door before walking away. Yes, I watch through the peephole. Guilty, completely guilty. Of course, I want a longer look at him.

"Savi, who is *that?* He's H-O-T. HOT!" My younger sister fans herself while stating the obvious.

Scarlett is a carbon copy of me when I was younger with her dark hair and light blue eyes. She's studying math and computer science at NYU. She's already in her sophomore year but may need five to finish her degree. She works as a hostess at a supper club as well.

"Thanks, Scar. That was Sam."

"He's your boss? How do you get any work done?"

Trust me, little sister, it isn't easy.

"Since when does he escort you home?"

"Since today. What's with all the questions?"

Scarlett isn't aware of Sam's status, only that he's my boss and owns the company. As long as possible, I'll keep that information away from her. The last thing we need is for reporters to show up here looking for information about Sam.

"You should consider dating him, Savi."

On it. I step out of my heels, setting my tired feet on the cool floor.

"How was school?"

"Ugh! Of my five classes, three are insanely boring, one is fun, and the last is difficult. However, my lab partner, Oliver, is adorable, even if he's a pinch nerdy."

"You know the deal. You need to maintain your GPA to keep your scholarship. Ask for help if you need it."

Scarlett is under the impression that she got a full ride to NYU. The truth is, I'm paying for it. I don't want her to struggle with student loans. After a brief break in schooling, I worked full time during the day and attended class at night. I barely slept for four years. After graduation I worked two full-time jobs and one per diem job. One job was simply to pay off my student loans as quickly as humanly possible.

"I know. Just venting. I have some work to do. See you in the morning."

"Okay." I continue shucking off my clothes as I climb the stairs. After replacing my dress with sleep shorts, a tank, and a thin hoodie, I hustle back downstairs in search of some dinner. My phone vibrates on the counter as I pass.

Sam: Random question. How do you take your coffee?

Me: Cream with one sugar for a medium. Why?

Sam: Just wondering. Sleep well, Savannah.

Me: You too, Sam.

I sigh. Aside from his insanely good looks, work ethic, and probably gym ethic too, I don't know very much about Sam. Well, he's remarkably close to his siblings. He would drop everything for any one of them or their significant others. In fact, earlier this year, he told me about checking on his sister-in-law because photographers camped outside Cash's home while he was away for work.

After inhaling some leftovers, I climb into my bed. Now that I can, I embrace sleep. Yet images of Sam keep crossing my mind. Hopefully, sleep will claim me soon. Otherwise, tomorrow is going to be rough.

SAMSON

I fully expect my presence first thing this morning to fluster Savannah. I'm leaning against the car as she steps out of her building. As always she's dressed perfectly. Today she opted for a navy, fitted dress with matching jacket. I didn't want to startle her or her roommate by knocking early in the morning. Although, part of me is dying to see her fresh from sleep.

"Good morning, Savannah." I sport a huge grin on my face as I hand her a homemade cup of coffee.

"Morning, Sam." Taking the cup, she takes a sip, savoring it before speaking again. Savannah may be a foodie. She certainly enjoyed that first sip. "Thank you, this is perfect. What are you doing here?"

"I came to bring you to work."

"You didn't have to do that."

"I want to." I would move her in with me if it were practical. It isn't, at least not yet. That notion should scare me, but it doesn't. Something about Savannah is different.

"How much earlier did you get up to be here?"

"Not too much. I go to the gym first thing every day. Instead of working from home for a bit, I came here." I have some time to spare for tomorrow and the next day, now that I know how long it takes to get here.

After closing her door, I round the car and buckle up. "I didn't know you had a roommate. How did you meet?"

She laughs. "We met on her birthday. Scarlett is my little sister."

I laugh at myself. "What else don't I know about you, Miss Clemons?"

"A lot, I imagine, Mr. Morgan. Exactly like I don't know very much about you. Well, not anything accurate."

"Meaning?"

"I only know what you've shared with me. All the headlines about you are false."

"You've read headlines about me?" Concern spreads in my chest.

"They're hard to miss. I mean, a girl needs to grocery shop at some point. It isn't as if I spend hours googling you. If I have a question, I'll ask."

"Do you have any?" I'm sure she has plenty of questions, but I'm not sure what she will ask first. My concern dissipates as quickly as it arose.

"Tons, but none that pertain to the headlines."

"We've got time. What do you want to know?"

"How do you take your coffee?"

"Same as you. Is that what you really want to know?" There must be something deeper she wants to know.

"How do you ignore the headlines?"

"That's easy, to date, not a single bit of it has ever been true." The last time a headline was true didn't even mention me by name. "We should talk about that though."

Our driver parks at the curb in front of our office building. Once we exit the elevator, I guide her into my office. I lean against my desk as she takes a seat in one of the chairs.

"Talk about headlines?"

"Sort of. I take extra precautions to protect my privacy. Agreeing to go on a date with me will take some of yours away. Would you prefer to stay in for our date?"

"No, I don't want to stay in. You and I have already been photographed together at business dinners and at the gala. Who cares if there are more photos?"

"I care."

My words are a bit harsher that I would like. If she notices, she doesn't indicate as much. Honestly, the press can go either way with me dating someone. I must admit, Cash and Noelle handled it well. They controlled the narrative by giving a legitimate, trustworthy reporter an exclusive.

"Sam." She inhales sharply before speaking again. "Why?"

"I want to protect you from all the things that come along with dating me."

"I can take care of myself."

"I know you can, but I don't think you realize how difficult the press can be." The phone rings. I ignore it.

"What do you suggest?"

She's giving me a little ground. I'll take what I can get. "Please be more cautious if you go anywhere alone."

She nods. The phone rings again.

"I should get to work." She stands from her chair, but I remained rooted in place. Savannah is as close to me now as last night outside her door. Like last night, her scent teases me, but it's stronger now. I smell jasmine, amber, and something else. She's alluring. Resisting the urge to kiss her requires epic restraint, especially considering I was this close last night and thwarted. She slides away, narrowly avoiding me.

Sitting in my chair, I turn to face the city. I've lived here my entire life. I can't imagine giving up the bustle like Cash has. Although I never considered finding someone to spend my life with after Meghan's death. Savannah is the first woman who's held my attention long enough for me to even consider it. Ironically, she wasn't trying to capture my attention. It doesn't matter, I'm already wrapped around her finger. She doesn't know it yet.

Savannah and I work the rest of the day as if nothing has changed between us. Other than spending more time together outside of work, nothing has. It will, soon enough. I made reservations for Friday. I hope she likes jazz. Right before six, I clear my desk and seek her out as she isn't at her desk.

"Looking for something?"

A warmth spreads in my chest. The sound of her voice runs over me, calming me. "You. Are you ready to go home?"

"Sure."

I refrain from reading into her tone. During the ride, I ask about dinner. "Do you want to go home before our date?"

"No, I can change at the office." After escorting her home, I finish planning our date.

As Friday afternoon approaches, I'm getting increasingly nervous. I haven't planned a date in years. Savannah buzzes around the office as usual. She's meticulous, organized, and capable of running this firm without me. Those attributes stood out when her resume graced my desk. When she walked in for her interview, my jaw hit the floor. Figuratively, at least.

Now, it takes composure to keep my jaw from gaping open. This morning Savannah wore a black, tailored pantsuit for work. After the workday is finished, she steps out of the bathroom wearing a red cocktail dress that hugs her body like a seamstress cut the fabric specifically for her. My body doesn't need more incentive to react to her.

"Savannah, you look gorgeous." I hand her a bouquet of colorful blooms of orange bi-color roses, yellow alstroemeria, orange lilies, and lemon leaf.

She takes them and lifts them to her pert nose. "Thank you. These smell wonderful. You look rather good yourself."

I smile, offer her my arm, and take a step forward. "Why are you shaking, Savannah?" Turning to face her, I rest my hand on the curve of her waist.

"Savannah, please talk to me."

"I'm nervous."

"It's just me."

"There is nothing *just* about you. I've wanted to be in this moment since we met. After the gala, my desire to be here, right now, has multiplied exponentially."

Before I think better of it, I draw her closer, my hand branding the exposed skin of her back. My other hand rests on her neck, my thumb grazing her jawline. A small sound of surprise passes between us, the air thick with unspoken desires.

"The same is true about you." Leaning forward, I set my forehead against hers.

Our mouths are barely an inch apart. She sucks in a jagged breath. As much as I want to kiss her, here isn't what I had in mind. Dragging my thumb backward along her jaw, I pull back, setting my lips on her forehead and looking down her wide, blue eyes staring up at me. She's scared. So am I. We feel… perfect.

Yet in order to give her an out, I ask again. "Savannah, will you go on a date with me?"

"Yes." I feel her shiver as my arm slides to rest at her waist.

A short ride later, we arrive at the Bistro on Fifth. The hostess guides us to a private elevator. When we arrive at the top, a dedicated server seats us at one of four tables on the roof. She hasn't uttered another word since we left the office.

"Mr. Morgan. Miss Clemons, my name is Ivan, and I'll be at your service this evening."

We order our drinks, and Ivan scurries away.

"Have you ever eaten here before?" I cover her hand with mine. The tremble has significantly decreased.

"No." Her quick response indicates she's still nervous about this date. My intention isn't to flaunt my wealth, the opposite in fact. I would have preferred to have Auggie cook for us at my penthouse.

"What's wrong?"

"Nothing." Her response is clipped.

Ivan returns with our drinks and immediately walks away. I rise from my chair, rounding the table, offering her my hand.

"Come with me."

Sliding her long, delicate fingers across my palm, she stands next to me. Electricity passes between us. I lead her across the roof to the observation area. It's chillier over here because there are no dedicated heaters. I release her hand long enough to shrug off my jacket. After wrapping her small frame with my jacket, I surround her with my arms. "Still nervous?"

She nods before resting her head against my chest. "There are two warring issues in my head. First, you're my boss, and dating one another is not the smartest idea ever. I need my job. Scarlett needs my job. Second, I want to be here. I'm insanely attracted to you, and that scares me."

"I'm drawn to you as well. What do you mean Scarlett needs your job?"

She exhales and lifts her eyes to mine. "Scarlett is under the impression that she's on a full scholarship to NYU. That isn't the case. While she did get a few small scholarships, I'm paying her tuition."

This woman is more than I ever imagined. Working her tail off to pay for her sister to go to a prestigious university. "What about your parents?"

"That's a long story."

"Well, isn't learning about one another what dates are for?"

She shrugs slightly. I lead her back to our table, where Ivan has placed the salad course at our seats as well as a blanket for Savannah. She covers her legs with the blanket.

"My parents married young and had me. By all accounts, they were happy. My mother had numerous complications during Scarlett's pregnancy, from diabetes to preeclampsia. She died a few hours after my sister was born."

"I'm sorry for your loss."

Savannah nods and looks off to the side briefly before responding. "Thank you. My dad checked out. He was in the house, but he wasn't truly there. I took care of Scarlett, from the midnight feedings to first day of school photos. She was near eight when I was deciding where to go to college. I took a few years to work until she was old enough to stay home alone after school. I went to community college for my undergraduate degree at night; then I completed as much of my graduate degree online while she was in high school. Now, she lives with me while attending NYU."

"You're even more amazing than I thought."

Redness spreads across her face. "No, I'm not. I did what anyone would do."

"You're wrong. There are very few people who would put their sibling before themselves at such an early age, if ever. Most would attempt to get their parent to step up. How is your dad now?"

"Since Scar started college, he has made progress personally by seeking counselling. With us, he's trying. He still doesn't realize that his grief necessitated me giving up a lot of my childhood. It doesn't matter; I would do it again if given the same choice. Scar is turning into a wonderful adult. I'm glad I didn't screw her up."

"You need to give yourself more credit. It seems to me both of you turned into amazing women with your gumption and guidance."

"Thank you."

Ivan returns, refills our drinks, and replaces our salad with soup. The rest of dinner passes with ordinary questions from favorite colors, mine is blue and hers is yellow, to hot or cold apple cider. We cover a bunch of topics, including sports and television. She loves football, dislikes baseball and stock car racing, and binge watches house flipping shows for décor ideas. Nothing as heavy as her family situation comes up again.

"Ready for our next stop?"

"Absolutely."

I direct our driver to the jazz club.

Her nervousness appears to have dissipated. She's sitting flush against me, our hands clasped atop my thigh. Unfortunately, the ride isn't far, and all too soon, I need to move away from her. A soft sigh follows me out the car door. Once inside the club, we're led to a private viewing area. The lighting is dim, the couch soft and comfortable. Shortly after sitting, our drinks arrive.

"Are you sure you didn't research me somehow?" she asks.

"Is that even possible?"

"No, but I love jazz. Aside from my initial concerns, I'm having a wonderful time."

"I am too."

The show starts. Soft jazz music surrounds us. The quartet features two trumpeters, a saxophonist, and a pianist. Savannah cuddles against me on the couch, my fingers drawing circles on the cap of her shoulder.

I press my lips to her temple before speaking. "Dance with me?"

I push the small table off to the side before pulling her into my arms and sliding one hand around her, resting our joined hands between us. This isn't the first time I've danced with Savannah, but this time I have permission to touch her like a date, not a business associate. Her curves pressing against me is a lot to take in. She fits in my arms like her body was molded for mine. Even with high heels, she's shorter than me.

Pulling back, I raise her chin with my forefinger. Her stunning cobalt eyes with long eyelashes lift to mine. As I drag the pad of my thumb across her lips, she inhales sharply. Her chest rises and falls faster against me. Tentatively, I lean closer to her. The importance of this moment isn't lost on me. This could be our last first kiss. Closing the distance, I press my lips to hers. Soft mewling sounds muffle in her throat. Her hand slides up my chest to cup my face.

Tightening my hold on her, I drop my other hand and reach for the couch. Slowly, I lower us to the cushion. Once seated, our mouths part for each other, our tongues twisting, exploring together. Every bit of desire I held back at the gala and earlier this week at her apartment, I give it to her. She's giving the same amount in return. Kissing Savannah is heavenly. The entire world around us falls away. It's only us. I could stay here in this moment indefinitely. However, here is not the place to take this further, despite the ache in my chest to do so. I draw back slightly.

"Sam… I have no words." Her lips are plump from our kisses and her skin is pink.

"Neither do I." *Everything was fine until I kissed you. It will never be the same again.*

Lost in each other and the feeling of our first kiss, we cuddle on the couch as the band finishes their first set

"Do you want to stay or go?"

"We can go."

I rise and escort her to the car.

SAVANNAH

The reality of Sam's lips on mine exceeds my imagination many times over. Until tonight, a date with Sam was a pipe dream. Now it's my reality, and I want more. So much more.

"Savannah, are you free tomorrow?" he asks after joining me in the car.

"Yes, I'm free."

"Will you spend the day with me?"

I smile and lean over to kiss him again. I intend a small, chaste kiss, but it morphs into something akin to two teenagers at make-out point. I didn't realize we parked in front of my building before we come up for air.

Slowly, I close my door after a shorter round of knee-buckling kisses with Sam in the hallway. I would invite him in, except I never know when Scar is going to be home.

"How was your date? Those flowers are gorgeous," Scar says as I turn from the door. "The look on your face says your boss can kiss and does it well."

Well doesn't begin to cover how melty I feel when Sam kisses me. Is that even a word? If it isn't, it needs to be.

"Seriously, Scar. Really, you can tell?"

Scarlett and I have talked about her dates before, but she has never been able to call me out until today.

"Savi, your lips look like you got a lip filler treatment, and your skin is blotchy."

"It was amazing. We went to dinner and then to a jazz club."

"Did you tell him you love jazz?"

"No, I didn't. Apparently, we have that in common as well as a love of priceless art and football. What are you doing home on a Friday night? Guy trouble?"

"Nah, I didn't feel like going out tonight. I'm turning in. Good night, Savi."

"Night, Scar." While searching for a vase, I hear my phone chime. While the water is warming, I check my phone.

Sam: I wish I were still with you.

Me: I do too.

Sam: Can I call you?

Me: I'll call you in a few.

I finish setting my flowers in water, hustle upstairs, slip out of my dress, wash off my makeup, and change into my pajamas. Nothing fancy, shorts and a tank top, and I twisted my hair into a messy topknot. I dress comfortably when I'm home. Settling into my bed, I call Sam. He switches it over to a video call.

"I want to see your gorgeous face."

"Sweet talker. Nothing gorgeous about me sans makeup."

"You would be wrong, Miss Clemons."

"Your sleepy eyes are messing with your vision."

"My vision is perfect."

I have no reply to his overly kind words other than, "Thank you. Where are you sitting?"

"In my bedroom, why?"

"Trying to orient myself. Is that the skyline behind you?"

"Yes."

"Wow, it's gorgeous." Sam is wealthy beyond my comprehension, but I can't fathom what a view like that would cost each month.

He stands, turning the camera toward his window.

"I would sit and stare mesmerized for hours at a time, if I had that view."

"I appreciate this view each morning when I wake and each evening. I'll show you." After a quick view of inlaid hardwood floors and bright white linens with a gray frame, I see Sam's grin before he turns the camera to the skyline. The lights twinkle and dance outside his window. A world of people spread throughout the buildings, going about their lives. It's stunning. "Were you born and raised in New York?"

"No, I was born in rural Pennsylvania. Why?"

"I'm finishing up planning our date for tomorrow while you admire the view."

I would prefer to admire it with Sam's arms wrapped around me. "You planned it already?" I ask as he flips the camera back to his face. Heat shoots straight southward as he removed his shirt before climbing into his bed. As predicated, Sam's chest ripples with ridges and curves from what I can see, at least six precisely cut abs. Refraining from fanning myself proves difficult. Even more now than before, I would prefer to be there with him.

"Yes, on the ride here. Can you be ready by eight?"

"Sure. What are we doing?"

"I'll take care of everything. Aim for casual dress with comfy shoes and probably a sweater."

"Okay. I'll be ready."

Sam sinks deeper into his bed, rolling onto his side. Even though we should get some sleep, we continue talking, covering all topics from current events to fashion trends to collections. Apparently, Sam collects original vinyl recordings of jazz legends. That knowledge makes me like him so much more. I snuggle deeper into my bed, rolling onto my side. It's as if he is lying next to me. It's too bad he isn't. It's crazy soon for me to think that way. Honestly, though, I have known Sam for almost a year at this point.

A few hours later, I groggily notice, we both fell asleep with the video connection still live. I watch him sleep for a few minutes. The rhythmic rise and fall of his hard-sculpted chest, the sheet bunched at his waist. If I'm not mistaken, he even has the V-shape that makes women drool. Me, I'm women. Not only does the man insure priceless works of art, he is one. I sigh softly and let sleep claim me again, knowing in a few short hours, I'll be with Sam again.

SAMSON

Near five I wake to the sound of soft breathing. Savannah and I never ended our call last night. Dressed in a suit and demanding information from clients or other insurance companies, she's a powerhouse. In comfy clothes with her hair crazy around her head, she's gorgeous.

As much as I would like to wait until she wakes, I dress for the gym. After an hour of weights and a long run, I dress for my date. Until last night, I haven't been on a date in years.

Losing Meghan was hard. While I never shared with my family, I knew Meghan was ill. I knew we may never make it to the altar. Unfortunately, I was right. Taking another chance on lifetime happiness never seemed right until Savannah. Even then it took me over four months to invite her to the gala, then another three to ask for a date.

After pulling in front of her building, I step out and knock on the door softly in case Scarlett is still sleeping. If I recall correctly, when I was in college, sleeping in on the weekends was a necessity.

When Savannah opens the door, I'm taken aback. Until this moment, I've never seen her dressed casually. She looks much younger in jeans, a graphic tee, and sneakers. While I notice her sexy heels and her legs at the office, I didn't realize that she's tiny without them until I wrap her in my arms.

"Morning, beautiful."

She smiles and hands me a cup of coffee.

I grin.

"Morning. What's with the grin?"

"I have a coffee for you in the car. Ready?"

"Yes." She grabs her purse and a cardigan from the side table near the door and takes my arm.

Our first stop is a ferry ride along the Hudson. We board the white-sailed schooner and find an offering of breakfast pastries. I may have purchased every ticket to make sure Savannah and I are the only people on this tour.

"Good morning, Mr. Morgan. Miss Clemons. I'm Walter. I'll be your captain today. Your guide today is Cassie. She will indicate points of interest once we're underway. Please make yourselves comfortable. We will depart in the next few minutes."

"Sam, did you rent this entire tour?"

The look on her face is hard to read. I'm not yet comfortable with her facial expressions to say whether or not she's angry.

"Maybe. Is that a problem?"

"Not necessarily. Why?"

"I'm not ready to expose you to the media yet. I know we have been photographed together, but then you weren't my…."

"Your what?"

I take her hand in mine, guiding her to the bench. We turn to face each other. "I'm not sure yet. I'm attracted to you. I like you. A lot. A whole lot." *Very eloquent, Sam.* "I would prefer to protect you from reporters as long as possible. When we need to, we can make a statement like Cash and Noelle's. For now, I want to shield you as much as I can."

"Okay. I'm not fancy, Sam." That's one of the main reasons I'm drawn to her. She works for everything she has. Even though she knows I have money, she isn't interested in five-star restaurants and events. "We don't always have to go out when we spend time together."

"I'll keep that in mind, after today."

She smiles, leans forward, and kisses me softly. Pulling back, she adds space between us as she lifts her dark blue eyes to mine. The look says she wants to continue kissing but isn't sure about me. *I'm right there with you, Savannah.*

Instead of moving away, I cup her cheek, drawing her close to me again. A soft sigh surrounds me right before I set my lips on hers. Her supple lips pressed against mine is as blissful as last night. We're so wrapped up in each other, we fail to notice our guide joining us until Cassie clears her throat. We rise and move near the railing.

"Mr. Morgan. Miss Clemons. The tour is about to begin. If you look out the starboard side of the schooner, you'll see…." Our guide continues talking as we pass the George Washington Bridge, the Cloisters, and the Little Red Lighthouse along with amazing fall foliage along the banks of the river. I'm more interested in holding Savannah than the scenery. Without heels, I can rest my head atop hers comfortably. It doesn't matter how tall her shoes are, her curves feel spectacular against me.

After the tour, we stroll hand in hand around Little Italy. We eat our way up Mulberry Street to Hester and Broome for the afternoon. After sharing spicy sausage, pastas, and even some zeppole, we opt to stop for the day and watch a movie at her apartment.

It's easy to talk to Savannah outside of the office. Not once has work come into our conversations since we left together last night. It was something that worried me about dating Savannah. Thankfully, that hasn't been the case.

After sending the driver home, insisting I would take an Uber, we step into her apartment. A woman who I assume is her sister, dressed in a slinky black dress is hopping around trying to pull on a high-heel shoe.

"Scar, those are mine," Savannah says, setting her bag on the small semicircle table by the door. She's meticulous with her home as well. Everything is neatly in its place. Shoes lined near the door, coats and handbags on hooks. A bowl for keys sits on the small side table.

"I know, but you weren't here, and I didn't want to interrupt your date, which apparently isn't over. Hi, I'm Scarlett. Her younger, meddling, shoe-stealing sister."

Savannah's description of her sister was accurate, except she's taller even without the stolen heels—black high heels with a strap around the ankle adorned with a small bow that I happen to love when Savannah wears them.

With a smile and a laugh, I extend my hand to her. "Pleasure to meet you, Scarlett. Your sister has told me a lot about you."

"Nice to meet you as well. Savi, I'm going to a club in Hoboken and then staying at Liza and El's." Scarlett kisses Savannah on the cheek and rushes to the door.

"Bye, Scar. Be safe."

It's endearing seeing her act like a mom to Scarlett. It's one thing to know she's paying her tuition, it's something else to see her acting like a parent.

"You too!" Scarlett replies.

I have never seen Savannah's face that shade of red. She tries to turn away from me.

Instead, I fold her into my arms, whispering near her ear, "Don't worry about her. You've met my siblings. She'll fit in well with comments like that."

She shivers in my arms. I'm not sure if it's from my proximity, my words, or my breath on her skin. I kiss her head before releasing her. She checks the lock before moving toward her kitchen.

"Do you want a drink?"

Her apartment is her. The beige couches are set in an L-shape facing a moderate-size television—not huge like mine, not even close. There's something to be said for the entire line of scrimmage emblazoned on your screen in ultra-high definition. A large chair is near the window with a small table nearby holding a stack of books.

"Whatever you have is fine with me. Who's the bookworm?"

"Me. I read a lot, mostly art history or suspense. Why don't you pick a movie? The remotes should be on the ottoman."

A small, gray cat prances down the stairs, curls up next to me, and immediately begins purring.

"What's the cat's name?"

"Mr. Gray Boots."

I literally laugh out loud. "Is it yours or Scarlett's?"

"He's mine, but Scarlett named him. I call him Gray. He usually stays upstairs when we have guests. You get the seal of approval if he curls up with you."

Ice teas in hand, she sidles next to me to watch the *The Avengers*. While the movie begins, she settles against me, my arm around her back. As the movie dances across the screen, my fingers draw circles on the exposed skin of her lower back. Hours later, the movie long over, I glance at Savannah. She's sleeping peacefully against my chest. No one has even made me pine for female attention until her. I never felt like I was missing it until her. I want her in my life as more than my associate. Cautiously, I shut off the television and recline further. Soft, muffled sounds escape her mouth as she snuggles closer.

SAVANNAH

Warmth surrounds me as a spicy man scent envelops me. Lifting my head slightly, I gaze up at Sam. His face is completely relaxed, his features softer than normal. His hand is flat against the small of my back. My chest is draped against him, one leg between his, and the other set alongside him. My fingers are beneath his shirt, splayed on his impressive abs. I narrowly resist the urge to peek.

My relationship history isn't complex. My focus was caring for Scarlett. I never really had a meaningful relationship outside of my best friend from high school. Bradley was always willing to forgo typical high school events to hang out with me and Scar at the park across the street from our tiny house. When he went away to college, we stayed connected, but we never moved past two fumbling teens sharing awkward firsts. Arguably, it wasn't a pleasant experience, though I gather most firsts aren't. Almost equally as awkward was teaching Scarlett to take care of herself and owning her choices.

Unwilling to move, I drift back off to sleep. After what seems like hours, Scarlett bursts through our front door. I push back onto my heels over Sam's leg. My eyes fly open, expecting a lecture from my little sister. Then I realize I haven't done anything wrong. Sam opens his eyes, looking over at me in my new position with my knees bent on the cushions.

"Savi, there are tons of photographers outside. What is going on?"

Crap! "Scar, why don't you put your stuff away while I make coffee. We need to have a chat."

As the words leave my mouth, Sam is scrolling through his phone. He shakes his head as he settles on an image. Turning his phone to me, he shares a photo of us at the jazz club on Friday, right before our first kiss.

The headline reads: *Insurance Titan Sam Morgan off the Market too? Who is this Mysterious Raven-haired Beauty?"*

His expression is hard to read.

"Sam, talk to me."

Before he speaks, he fully sits up, caressing my face before kissing me softly. Every kiss makes me gooey inside. *Very respectable, Savi.*

"I'm trying to collect my thoughts, which are opposed to each other. *Cara mia,* I care about you. We need a plan to handle the photographers. Is there a back way out of here? Also, what do you plan on telling your sister?"

"I plan on telling her the truth. I can't believe I have been able to work for you for almost a year without her figuring it out. There isn't another way out of here. If I leave, will they bother Scar?"

He pulls me into his lap, his arms engulfing me. His lips press against my temple. "I don't know if they will leave her alone. Let's make that coffee."

I inhale as he sets me on the floor. It takes a lot for me to ignore the rush southward that his manhandling me causes.

As the coffee starts to brew, Scarlett returns downstairs. Sam leans against the counter near the stove within arm's length of me.

"I assume they're here for you?" she pointedly asks Sam.

"Yes."

"Who are you?"

He looks over at me, I nod tightly. "As you know, I'm your sister's boss. I own Morgan Insurance. We specialize in insurance for priceless art. They're here because my family is well-known, and since my brother's marriage, I'm now New York's most eligible bachelor."

I set a cup of coffee near Sam. As he takes it, his fingers glide along mine. I look up but say nothing. Content that he feels it too, I start work on mine.

"Okay. What have you done when your past girlfriend's homes were surrounded?" Scarlett asks.

"I haven't had a girlfriend in years," Sam replies, and his expression doesn't flinch at calling me his girlfriend.

A look of surprise crosses Scarlett's face. "How is that possible considering you're successful and good-looking?"

I wonder that myself, but never felt it was my place to ask until recently. I suppose now is an appropriate time.

"I need to share those details with Savannah first. If she chooses to share with you, that's her choice."

"Fair enough." Scarlett doesn't press. Honestly, I'm surprised she isn't digging for more information.

"Did the reporters recognize you?" Sam asks Scarlett while I take the first sip of the day. I would much rather still be lying with Sam on the couch than having this conversation.

"No, they didn't. How long will they stay outside?"

"Until I leave. If they didn't connect you and Savannah, that's good for you. Until they do, you should be able to move freely. When they do, you can simply say 'no comment.' Savannah, they won't believe me if I make up an excuse since there's a photo from Friday. What do you want me to do?"

"Scar, are you good with all of that?"

"I'll be fine, Savi. I have some work to do. I'll be down later." Scarlett turns to Sam. "Thank you for your honesty. As long as you're good to Savi, we won't have any issues."

"You're welcome. I will be."

Scarlett takes a cup of coffee and climbs the stairs. Once she's out of sight, Sam tucks me into his body, his head resting on mine. His large hands slide up and down my back in opposite directions.

"I'm sorry. I should have left last night, but falling asleep with you was downright perfection."

"There's nothing to be sorry for. It was amazing. I could get used to it."

"Me too." Adding some space between us, he exhales sharply. "Meghan was my childhood sweetheart. We hated one another even though our teachers paired us together for project after project; we were even lab partners. Despite our initial dislike, we became inseparable. One night during freshman year at boarding school, some classmates were mean to her because she was a scholarship student. Regardless of curfew, she stayed in my room. We shared our first kiss that night. Fast forward through boarding school, we selected our colleges so we could be near one another. I proposed the summer before our junior year." Sam pauses to regain a grip on his emotions.

"What happened to her?"

"Meghan had a congenital heart defect. She went in for surgery over Christmas break but didn't survive. My family doesn't know I was aware of her heart condition. I presume they would've had me refrain from proposing knowing she might never make it down the aisle. I wouldn't have changed anything."

"Why are you telling me?"

"Until you, I haven't felt the pull of someone else's heart. Until you, I haven't wanted to try again." He leans forward, brushing his lips across mine.

Immediately I rise on my toes, sliding my hands to his face to kiss him. From the times they call and the limited time I spent with them after the gala, I noticed Sam and his family are incredibly close. He puts everyone before himself—everyone apparently includes me and Scarlett now.

"I want you too."

Sam wraps his arms around my waist and lifts me to the counter. Stepping between my thighs and tilting my face upward, he kisses me, his tongue exploring the depths of my mouth as if it's the first time. The desire flowing from his kiss is heavy and so easy to succumb to—not that I'm resisting anymore. My resistance started crumbling at the gala when his fingers branded my back.

Sam travels down my neck and outward as far as my shirt will allow. Sliding my fingers beneath his shirt, my fingers meet sculpted peaks and valleys of muscle. His fingers grip the hem of my shirt, lifting. It yanks me back to my senses. "We aren't alone," I whisper.

With that reminder, Sam sets his hands on my upper thighs, his thumbs pressing against my core. That slight skim of his fingers makes my muscles clench in anticipation. His forehead meets mine.

"I should get going to make them leave."

I frown.

"It isn't what I want, but I don't see another option right now. Do you?"

"No, but that doesn't mean I like it. Please call me later."

Slowly, he pulls on his shoes near the door. "Of course. If it gets to be too much, the three of you are welcome to move in with me. I have plenty of space, more privacy, and security."

"I'll talk to Scarlett if it gets worse."

"Thank you, *cara mia*. I'll call you later. Also, I'll be here to pick you up in the morning, but I'll stay in the car." Pulling me into his arms, Sam presses his lips to mine, then my forehead before sliding through the door.

For a few long moments, my hand remains on the door.

"Savi, we need to talk." Scarlett's voice pulls me out of the memory of sleeping in Sam's arms and his deliciously talented mouth.

SAMSON

Cash: Is that Savannah? Do you need anything?

Billie: I'm so happy for you. Love you bunches.

Auggie: Do you need some food? Caro can bring some over.

Those are the texts from my siblings since Page Six released this morning. We have a sibling group text. If something needs to be private, we don't talk in there. Rarely do we not share with everyone eventually. Initially, Cash only shared with me about buying the airline only because of my expertise with our family trust.

Me: Yes, that's Savannah. Currently, about ten photogs are camping out at her apartment.

Me: I'm good, Auggie.

Billie: Is she okay? That will take some time to get used too.

Me: Her sister wasn't fazed, but it isn't something I want them to deal with.

Billie: Sister?

Me: She has a younger sister, Scarlett. She's a student at NYU.

Cash: Do you need to talk to Jacob from Blackthorne?

Me: Not yet. Savannah is like Noelle. I might get away with a dog. I left offering "no comment."

Auggie: Do you want company today?

Me: No, thanks. I'm good. I'll bury myself in work.

At my direction, my driver pulls into the garage of my building. I advise him of the schedule for tomorrow, and he leaves. My phone chimes with another text. This one is private.

Cash: If you need to talk, I'm home all day.

Me: Thanks. This is new for me. Paparazzi was never an issue when we were younger.

He knows I mean with Meghan and before our success in business.

Cash: I know. I will say, York Beach is fabulous. No one cares who I am, and it's peaceful.

Me: I don't know if Savannah will leave her sister. It's also crazy soon for me to approach that.

Cash: Can't you issue your policies from anywhere?

Me: Probably. Worth looking into. Never had anyone worth protecting before.

Cash: I understand. Don't let the crazy panic about her safety push her away. Trust me, talking to her is a much safer option.

Me: I'll do my best.

If anyone understands how I'm feeling right now, it's Cash. Not only was he New York's most eligible bachelor, but his wife, Noelle, is the younger sister of one of Hollywood's hottest commodities, both as an actor and director, Ellis Barnett. While Noelle was somewhat aware of the paparazzi, Savannah and Scarlett aren't.

After a scalding shower, I change into sweats and a graphic tee before opting to watch football pregame instead of working. My mind races about Savannah, our dates, and my visceral reaction to having her in my arms. Her lips on mine feel as if they were meant to be there. At least a half dozen times, I pick up my phone to call Savannah. I would prefer to have her curled against me watching the game.

"Mr. Morgan, Mr. Ramon Santiago is here to see you," Jimmy announces through the intercom.

"Thank you. Please send him up."

Ramon is my childhood nanny's son-in-law. His wife, Marisol, was always around when we were younger. Before they were married, and twice after, Marisol and I have been intimate. I'm not proud of that fact, but whenever they separated, she would cry on my shoulder. Their relationship is tumultuous at best. Marisol never indicated that Ramon was physically abusive, nor did I see any signs. Emotional abuse, I would bet on.

Ramon steps off the elevator.

"Good afternoon, Ramon. What can I do for you?"

"Marisol has been in an accident. She sent me to bring you to the hospital." Question after question zips around in my head. I'm surprised that Ramon heeded her request as well.

"Give me five minutes to change. Would you like a drink?"

He shakes his head. "No, thank you."

After an agonizing car ride, we arrive at Lennox Hill, and Ramon is ushered back to Marisol. Her condition has deteriorated since he left. I settle into a chair to wait for his return.

Me: Cara mia, *I'm at Lennox visiting an injured friend. I'll call you when I can.*

I'm not a fan of hospitals in general. Rarely, do good things happen at a hospital. A young nurse calls my name in the waiting area. I rise from the stiff chair and follow her. The tag on her green scrubs indicates her name is Shelley.

"Mrs. Santiago needs additional surgery. She requested to speak with you beforehand."

As I round the corner, Shelley ushers me into a small, windowless room. Tubes and wires surround Marisol. She looks tiny in the huge hospital bed and markedly pregnant. The monitor indicates two strong heartbeats, hers and her baby. Nothing like Billie's, but nonetheless, lacerations mar her olive skin. Tears have fallen down her cheeks, the trails evident.

Marisol raises her hand toward me with significant effort. I sit on the edge of her bed, covering her tiny hand in mine.

"Sam, I'm sorry. She might be yours. Margaux paid me to say it was Ramon's. I took the money; I needed to secure her future. Ramon knows about us." Her voice is raspy and cracked as more tears stream from her eyes. "I'm so sorry. I wasn't strong enough."

"I would have taken care of you and the baby if I knew. I would have helped you."

We've been together twice in the last three years. Before then, before her marriage, it was more frequent. Easy, no strings. That isn't an "us." It's a hookup.

"I know, but you and I aren't meant to be more than friends."

"Were you ever going to tell me?"

"I don't know." More sobs wrack her injured body. The monitors beep, and nurses flood into the room.

"Sir, I need you to step outside," a male staff member informs me.

I back away from her bed as they work on Marisol, my gaze stuck on the monitor, watching the line that follows the baby's heart rate. A baby that could be my daughter. My emotions ping back and forth from elation, devastation, fear, and downright hatred. I may be a father in a matter of weeks. I didn't know she was pregnant.

Savannah.

I just started a relationship with her. My mother has done some atrocious things, but preying on Marisol and possibly keeping my daughter from me is reprehensible. The walls of my chest squeeze as I walk back into the waiting room. As I search for a seat to wait, my newly minted, raven-haired girlfriend rises from a chair with two cups of coffee.

SAVANNAH

After a few minutes to center my emotions and push away the notion of what could have happened if Sam and I were alone earlier, Scarlett trudges downstairs. Grabbing a water, I lean against the counter. I've wanted to be with Sam since the moment we met, but I didn't know the lengths the media would go to for a story.

Scarlett plods into in the kitchen. "Were you ever going to mention that your boss is uber rich?"

"No, it isn't important."

"Savi, your boss is splashed across covers in the corner market and the grocery store."

"Scar, it doesn't matter. Yes, he's wealthy. So what?"

"He can take care of us."

"Scarlett Mae! We don't need Sam to take care of us. I have been taking care of us for a long time." I can't believe those words came out of her mouth. "Have you ever not had everything you needed? Do you really think you need a man to take care of you?"

"No, but—"

"But what?" Still I'm in disbelief.

"Did you see the reporters outside? He's a big deal."

"Yes, he is. I thought there would be more time. Sam warned me; we have been out only twice. Again, so what? I can't believe you're truly that ungrateful. If you take anything from this, know you do *not* need a man to take care of you. I don't need Sam, or any man for that matter, to pay my way. I only want his time." And affection, but I would prefer not to talk about that with Scarlett right now. I shake my head before continuing. "Scar, the reporters likely won't go away until Sam and I decide to acknowledge our relationship—not that I know what that is now."

"You looked pretty cozy this morning on the couch."

It felt amazing too. That isn't the point though. His whole life he has been dealing with protecting his privacy. Now I need to worry about mine and Scarlett's.

"We fell asleep watching *The Avengers* probably because we've both seen it before. I'm asking you to simply ignore the reporters. If you need to, please say 'no comment' and go about your business."

"Fine. Is there anything else?"

"When I have more time to talk with Sam or if the attention becomes too much, I may need to take additional precautions."

"Like?" she asks as if at this point I care what her opinion is on the matter. Her statements have made me question how well, or more accurately, how poorly a job I have done raising her on my own.

"If they refuse to leave us alone, we may need to move or get personal security."

"Yes, please. I'll take a hot bodyguard with dark hair and light eyes."

"Scar, this is serious."

"I'm sure you think it is. Either way, if I need a bodyguard, he must be hot as hell."

"I can't with you."

"Savi, if you need personal security in addition to the smoking-hot man who slept on the couch last night, I'm not feeling bad for you."

I agree with her assessment. Sam is beyond gorgeous. His dark hair and eyes are delicious. That doesn't even begin to consider the sculpted, hard muscles I have only barely touched with my fingertips.

"Savi. Earth to Savi."

"Sorry, please do what I ask about the reporters and please don't make it harder by sharing the information with your friends."

"Fine, I have homework to do." She walks away with a snicker. Goodness knows what that means.

Sam: Cara mia, *I'm at Lennox visiting an injured friend. I'll call you when I can.*

Needing a reason to leave, I decide sitting with Sam is as good a one as any. I tell Scarlett I'm leaving and step outside. Walking though the photographers to get to Sam doesn't even cross my mind. I want to support him, comfort him.

Seeing the anguish on his face as he steps into the waiting room is heart-wrenching. It tells me I made the right choice.

He motions to a small alcove off to our right. I follow him there. Setting the cups down, I encircle his waist with my arms. His body is taut and fraught with tension. While the tension doesn't dissipate completely, it lessens some while I hold him in the dim room.

"What are you doing here? You braved the reporters outside your apartment for me?"

"I thought you might want some company. I can leave if you would prefer."

"Yes. No." He draws his fingers through his hair. "I need to process everything. Will you sit with me?"

"Of course."

We sit on the sofa side by side, his leg bouncing on the floor.

I set my hand on his thigh, stilling him. Heat from his skin warms my fingertips. "Do you want to talk about it?"

He opens his mouth to speak but immediately closes it. The look in his eyes tells me somehow this could affect me. "Marisol is my childhood nanny's daughter. She was in a car accident earlier today. She and I have been close since we were kids. Her parents didn't mind that she spent time with my siblings and me. Truthfully, it was mostly me. She and Ramon married about four years ago—"

The doors across from us slam against the frame with a harsh bang.

"This is your fault!" an averaged-sized man yells at Sam, approaching him in anger.

Sam rises from the couch, stepping in front of me. I don't understand why until the man throws a punch, but Sam blocks it. He fends off two more punches before the man steps back.

He mumbles, "Marisol is gone," before crumbling to the floor.

"What about the baby?" Sam asks so softly with a hint of fear in his tone.

"She was born via C-section a little bit ago. They're working on her."

"Mr. Morgan," a nurse calls from the doorway that Ramon exited. The look on his face is hard to discern.

"Savannah, I'll explain everything. Please wait." He leans down and kisses me softly. Anguish and anger roll off him as he follows her back toward…. Toward what? Didn't the man say she died.

"Mr. Santiago, this way please." A male nurse escorts him through a different door.

I lower myself onto the bench, finish my now cold coffee, and flip through an outdated *InStyle* magazine from the side table. Three issues later, the doors open and Sam walks through, visibly shaken.

SAMSON

I'm an intelligent man, but what happens now? I have so many questions. Why is Ramon out here if the baby is still being worked on? Does he know for sure she's mine? In the next few days, I'll know whether I'm a father. Shelley leads me back to an exam room to take a DNA test. Never did I ever think I would be in this position. Thankfully, Marisol requested the test before her surgery. They won't let me see Marisol, but I'm able to peek at her little girl through the nursery window. She's perfect, wrapped in a pink blanket, wearing a hat with a huge bow. Even though she was born a little early, the only thing she needs right now is supplemental oxygen. Shelley, even though she shouldn't have, indicates that she should be out of the woods in the next day or so. *Our* little girl. Marisol is gone. *My* little girl. All these thoughts and emotions in my head and in my heart, while knowing I need to tell Savannah. Then I need to have a serious conversation with my mother and completely cut her out of my life. She'll never see me, this gorgeous bundle of joy, or woman, or future child I'm lucky enough to have in my life.

I'm done.

Simply *done.*

Margaux Morgan has gone too far with Billie, Cash, and now me. It begs the question, what has she done or what will she do to Auggie.

As gently as possible, Shelley indicates I need to leave. I'm sure she broke some rules allowing me to stand here.

"Thank you, Shelley."

"You're welcome, Mr. Morgan."

"Please, it's Sam."

"I hope things work out for her. She's lovely. I'm sorry you found out she may be yours today of all days. May your friend rest in peace."

"Thank you, Shelley. Marisol was a wonderful friend. I would have been involved from the beginning if I knew."

She nods and points me to the exit. As I step through the doors, Savannah's gorgeous smile greets me. I'm about to find out how much loss I can endure in one day. While Savannah and I have only technically been on two dates, we've been coworkers and friends for almost a year.

As I approach her, she rises from the chair, her arms circling around me tightly.

"Will you come to my place with me? I need to finish explaining and share something with you." Even though I wasn't supposed too, I took a photo of the most beautiful baby girl I've ever seen, one who may be my daughter.

"Sure, but can we order some food once we get there?"

I nod, intertwine my fingers with hers, and step into the elevator. "How did you get here?"

"Uber."

The ride to my building is largely quiet aside from ordering food. Savannah's fingers stay twisted with mine.

"Good afternoon, Mr. Morgan," Jimmy says as I step through the glass doors.

"Jimmy, good afternoon. This is Savannah Clemons. She's already on the list. I would like to add her sister, Scarlett Clemons. Both are welcome here even if I'm not."

"Absolutely, sir."

"Also, some food will be delivered in the next thirty minutes or so. Please send it up."

"Pleasure to meet you, Miss Clemons. I'll send the food when it arrives."

Sliding my arm around her slender waist, I lead Savannah onto the elevator. As the doors open, I step out into my foyer area and remove my shoes, lining them against the wall. Savannah sets hers next to mine and her purse on the small chest near the door.

"Would you like a drink?" I move into the living room, offering her a seat on the couch.

"Whatever you have is fine."

"Scotch?"

"Sure." I'm even more intrigued by her after that answer. Handing her a glass, I take a seat facing her on the ottoman, my legs bent around hers. "Please finish the story."

After a healthy sip, I place the glass on the floor before setting my hands on her outer thighs, and I continue where I left off in the waiting room.

"Marisol and I have been friends since childhood. We were more than that until about five years ago. Dating, not really. I wanted nothing to do with the scrutiny of dating, especially after Meghan's death. Marisol was there for me, like I was for her. As crass as it sounds, especially today, we were friends with benefits. She married Ramon about four years ago. Twice over the course of the last three years, Marisol asked for a separation. I'm not proud to admit that we were together both times she separated from him. Technically, she was still married. The last time was about eight months ago. Her daughter, that was born today, could be mine."

"Oh, Sam. You didn't know she could be yours until today?"

"No, but my mother did, and she… I can't even fathom that portion of this. When I arrived at the hospital, I spoke with Marisol briefly. She admitted that my mother knew about the pregnancy and urged her to agree the baby was Ramon's. How my mother knew or why she asked Marisol to hide it is beyond me. I thought Marisol and I were friends. That she may have kept my daughter from me is unforgivable."

"What happens now?"

As the question leaves her lips, Jimmy announces he's on his way up with our dinner. Take-out bags in hand, I set them on the granite island.

"Where are the dishes?" she asks from beside me.

"Plates are above the stove to the right, glasses to the left. Silverware is in the drawer right in front of you."

I pull out the food, the amazing aroma filling the kitchen. She sets the plates and silverware out before moving around me to sit. Settling beside her, we start to eat. I ordered Italian from a family-owned hole-in-the-wall around the corner. Mama and Papa Romano never fail. Their copious amounts of savory food are always fantastic.

Halfway through my plate, I muster the courage to answer her. "Just before she went into surgery for internal bleeding, Marisol signed a request for paternity testing for her daughter. When the nurse called me in, I took a test. Now, I wait for results. Aside from that, I don't know what to do for her, if anything. I plan to deal with my mother tomorrow." I look over at her, her eyes searching my face, looking for a crack, a break, a tell—I don't know. "How is it you're still here? Why haven't you run from me?"

"I believe you. I have no right to be upset about your relationship with Marisol. It was before my time. I have no right to judge you, same as I know, without question, you wouldn't judge me if the situation were reversed."

I close the distance between us, turn her face toward mine, and kiss her soft, pink lips.

"Thank you, *cara mia*. However, I can't ask you to be with me if she's mine. I won't put you in the same position that your father did."

"What are you saying? You don't want to date me anymore?"

"I don't know. The last thing I want is to hurt you, but I need to sort this out on my own."

She sets her fork down and swivels on the stool to face me. "Do you want to date me?"

More than anything. I haven't felt this deeply since Meghan. Even those feelings don't reach what I'm starting to feel for Savannah. "Yes, but I don't want you to feel like I'm using you."

"What kind of woman would walk away when things get tough?"

I'm pushing her away, that's different. Isn't it? "I'm asking for some space to figure this out."

"Why bother inviting me here and telling me about Marisol and her daughter if you were going to ask me to step away?"

"I don't know. Shocked is the understatement of the day. At least shocked as it pertains to Marisol and my potential fatherhood. Margaux, well, this doesn't even make my meter move. It's absolutely something she would do to protect what she thinks the Morgan name embodies."

"I'm not this woman, Sam. I don't run away when things get hard. I stick them out and put in the work. I'm offering you… me. I realize we just started dating, and this hurdle isn't conducive to learning about one another in the best circumstances, but I'm willing to try. I'm offering to help you. I want to be with you." A heavy sigh falls from her lips, a choice made. "You know how to reach me. Good night, Sam." She tugs on her booties, grabs her purse, and waits for the elevator car without a look back.

What have I done?

SAVANNAH

Well, that was short-lived.

First thing the next morning, I dress for work and follow my old routine. Coffee in hand, I empty my inbox and sort through the policies that need to be addressed. Most are simply waiting for Sam's signature. As the clock ticks, Sam doesn't appear. Near eleven, I send him an email.

Moments later a response indicates that he won't be coming in today. *Fine, you can't come here, I'll come to you. Things still need to be done.* Near four, I enter the grand foyer of his building.

"Miss Clemons. It's a pleasure to see you today."

"You as well, Jimmy. Is he home?" I wonder if he's even allowed to tell me that.

"No, he isn't."

"That's fine. I'll leave this and come back to pick it up tomorrow." I ride to Sam's and set the stack of files on the island with a note. Sighing deeply, I push the button to return downstairs for my trek home.

As far as early dates go, ours were spectacular. Once I got past my initial nervousness, everything went well. Now I have no idea what's going on. Either way, I can't sign certain things for him, so if I must bring them here, I will.

"Have a good night, Jimmy."

"You too, Miss Clemons."

The subway passengers were fewer today than normal on my ride home. After dropping my tote by the door, I pluck off my heels and sink into the couch. Unfortunately, vivid memories of Sam's big hands caressing my skin invade my thoughts. Shaking my head, I rise and change into more comfortable clothes.

While I start dinner, Scarlett arrives home. As much as I share with her, this is something I can't. For now, I need to suffer in silence, at least about his potential fatherhood.

"Hi, Savi," she says with a chipper tone.

"Hey. How was class?"

"Fine. How was work?"

"Boring. It was just me today. I dropped a stack of files off at Sam's before I came home."

"Is his place amazing?"

"Scar, what is it with you and Sam's wealth? Who cares if he has money? We have everything we need."

"I note you didn't answer my question. True, we don't need anything, but I'm sure there are plenty of things you want that he could afford."

"Nothing I want from Sam will cost him anything." I want his time and affection. I realize that at any time in the next few days, his available time may decrease exponentially, but either way that's all I want from him.

"Does he know that?"

"I believe that he does. What is this truly about?"

"I'm moving in with Liza and El."

I try to mask my hurt and pride. "You have been considering this for a while? What about rent?" She's my sister. If she wants to move out, that is up to her. Honestly, I'm surprised she hasn't moved sooner.

"Yes, I have been saving since last year. I have enough to cover six months' rent in my account. Plus the split is three ways. Liza and El are a couple, so they have a spare room."

"Scar, I'm proud of you. When do you plan on moving?"

"Over the long weekend."

"Please make sure you know what the lease says and follow all the rules. It shouldn't be too difficult for you; you do fine here."

"Wow, Savi. I'm shocked. I honestly thought you would lose your mind."

"Scar, you've embraced college life. I understand that you want to go out and experience it fully without your sister/mother figure as a roommate. The only thing that concerns me is your grades. As long as you keep them up, you'll be fine."

"Thanks, Savi. Love you." She throws her arms around me and hugs me tightly.

The moment she releases me, I want to call one person. I can't. I can, but I'm not sure how a message would be received. He asked for space, so I need to give it to him. Even if I don't want to. Even if I know for sure I can help and I'm willing to do so.

"Let me know if you need any help. You may need me to rent a moving truck."

"Thank you so much!" She scales the staircase, three steps at a time.

I hear a shriek as her door closes. I decide on breakfast for dinner. Nothing soothes the soul like greasy spoon food in your own home. Diner food is equally as awesome, but I don't want to drive now.

I curl up in my chair with my plate holding a ham and cheese omelet, fried potatoes, and four strips of crispy bacon from my toaster oven. I would add sourdough toast, but we don't have any. I enjoy my meal and consider next week at this time. This will be how it always is. Me alone.

My phone chimes with a few notifications while I eat, but I ignore them. Nothing of importance for work comes through in the evening. After cleaning my dish, I check my phone.

Sam: Thank you for bringing the files. You don't need to do that for me.

Me: It's no problem. I'll pick them up in the morning.

Sam: I'll sign them tonight and leave them on the island.

Me: Thank you.

Sam: If I come in, it'll be in the afternoon. Thank you again.

Me: You're welcome.

Resigned that my chance with Sam rests completely in his hands, I grab a book and read for a bit before turning in.

SAMSON

Since the moment Marisol shared that Margaux knew about my potential fatherhood, my mind has been spinning like a top without the possibility of slowing. True, this isn't low for her. I don't believe there's anything she won't do in the eyes of protecting the family legacy.

Last night, I reviewed the files Savannah left for me. The entire time my mind drifted to her. Asking for space is a double-edged sword. I care about Savannah, but I won't put her in the same position her father did. If that gorgeous baby is mine, I'll have to wait to build something with Savannah. If I'm lucky, there won't be another guy in her life when I figure all of this out.

After setting the files on the island with a note thanking her, I ride down to the gym in my building. A grueling workout later, I return home and find the files gone. Relief and anguish flow through me. Relief that she was here but also anguish that I missed seeing her. *Isn't that what you asked for?*

The ride to my parents' is longer than necessary since the roadway is packed with cars, buses, and trucks.

Generally, I call ahead. Not this time.

"Good morning, Samson," Henry, my parents' butler greets me cheerfully. The portly man, who has been working for my family as long as I can remember, ushers me inside.

"Morning, Henry. I apologize for arriving unannounced, but I need to speak with my parents urgently."

"Of course. I'll tell them you're here. Please use the solarium. It's already set for morning coffee."

"Thank you, Henry."

He walks away to inform my parents I'm here. Stepping into the solarium, I find Salma completing the buffet.

"Samson, it's lovely to see you."

Leaning down, I hug her. "You as well."

"I take it you aren't here for a friendly visit."

"No, I'm not."

"Be strong, Sam. Maria-Luisa, Henry, and I taught all of you to stand on your own despite her."

"Thank you. Her actions this time are unfathomable."

As I finish my sentence, my mother breezes into the room perfectly dressed in a tailored suit. Salma nods and politely walks away. At the threshold, she meets my gaze, offering a show of support. The staff acted more like parents than our actual parents ever did.

"Samson, lovely to see you this morning. Your father will be down momentarily."

My blood is boiling. Refraining from yelling at my mother is increasingly harder each moment we're in the same room. Henry arrives with the morning paper, which takes my anger down a notch or two. Shortly thereafter my father joins us.

"Son, to what do we owe the pleasure of your visit?"

"Good morning. I'm here to talk about Marisol."

"The poor girl. We heard she died over the weekend." Margaux feigns sympathy for Marisol's family.

I'm seething. Margaux never cared about Marisol. She let her hang out so that Maria-Luisa could care for my siblings and me longer.

"How dare you?"

Both of their heads snap in my direction.

"How could you, Mother?"

"I have no idea what you're referring to, Samson. I don't appreciate your tone. Show a little respect."

"No, Mother. I will not. You threatened her. You bought her silence. How could you insert yourself into my life like that? I thought your treatment of Billie and Noelle was bad enough, but this? This is a whole different level of evil manipulation."

"Margaux, what is he talking about?" My father's voice is stern.

At my mother's inherent disregard for my siblings and me having lives of our own, my father has become increasingly disenchanted with her. I recognize they have a marriage of convenience, a business deal, but that doesn't mean he endorses her behavior.

"About ten months ago, I learned that Samson and Marisol were spending *time* together. I approached her asking her to stay away. Reluctantly, she agreed."

"Keep going." Anger seeps deeper into my tone.

"There's more?" my father inquires, a hint of disgust lacing his voice.

"About two months later, Maria-Luisa came to visit, announcing that Marisol was pregnant. We had tea while she gushed about how happy she was and that Marisol was absolutely ecstatic."

"Margaux, please tell me you didn't."

Margaux clams up and refuses to finish the story.

"As Mother seems to be rendered mute, she approached Marisol again, strong arming her into saying her daughter was Ramon's without determining the actual truth. I saw Marisol right before she died. She admitted that her baby could be mine. I'm awaiting results of a paternity test."

"Margaux, is all of that true?"

"Warren, I…." She turns and gazes out the window. "I was trying to protect him from that opportunist. Clearly, she only wanted money since she took it from me. Samson, please understand, she wasn't good enough for you. Neither is that new woman you've been seeing."

"You don't even know her." I was only beginning to know her. The traits I do know are exceptional. Despite my stupidity, she keeps my business on task.

"Being cut off by Cassius and Wilhelmina wasn't enough for you? How dare you risk our other children, Margaux?" Anger and disdain drip from my father's voice.

"Mother, don't come near me, my home, my office, or Savannah. I never want to see you again."

Not that Savannah is in my life outside of work, but either way, the warning seems prudent. Although, I don't think Margaux hears what we say. She simply does what she wants to protect the Morgan name. Often she does more damage than damage control. Rarely, if ever, does she get the desired outcome. Turning on my heel, I attempt to leave.

"Son, can I have a word?" My father escorts me into his private office, locking us in.

"I didn't know she sought out Marisol or the money." His reaction leads me to believe him. He didn't know. "When will you know the results?"

"Later today or tomorrow. Father, I don't want to see her ever again. I won't step foot in this house or attend any event if she'll be present."

"I understand. I would appreciate a call when you know."

My father has changed over the course of my life. He was part of attempting to get Billie to marry a competitor's son. However, when Billie thwarted the arrangement with Peter, he softened quite a bit. Warren had no idea Margaux was fooling Noelle. Since then he has distanced himself from her and her schemes. Hopefully this saves Auggie from dealing with Margaux's plans and choices she would prefer him to make.

"How does Savannah feel about all of this?"

"I don't know. I pushed her away." The tightening in my chest reminds me I likely made the wrong choice, at least wrong for me.

"Son, she has been working for you for almost a year. I saw you with her at the gala; you have real feelings for her, more so than Meghan. You're in a difficult position, but don't let your mother mess up something else in your life because of your need to put everyone before yourself. You deserve happiness too."

"Thank you. I'll keep you informed." I show myself out and decide to walk around Central Park before heading into work. Margaux's reaction was expected. I never thought she would own up to her role in this scheme. Aside from failing to share about the baby, Marisol and I have always been honest with one another. She offered a shoulder and other comfort when I needed it. I did the same for her. I resolve to wait until the results before sharing with anyone else.

While I should go to the office, I head home instead. Even though I shouldn't rely on her, Savannah will bring the files to me tonight.

SAVANNAH

Near three I finish gathering the files for Sam. Like yesterday, Jimmy greets me cheerfully before I ride upstairs.

As the doors open, Sam is standing near the island downing a bottle of water. I have seen Sam dressed in a tux, a suit, and business casual. Never have I seen him dressed comfortably. Tonight he's in low-slung sweatpants and a graphic tee with Dave Matthews Band emblazoned on the front.

"Hi, Savannah."

"Hi. I'm sorry. I don't mean to disturb you. I wanted to drop these off for your review. I'll get going." I turn and push the down button immediately.

"Don't go."

Confused is an understatement. He asks for space, yet less than two days later, he asks me to stay.

"Do you have somewhere to be?"

I turn to face him. He scrubs his hand down his face.

"No, I was going home."

"I miss you. I miss seeing you every day. I know that almost two days doesn't seem long. However, for the last year, I have spent entire weeks with you at the office unless I was travelling. Add in the fact that our dates were amazing, and I'm twisted up in knots."

You forgot your potential fatherhood, your status in this city, and the fact that I'm a normal girl who happens to work for you. "I don't know what to say except I miss seeing you too." A glimmer of hope pierces the armor I surrounded my heart with while riding the elevator. "If you genuinely want me, then you know where I stand. However, I can't go back and forth between dating you and working for you to simply working for you."

"I do." His gaze burns into mine. Uncertainty reflects in his dark eyes—eyes that I could lose myself in as easily as I can in his arms.

"But…."

It took him months to ask me on a date, now his life is upside down.

"I won't be able to give you all the attention you deserve, especially if she's my daughter."

"I understand. Please know that I wouldn't expect to be ahead of your child. I'm sure you're petrified with the unknowns right now. I'll handle the office and bring the files to you as long as necessary. Have a nice evening."

The elevator doors open, and I step inside, dropping my head. He doesn't stop me—not that I'm sure I would have stayed if he tried to.

As the doors open in the lobby, flashbulbs go off. Jimmy hops into the elevator with me and closes the door.

"Miss Clemons, I was about to call up to Mr. Morgan. We have a situation."

When the doors open upstairs, I see Sam, glass of scotch in hand, staring out the window, his features drawn and weary.

"Savannah. Jimmy. What's going on?"

"Photographers are camped out at the entrance, Mr. Morgan. Most are inquiring about Miss Clemons and a baby," Jimmy answers quickly.

"Damn him!"

I set my hand on his forearm, not only for me, but for him. The familiar tingles up my arm have me removing it much sooner than I would like. He looks over at me, his expression unreadable.

"Thank you, Jimmy. Savannah and I will discuss our options and let you know. If you can ask them to leave, we would appreciate it."

"Absolutely, Mr. Morgan. Please let me know if you require any assistance."

Once the doors close, he pulls me into his arms. One hand around my back while the other is at the base of my neck. At first I'm tense because I don't know what this means, if anything. My resolve crumbles within moments. I sigh softly, memorizing him again. Taking in the smell of his cologne and the feel of his muscular back under my fingers. His shirt is threadbare; he might as well be shirtless. This feels amazing. I rein in my thoughts and slowly step back.

"I shouldn't have…. This is my fault. Let me figure out how they know who you are and how to get you home."

"Sam, there's no need to be sorry. I knew this was a possibility simply working for you."

"Please make yourself comfortable, then join me in my office."

"Sure. But, Sam, where is your office?"

"I'm sorry. My office is the first room on the right off the kitchen."

I nod, unsure what to say. I step out of my heels, line them by the door, pull my phone out of my purse, and check my messages.

Scarlett: I have a late shift. I'm going to stay at my new place tonight.

Me: Okay. LY

I pour a glass of white wine. Along with the scotch, Sam's wine selection is impressive as well. After a few healthy gulps to settle my nerves, I refill my glass and pad to his office.

It's exactly as I would picture it. Light, neutral colors are splashed on the wall. Built-ins surround a massive granite fireplace. There's a set of chairs situated around the hearth. His desk faces the large windows.

"I found the story that led them here." He motions for me to join him to see the screen. *Sam Morgan, The Nanny, and a Baby.*

Being this close to him isn't good for me. I crave his lips on mine again. The wine surely isn't helping.

"It appears Ramon gave an exclusive to the paper saying that the baby is mine. I don't have the results yet. Either there has been a violation of my privacy or he's lying. I would lean toward the lying, considering how much someone would pay for dirt on me."

"What about me? I didn't talk to any reporters. Is it because I came to the hospital?"

"I know you didn't. I trust you, Savannah. It might be because you came to the hospital. I'm not upset about that. I'm concerned for your safety and Scarlett's."

"Don't worry about Scar. She isn't coming home tonight. Well, it isn't really her home anymore."

He turns his eyes to mine, setting his hand atop mine. "What do you mean?"

"She's moving out this weekend."

"When did she tell you?"

"Last night."

"Why didn't you call me?"

I open my mouth to respond and immediately close my mouth. I wanted to. So much, but I couldn't do it. "I didn't want to impose on your space. Yet, here I am."

"You did nothing wrong bringing the files here. This isn't on you. That gauntlet of reporters is on me and likely Ramon Santiago."

My stomach growls loudly. I giggle.

"Why don't I cook something for us? Maybe you can outwait the reporters."

"If it isn't too much trouble, I would like that."

"No trouble at all." He rises from his chair, pressing his lips to my temple. I sigh inwardly and follow him to the kitchen. Despite my offers to help, Sam prepares the meal himself. It smells delicious.

SAMSON

Plating the chicken with risotto, I set a dish in front of Savannah and the empty spot next to her.

"Thank you for staying for dinner. I'll escort you home after we eat through the garage, to make sure they aren't camped at your place as well." I dig into my meal and savor a few bites.

"That isn't necessary. No reason for you to ride with me. I'll be fine."

"It's not optional. If you want to go home, I'll escort you. This is about me. It's partially why I waited so long to hire someone. Despite your qualifications, I should have hired someone named Joe who isn't gorgeous like you." My words come out a bit more forceful than I would have liked.

"I—"

"Mr. Morgan. You have a few urgent visitors," Jimmy's voice echoes through the intercom. His tone indicates asking for more information isn't necessary.

"Send them up."

When the doors open, three people step into my home.

"Mr. Morgan, I'm Officer Peters. This is my partner, Officer Jetty, and this is Pamela Torcher; she's a social worker with the Office of Children and Family. Could you please provide photo identification? Who are you?"

"Savannah Clemons. Mr. Morgan is my boss. I came to bring some files, and the mob of photographers delayed my departure."

"I need identification from you as well." Both Savannah and I show our licenses to Officer Peters. After a cursory look between the cards and our faces, he continues. "Mr. Morgan, we're here to inform you that Baby Jane Doe at Lennox Hill Hospital born of the late Marisol Luisa Santiago is your daughter. Ms. Torcher is here to explain the process for custody."

I open my mouth to speak, but the words get caught in my throat. After two more failed attempts, finally I reply, "Thank you. Could you give us a moment?"

"Of course, Mr. Morgan," Officer Jetty replies.

"Savannah, will you come with me?" I barely resist the urge to take her hand.

Back in my office, I'm shaking like a leaf. Tears prick my eyes, and I'm markedly overwhelmed. Her hand cups the side of my face. I turn my head, kissing the inside of her palm.

"Breathe, Sam. You can do this."

I pull Savannah into my arms to draw comfort and strength from her. Without trying, she calms me.

"Do you want me to stay here?"

"You can't leave with those reporters downstairs." My quick reply gets me a raised eyebrow.

"I meant in your office. Would you prefer to talk to Ms. Torcher privately?"

"Honestly?"

"Absolutely."

"I would like you to be there with me."

Slowly I release her from my hold and return to the living room. After I offer drinks, Ms. Torcher explains what I need to do, how the process works under these circumstances, and when I can see my daughter. Savannah sits beside me listening intently. We're sitting side by side on the couch. Her body pressed against me helps and hinders my focus. She calms my mind but drives my heart and body to distraction.

A little under an hour later, I'm pacing the floor of my home after my guests leave. Savannah is calmly writing a list, probably of immediate needs for my daughter. My head is spinning. *I'm a father*. I'm responsible for that beautiful, little, pink bundle of joy. There are so many things to do. Most people have months and months to prepare for this, I get one day, two tops.

"Sam."

I hear my name in the recesses of my brain.

"Sam."

Again, but I don't reply. As I pass, Savannah sets her hand on my forearm and calls me again. I stop walking and look down at her. The heat from her touch shoots over my entire body. It's the last thing I should be considering right now. Yet I crave her. Once she has my attention, her soft skin slides away. "How can I help?"

"Believe it or not, you are simply by being here. I need to make a list of things she'll need. Maybe there is a list on Google that I can use as a starting point. I need to prepare a statement. Call my family. Do you mind bringing files here as necessary? I know it isn't part of your job, but…."

Savannah is furiously typing on her phone. "No, of course not. Anything else?"

"She needs a name."

"Have you ever given any thought to your future daughter's name?"

"No, I was waiting for the right woman." I found the woman, but now my life is in chaos and I can't devote enough to her to grow our relationship. Savannah doesn't react to my statement.

"I'm sure there are lists upon lists on the internet or even books to purchase," she softly suggests. "Why don't you go to your office and get started on this list? I emailed it to your personal address. I'll make some coffee and join you. Maybe after a bit more time, the crowd will have dispersed enough for me to go home."

I nod and move slowly to my office, opening our group chat.

Me: I need to talk to all of you and your better halves asap.

Cash: We're here.

Billie: Us too.

Auggie: Give me five. I'll call Caro.

I open a video chat room and invite my siblings and Caro, simply because she and Auggie don't live together, at least not yet. Soon my siblings and their better halves start gracing my screen. Once they all join, I take a deep breath and share my amazing and scary-as-hell news. At some point during the conversation, Savannah sets a cup of coffee near me and leaves my office. That spurs an entirely different conversation that I push off. After many well wishes, offers of help, and shelter away from New York, I sign off with my siblings and reach out to my father. I share the same news with him and my game plan, at least for a press statement. I ask that he attempt to stifle Margaux at least until my statement is made and my daughter is safely home. The rest… I'm still swimming in details. After my call and a scan of the email Savannah sent, I search for her.

Not only did she make me coffee, but she cleared and washed the dinner dishes and pans. She's staring out the window toward the skyline. While my instinct is to wrap my arms around her from behind and press my lips to the curve of her neck, I refrain. As I approach, she looks over her shoulder at me.

"Thank you. You didn't have to clean up."

"You're welcome. It's no problem. You cooked. I washed. What did you tackle first?"

"I called my siblings and my father. I'll work on a press statement for release after I bring you home and order some necessities."

"Honestly, I don't need you to come with me."

"I insist." Eventually, she will realize that arguing with me about her safety isn't going to get her anywhere.

"Fine, I give."

We ride straight down to the garage where we slide into a waiting car. The ride to her apartment is quiet. When we arrive, there are no reporters milling around. I ask the driver to wait while I walk Savannah to her door.

"Good night, Sam."

"Good night, Savannah."

She steps inside and closes the door. I hear her exhale sharply from behind the closed steel. I hope when I'm settled into my new role as a father, she'll still want me. Want us.

I direct Eddie to my next stop, Lennox Hill. My palms are sweating, my head is spinning, and I feel wholly inadequate as Shelley helps me gown up to meet my daughter.

"Congratulations! You're welcome as often as you like. She's doing well. Her formula intake is sufficient, two ounces every two hours. Her oxygen levels are stable. The doctors will try to ween her off the supplemental oxygen starting in a few hours. If her numbers hold steady, you can take her home tomorrow."

"Thank you."

"Have you decided on a name?"

"Still working on it. I've only known for a few hours. At a minimum, could you change that to Baby Girl Morgan for now?" I point to the card on her bassinet.

"Of course."

I sit in a comfortable rocking chair as another nurse, Kyla, instructs me how to hold my daughter. The successful businessman in me wants to rebel, but I'm not equipped for this. I take her guidance and words to heart.

"Everything you feel right now is completely normal—the fear, anxiety, lack of knowledge," she assures me after setting my daughter in my arms.

She's so tiny. Although from the information Savannah sent, she's appropriate size for a baby born at thirty-six weeks. My heart feels like it's going to burst. Yet I wish Savannah were here too. No matter how hard I try, I can't ignore my feelings for her. For the next hour, I chat with, cuddle, and study my daughter, imagining how I got to this point. How inexplicably I feel like she was meant to be.

SAVANNAH

Navigating my relationship with Sam just got a bit harder. I'm not upset about Marisol or their daughter at all. I have no right to be, but resisting my urge to kiss him again is more difficult that I imagined it would be.

Thankfully, there were no reporters camped out at my apartment. Unfortunately, I'm here alone counting the divots in my ceiling because I can't sleep. Tossing and turning, I finally give up and flick on the television. Nothing good graces the screen in the wee hours of the morning.

Hours later, I pull myself up, dress for a run, and take off out my front door. A run usually clears my head a bit. Turning the corner to my apartment after a sunrise run, there are photographers leaning against the stoop of my building.

"Miss Clemons, care to comment on your relationship with Sam Morgan?"

"Are you the nanny?"

"Is the baby his?"

"Who is the baby's mother?"

After a slew a questions as I approach, I stop on the stoop and address the reporters. I understand they simply have jobs to do.

"At no time will I answer any of your questions, now or in the future, except to say no comment." I enter the foyer and hurry to my apartment to dress for work. Hopefully if I vary my schedule, I can avoid their daily inquiries.

As my Uber approaches Sam's building, I note the swath of reporters still camped out there. Unfortunately, I need to get the files from last night. More questions hurl in my direction as I step inside. I ignore them, walking directly inside.

"Good morning, Jimmy."

"Miss Clemons. Good morning. He returned a while ago. He's likely in the gym."

"Thank you." I ride up to Sam's. Setting my bag on the island, I see a stack of files. Opening the top one, I note it isn't signed yet. No problem. I'll come back later with more and collect these. Regathering my bag, I push the down button on the elevator.

When the doors open, Sam is stepping into his home. *Holy hell!* Sweat is dripping down his sculpted chest and abs. His form could be used as model for others. Broad shoulders, lean waist…. My mouth is watering as heat rushes southward. I squeeze my inner thighs to tamp the sensations building in my core. Thankfully, I'm wearing a skirt and he doesn't notice. I resist the urge to fan myself by the slimmest of margins.

"Hi. You're here already? Did you sleep at all?"

"No, actually. I didn't sleep well. Did you sleep?"

"I didn't sleep. I went to the hospital after I left your apartment. I couldn't help myself. She and I have come to an understanding."

Why does that feel like a gut punch? I have no right to think I deserve an invitation to meet his daughter. We're colleagues who shared two amazing dates and a few toe-curling, knee-weakening kisses, that's all. *Wrap your head around that, Savi.*

"What kind of understanding did you come to with a newborn?"

"She agreed to be an easy baby so I can pull off being her dad."

I smile. "I hope you got that in writing. Either way, I have no doubt you will pull it off with grace."

"Thank you, Savannah." He grabs a water. The movement of this throat catches my attention. Never found that attractive before.

"I was on my way into the office. I'll come back later for those. I understand you're busy."

"Thank you, Savannah. I appreciate your help."

The office is literally four blocks away; it's not a major inconvenience.

"It's no problem. I'll see you later." I hurry around him, recalling the elevator car. As the doors close, I lean against the wall of the car and exhale sharply. As I exit, no questions come my way.

Waking my computer at the office, my brain flashes back to shirtless, sweaty Sam. Dear God, his chest is flawless. While his body is impeccable, it's his dimples that hooked me. I push the memory away. He has made his position clear. He doesn't want to date me right now. His focus is his daughter.

"Morgan Insurance. How may I direct your call?" I answer as the phone drags me out of my thoughts.

"Good morning, this is Billie Morgan. Is Sam available?"

"Hi, Billie. It's Savannah. He's working from home today. Would you like me to give him a message?"

"Hi, Savannah. How are you?"

"I'm well and you?"

"Peter and I are amid wedding planning. It's coming up fast. Will you be accompanying Sam?"

"He hasn't asked me to accompany him, Billie." I would love to attend, but with his self-imposed dating moratorium, I highly doubt that's a possibility anymore.

"I thought you two were dating. That was you at the jazz club in the photo, right?"

As did I. That night was simply magical.

"Yes, it was me. He asked for space when he learned about Marisol and her baby."

"I see. My brother is back to putting everyone before himself without regard for his personal happiness."

"It would appear so. It's okay, Billie. I imagine he's in an awkward position right now. I was upfront with him. If he wants me, he knows where to find me."

"I'm sorry, Savannah. I thought he finally saw what was right in front of him. You're smart, funny, don't take his crap, and you're gorgeous."

I don't know about all that, but I'll take the compliment from his sister either way. "Thank you, Billie. I'll let him know you called."

"No need. I'll call his cell. Bye, Savannah."

I hope she doesn't make this worse. Sam needs to realize he wants me even though he's a father now. He doesn't realize it yet, but he'll need some help if his daughter breaks the deal brokered in the hospital nursery incredibly early this morning, despite his belief it's a binding agreement.

I spend the next few hours handling my work and Sam's. I sit in his chair and wake his computer to check for the online inquiries. Immediately I forward them to my desk and get them started.

A few hours later, I bundle today's files and stroll back to Sam's. A different group of paparazzi are there to greet me. I ignore them too. I'm floored by the condition of Sam's home when I step off the elevator. The entrance and living room are filled with boxes, packages, and shopping bags. Did he buy half of Manhattan? I set down my stuff, shuck my shoes, and search for Sam.

If I thought the packages were a shot to my heart, Sam shirtless on a fluffy white area rug, staring at what appears to be instructions surrounded by the parts of a crib. For all that is holy, hot, single dad-to-be doesn't begin to cover it.

SAMSON

In less than a day, I'll be solely responsible for a tiny human. After Savannah left this morning, I ordered everything my daughter could possibly need. Certainly I have purchased way too much, but I would rather have it and not use it than need it and not have it. After a whirlwind of shopping, I went to the hospital to spend time with her. She's extraordinary. She's a fighter.

After returning, I haul the stuff into the living room I purchased to decorate her nursery and fill her closet. Well, I have all the pieces scattered around my home. I have been working on assembling this crib for the last hour, and I haven't made much progress. I hear my door open and know that she's here. *Savannah*. I can't believe it's already the end of the day. I don't have much time to finish this.

To protect my privacy and my daughter, Ms. Torcher agreed to meet with me extremely late this evening to transfer custody to me. I need to finish this and clean up.

"Hi. Thank you for coming back."

"Of course. Would you prefer help with that or something to eat?"

"I need to get this done before I have to go to the hospital."

"No problem. I'm pretty handy." Even after working all day in the office, she looks beautiful. "Do you have shorts I can use? Building a crib in this skirt isn't going to work."

She's absolutely right. The fitted pencil skirt hugs her hips perfectly. My attraction to her has never been an issue. I'm also sure she doesn't care about my wealth. She's secure in who she is and doesn't need me to fix anything for her. The fact that she takes care of herself, Scarlett, and her tuition is sexy as hell. I can't allow her to feel less important than she is to me. Yet pushing her away isn't the right answer either.

"Sure, I'll be right back." I rise from the floor, hoping to discreetly mask her effect on me. That small smile and lip pulled between her teeth tells me I failed miserably. I can conjure up thoughts to decrease my arousal, but it won't matter. The moment she and I are in the same room again, my efforts will be a waste.

When I return to my daughter's nursery, I find Savannah jacketless, reorganizing the pieces on the floor and sorting the hardware. Like I said, painfully aroused yet again. *Damn she's gorgeous!*

"Here you go," I say, reaching the shorts in her direction purposefully in front of me. Her hand grazes mine as she takes the shorts. The warmth of her touch is too much. Grabbing her wrist, I draw her against me. She inhales sharply, unsure of what I will do next. Like every time before, her flush against me is perfection. Looking down into her eyes, I see it. Her feelings screaming at me. Impossible to miss. I'm sure mine are as well. I want her. "*Cara mia.*"

"Samson." My name falling from her lips makes my heart pound harder.

"I want you." That is an understatement of epic proportions.

"I want you, but you don't believe you can handle me and your daughter."

"You deserve all of me. I can't give it to you while embarking on fatherhood alone. You deserve romantic dates, flowers, and most importantly, my undivided attention."

"Don't do it alone. I understand that you feel like it would be using me, I don't. She's part of you. It won't be easy to do both, I know it won't, but that doesn't diminish my feelings for you. I want to see what we could have together."

Before I can answer, Jimmy calls up from the lobby.

"Yes, Jimmy. Ms. Torcher is here. She says it's urgent."

"Thank you, please send her up." I snatch my shirt from the floor and tug it over my head. Concern rockets through me. Savannah is close behind me, pulling her jacket back on.

As the door opens, my eyes pin to the tiny pink bundle in the carrier. We agreed to meet later.

"Mr. Morgan, I apologize for the departure from our plans. However hospital policy states that babies leave the nursery once cleared to do so." Pamela sets my daughter on the island and begins to remove the harness.

"May I?"

"Of course."

With shaky hands, I unclasp the buckles, lift her, and tuck her against me. Savannah ushers a bit closer, her fingers grazing mine in a show of support. I glance down at her and nod tightly.

"There are two forms to fill out." Ms. Torcher sets them on the island and offers me a pen. I shift my daughter to the other side to take the pen in my left hand.

"This is the discharge paperwork from the hospital." She points at the bottom, and I scribble my name. "This is her birth certificate. Please review it, fill out her name, and then sign."

I have been considering options since I took the test. I fill in her name, Emerson Sarah Morgan, verify the remaining information, and sign at the bottom.

"Congratulations, Mr. Morgan."

"Thank you. When did she eat last?"

"Here is her chart from today. Shelley sent along well wishes and added her number in case you have questions. Kyla as well."

"Thank you for your assistance and discretion. I appreciate it."

"You're welcome. Have a nice evening."

Once the door closes, I lean against the island holding Emerson. The fear is less, but not by much. Savannah is standing beside me, her eyes cast down at my daughter.

"Sam, she's gorgeous."

She is. I have spent my time with her examining her perfect fingers and toes. I'm amazed.

"Thank you."

"What do you want to do now? I gather this wasn't the plan."

"No, I want to call my siblings. Then I need to finish her crib, so she has somewhere to sleep tonight."

"I'll make something to eat while you call them. Then we can tackle the crib."

"Thank you."

"Are these organized in any way?" She points toward the packages strewn in my living room.

"No, why?"

"Just wondering. Go, I'm sure the Morgan clan is dying to meet her."

I press my lips to her forehead and linger longer than I should. In a matter of hours, it'll be only me and Emme. I have no right to ask Savannah to stay. Yet I want her here with me, with us. It's unfair to even ask.

"I…." Clueless as to what to say next, I turn toward my office. This is a mess. I want Savannah. We have been interrupted every time with get close to choosing one another. Close to me choosing her and my daughter.

The mixture of joy and terror isn't a pair of emotions I thought would mesh. Yet, here I am feeling both at the same time—joy that I have this perfect little girl, terror that I will fail her, that I don't have what it takes to be her father.

Me: Ready to meet your niece?

Cash: Logging on now!

Billie: OMG! So excited.

Auggie: Give me two minutes to get into my office.

One by one, my siblings and their significant others join the call, all their voices fighting for supremacy through the speakers. Well wishes, statements of joy, and literal gawking at Emerson ensue. As if she senses my unease, she starts to squirm and cry in my arms.

"I need to feed her and finish her crib. I'll talk to you soon. Love you bunches." I close the screen and return to the kitchen. I'm floored not only by how much work Savannah has completed in the brief time I was talking with my family but also her in my shorts and a tank top she had under her blouse. True, the shorts are too big, but the tank molds to her frame, displaying her full breasts. *I'm screwed.*

She sorted and organized many of the items. The assembled pack and play is near the island, along with the changing area attachment. The carrier is open and ready for installation in my car. A few outfits are neatly folded. The far counter in the kitchen is set up with a drying rack, bottles, and formula.

"You didn't have to do all of this." Emme cries in my arms.

"I know, but she needs you to know where everything is. Once the crib is together, you can set up the rest of her nursery tomorrow. I'm sure there is one, but I couldn't find a monitor."

"There is. Where? No idea." I set her on the changing area and attempt to change her diaper.

"Do you know how to do that?"

"I haven't changed a diaper since boarding school when Suzette and I were parents of a doll for a long holiday weekend. That was comedy at its finest. Maria-Luisa was watching us like hawks as we slept in the living room with our *baby*. I need to call her." Once I have the wet diaper away from her skin, Emme is back to quiet instead of crying. I set the dry one beneath her and successfully fasten it at her sides. "Why is the stripe yellow?"

"The stripe is yellow if the diaper is dry. Blue means she's wet and needs to be changed."

"Helpful. Although her cries kind of make that useless."

Savannah giggles. It's a sweet sound. "The food is ready if you want to eat before she needs to."

"Sure."

Savannah sets the plates on the table and starts to sit. As I fumble holding Emme in one hand and my fork in the other, she stands and reaches out for my little girl.

"May I?"

I give her a short nod. She scoops her from my arms. In a few steps, sets her down in the swing thing I bought, and buckles her in. I didn't even notice she put that together too. Sitting back down, she starts to eat. Although it's delicious, I shovel the food into my mouth. I don't recall eating anything since after my workout this morning.

"Slow down, Sam. There's plenty."

"I haven't eaten since this morning. It's exceptionally good."

She nods and finishes her plate.

After eating we assemble the crib with relative ease. It's much easier to pull off with her help. Savannah shows me how to swaddle Emme and set her on the positioner in her crib after I feed her. I use a plain white sheet for tonight since her bedding is in the wash. Quietly, we set up much of her nursery while she sleeps. So many times, I think I can share my feelings with Savannah, each time I fail. Near ten Savannah leaves for the night.

As much as I want her to stay, I realize she has drawn a line—a line that delineates she's simply my employee and friend despite our feelings for one another. That line exists because of me. It's up to me to make it disappear.

SAVANNAH

As if Sam wasn't perfect on his own. I don't mean perfect as in flawless. Everyone has flaws, except Emerson. She's simply angelic. I couldn't sit around while he was sharing his daughter with his family. He has made his position clear. His focus is Emme. While I understand he's overwhelmed and his belief—incorrect as it may be—that he can't handle both, we aren't a couple, which is precisely why I'm crawling into my cold bed alone. Not even Gray joins me tonight.

Sam: Are you still awake?

I consider whether to answer. I decide against answering now. My heart can't take it.

Sam: I can't thank you enough for your help both at the office and here.

Sam: I'll see you tomorrow. Good night, cara mia.

After a restless night's sleep and zigzagging around photogs, I arrive at the office. I didn't even stop by Sam's this morning. I figure he hasn't had time to sign those files. Clearing my inbox and his, I get to work. Midday I text Scar.

Me: How are things going? Classes? Do you need anything for the move?

Scarlett: Good. Classes are the same. No, I don't think so. LY.

I have another stack of files, so I leave the office and walk to Sam's. This time and going forward, I walk a block further and use the side entrance into the garage.

Quietly, I set the files on the side table and remove my shoes. Aside from the relief it provides my arches, the noise might wake up Emme. I note that the living area is empty of boxes save for a small pile in one corner. Either he bought duplicates or determined he bought too much. The latter is most likely. I search for Sam. He isn't in his office, the living room, or the nursery.

The nursery is complete with pristine white furniture fit for a princess. The linens Sam chose are white with large pink peonies. The accent color is a light flax. It's feminine but not overly so. The fluffy white area rug is a nice touch, along with the small chair in the corner. The only thing left to do is hang the curtains.

Is there another room I missed? I pass three other guest rooms. I continue my search until I'm at the threshold of the only remaining possibility, the master bedroom.

I peek inside. Sam is sound asleep on a leather couch with Emme curled against his bare chest. My ovaries exploded. My heart squeezes in my chest, not only for him, but for her too. She doesn't know it, but she hit the dad lottery. I'm not surprised. Sam gives everything his full attention. Sighing softly, I pad back to the kitchen.

After leaving a note on the stack of files, I ride to the garage. As I step out and turn right to exit the building, I ponder what to do with the rest of my day.

"Miss Clemons?" a deep voice behind me calls. A fit, older man is approaching the doors.

"Mr. Morgan. A pleasure to see you again."

Strained is the best way to describe Sam's relationship with his parents, especially with his mother.

"Is Samson home?"

"Yes. Have a wonderful visit." I attempt to turn to leave, but he touches my arm to stop me.

"Savannah, I realize you don't know me well nor do I have the greatest relationship with my children. I'm working to remedy that. However, I know without a doubt that my son cares for you deeply. I saw it at the gala. His daughter's arrival and my wife's role in the cover-up threw him. Please give him some time. Eventually, he'll get out of his own way."

"Have a wonderful visit with your son and granddaughter, Mr. Morgan." I turn to leave. This time he doesn't stop me. Wallowing in my emotions, I almost miss my stop on the subway. Thankfully, my stoop is clear of loiterers with cameras. I strip out of my work attire and pull on yoga pants, a tank top, and a thin open-back sweatshirt. Piling my hair on top of my head, I search through my menus.

After placing my order, I realize I ordered way too much. Huge order for one person. *Well done, Savi.* I throw in a load of laundry and flip through the local paper, looking for something to do this weekend since Scar doesn't need my help. Before I finish, my doorbell rings. It's too soon for the food; plus they don't have access to the foyer.

I check the peephole, and familiar eyes stare back at me.

SAMSON

The visit from my father isn't awful. I've never seen him with a baby. He watches Emme, talks to her, and briefly touches her tiny hands. It makes me wonder how he was with us when we were young. Only a handful of people know the answer to that, one of whom I need to reach out to once my father leaves.

"I saw Miss Clemons leaving when I arrived."

"She brought some files from the office before going home."

"Don't wait too long, son. I'm sure you feel like everything is in chaos, but she's a stabilizing force for you."

It surprises me that my father sees how a relationship could truly be considering the path of his. "I refuse to rely on her for Emme as well as my business, which she has taken on without me even asking."

She has been singlehandedly running my business since Marisol's accident. An increased salary doesn't even come close to what she deserves.

"I'm only suggesting that you can do it all; you need to find the right balance for the three aspects of your life." Sage advice from my father who never had to balance anything in his life. Maria-Luisa, Salma, and Henry took care of my siblings and me. Mostly, Maria-Luisa. He's suggesting I can run Morgan Insurance, successfully raise Emme, and have a real relationship with Savannah. Either he's off his rocker, overconfident in my abilities, or both.

"Thank you, I'll consider it."

"Have you spoken with Maria-Luisa yet?"

"No, it's on today's agenda."

"Thank you for allowing me to visit. Will you be attending the wedding?"

"Yes, we'll be there. Will you?" The unsaid question, more pressing anyway, is will Margaux show up?

"I'll be there without your mother. Billie has been adamant that she's unwelcome, and frankly, I don't blame her one bit. I'm simply happy to be in her life even the slightest bit at this point."

"I'm sure she appreciates your efforts."

He nods and leaves as quickly as he came. After a quick call to Maria-Luisa, I call for a ride, pack a bag for Emme, and leave for Savannah's. I lightly knock on her door and wait.

"Hi," She murmurs as the door opens.

"Hi. Can we come in?"

"Of course. Sorry, I'm surprised."

"Expecting someone else?"

"Yes."

"Oh, we can leave."

"I ordered food. I didn't feel like cooking. I over ordered, so you're in luck, there's plenty for you."

An unexpected take-out picnic indoors works for me. I set Emme on the counter and lift her out of the carrier. As if I'm a veteran dad rather than a rookie, I pull a medium-sized blanket out of her pink ruffled bag and spread it on the floor, then unfold another on top of it before setting Emme down.

"Why did you leave earlier?" I ask as she turns from pulling glasses out of the cabinet.

"I didn't want to intrude. You were both sound asleep."

"You could never intrude. I meant what I said."

"I'm sure you did, but—" The buzzer for the foyer interrupts our conversation. Why can we never finish this conversation? "I'll be right back."

Once she returns, we sit on the floor near Emme and unpack the food.

"How many people were you planning on feeding?"

She ordered Kung Pau chicken, teriyaki skewers, pork fried rice, eggrolls, and some General Tso's as well.

She smirks at me. Lighthearted, comfortable Savannah is everything I ever dreamed my future partner would be. While I've taken time away from dating, I always knew what I was looking for. I never found her until Savannah. Setting aside how a custom-made cocktail dress accentuates her assets and her work clothes cling to the contours of her body, her comfy clothes leave nothing to the imagination. Her yoga pants surround her legs and ass like a second skin; the sweatshirt is thin and open in the back, revealing a cropped maroon tank. My fingers itch to touch her skin again. Hell, my lips ache to feel hers against mine.

"This is my normal order with Scarlett. We usually have enough for each of us to eat twice. I'm still adjusting to her being gone."

I fill my mouth with food. Savannah does the same, occasionally looking over at Emme. We eat silently, likely because each time we talk about us, we get interrupted.

"Those files that you left, is that everything from this week?" As soon as I ask, Emme starts crying. Leaning forward, I lift her into my arms. Even though I'm holding her, she's still whining.

"Those are from Tuesday through today—renewals, binders, and quote inquiries. They just need review or signature. Does she need to eat?"

I glance at my watch.

"Probably."

"Can I do it?"

I attempt to hide my surprise at her question. Honestly, I shouldn't be. She has never once given me the impression that Emme is an issue for her. The issue is me.

I'm solely responsible for Emme, but I feel okay with allowing Savannah to feed her. Maybe this is what my father means, accepting help at face value without looking for a sinister meaning behind it. I never would have asked Savannah out if I didn't trust her with my heart. Trusting her with my daughter should be the same. Yet my instincts are screaming—not only for Savannah but for everyone.

"Sure, the formula and bottle are in her bag."

Rising, she prepares her bottle, setting it on the side table near the couch. I walk to where she settles in the corner of the couch and set Emme in her arms. After some fussing, she takes the bottle. I sit staring at them for a bit. Savannah with a baby, *my* baby is breathtaking. Would it be even more if it were *our* baby? That thought sends darts straight to my heart. I decide in this moment to court Savannah properly, as I intended before I learned about Emme.

Rocking onto my feet, I lean down and kiss Emme and Savannah softly before clearing our dinner remnants, setting aside our fortune cookies. When I finish, I retake my seat near my ladies. I like the sound of that in my head.

"Savannah, are you free this weekend?"

"Yes, Scarlett doesn't need any help. She has been slowly moving her stuff out little by little. Why?" She lifts Emme to her shoulder, tapping her back for a burp.

"I want to try. I haven't been… I miss you. I miss us. I realize two dates doesn't make an us, but we were… I'm failing at this. I want you. I want to get us right."

She hasn't uttered a word. Emme's perched on her shoulder, but Savannah's hand stops midair.

"Will you come visit Cash and Billie with us?"

"I would love to."

Her response is without hesitation, without even the slightest note of concern. I'm not worthy of this woman, but I'll try like hell to become what she deserves.

"Also, will you be my date for Billie's wedding?"

"Yes. Do I need a new dress?"

"Up to you. That blue dress you wore to the gala is stunning on you. Or I'm sure Billie or Kelly have some designs at the store for you to try."

"I'll visit the store while we're there. When are we leaving? Where are we staying?"

"Tomorrow morning. I'm meeting with Maria-Luisa, and then we can leave. We're staying with Cash and Noelle."

"How do you feel about that?"

"Mixed, honestly. Marisol and her mother were remarkably close. After everything Maria-Luisa taught us, if she knew about the money, I hope she would've told me. Although I don't know if she knew about Marisol and me presently."

"She knew you were together before?"

"Yes." I move the blankets over near the couch. Before joining her on the couch, I grab our drinks and fortune cookies. "Let's open these before I need to go home to pack. I'm so happy you agreed to join me." If I'm lucky, I'll be able to spend some time with Savannah alone.

"Me too."

"What does yours say?"

After popping half of the actual cookie in her mouth, she reads aloud, "'A truly rich life contains love and art in abundance.' What does yours say?"

I crack the cookie open, hoping my fortune is as perfect as hers. Inhaling, I scan the narrow paper before reciting, "Embrace this love relationship you have." I'm speechless, and so is Savannah.

"That's… disturbingly accurate."

"It is." I gaze over at her still holding Emme. If I'm going to jump in, I'm going into the deep end. "Is there any reason that you can't come with me tonight?"

She lifts her eyes to mine. I see the wheels turning in her mind, mentally ticking off the pros and cons of staying at my place tonight.

"No, I need to pack some things. Come up with me."

I follow Savannah with Emme in her arms up the stairs. Ignoring my reaction to her body is futile. I'm already at half-mast by the time we get to the top of the stairs. In an instant, I'm rock-hard as she sets my daughter in the middle of her bed, surrounding her with pillows, especially with the image of taking her from behind flashing through my mind.

SAVANNAH

Well, so much for not being sure about his feelings for me. That isn't true. I never doubted his feelings for me. He doubts his ability to juggle his business, his daughter, and me at the same time. I don't blame him; it's a lot for anyone. Plus, fatherhood became part of his life in an extremely unusual manner, at least as far as being the sole caregiver.

I set Emme in the middle of my bed and surround her with pillows, even though she can't roll yet.

"Why did you do that?"

"It's an extra precaution. I know she can't roll yet, but I feel better since she isn't on the floor."

Sam smiles, leaning against the doorframe. Hurriedly, I pack a bag for the weekend. After securing Emme in the car, Sam takes my hand in his, linking our fingers.

I'm stepping back into dating Sam. It isn't as if he hid Emme from me. I'm dating my boss, a single dad, and a disgustingly gorgeous one at that.

He buckles a sleeping Emme into her swing and switches on the monitor after we step into his home.

"Let's get you settled." Taking my bag and then my hand, he leads me to his bedroom.

"Are you sure about this?"

"Why not? We already slept together on your couch. Plus, my bed is huge, and I promised to share my view."

I walk over to the massive windows and take in the view; it's more spectacular in person. "The view is stunning."

"She is." His big hands slide around my waist, his fingertips grazing my abdomen. His head rests on my shoulder.

"Sam." Holy hell! He makes me want to strip his clothes off and follow each inch with my tongue. Slowly, I turn in his embrace, looking up at him. He lowers his head toward mine, waiting for an objection.

He won't get one. Rising on my toes, I meet his lips urgently. After the first hard press, he lightens his kiss like at the jazz club. Taking advantage of the space between us, I draw my tongue along his lips. A groan escapes his lungs as he lifts me into his arms. In two strides, he sits on the couch near the granite fireplace. I straddle him as he lifts my sweatshirt over my head.

"Do you have any idea how many times I thought about this moment?"

As he asks, I slide my hands beneath the hem of his hoodie. Sliding upward, I feel his rock-hard, finely sculpted abs contract under my fingers.

"About as long as I have wanted to do this too." I tug his hoodie over his head and run my fingernails down his pecs and abdomen, raising goose bumps along the way. Once I reach his waistband with my fingers, I set my mouth to the center of his chest, kissing upward to the sexy cleft in his chin. His hands glide from my thighs to my back beneath my tank top.

"I need…."

"What do you need?" he murmurs against the curve of my neck.

"Off. Take this off. I need to feel my skin against yours."

The look in his eyes dives even deeper into the well of lust. Within seconds I'm naked from the waist up, and he pulls me closer to him. The softness of my breasts against his hard chest feels like heaven, but that has nothing on the heat of my core sliding along his hard shaft. A moan escapes my lips.

Sam twists on the leather couch, lowering us flat. I take the opportunity to press my mouth along his chest, draw circles around his nipples with my tongue, and kiss down his flank to the divot in his hip that drives me absolutely insane. Each time my tongue touches his skin, a low growl echoes around us. To elicit more satisfied sounds, I continue peppering his skin across his taut abs all the way back up to his lips.

"Hi there."

"Hi."

"My turn." He swiftly switches our positions on the couch so that he's hovering over me, pressing his mouth to my temple, along my jaw, and over my chin. Sam pauses, savoring the valley between my breasts while rolling my nipple to a tight peak. Without discontinuing his fingers, he nips and sucks one nipple with his mouth, causing me to arch off the couch. Sliding my hands southward, I dip them under the waistband of his boxer briefs, cupping him. He's... wow! I wasn't sure before. Now I am. He's—

"Savannah."

I close my hand around him. Feeling him lengthen with each stroke wets my panties even more.

"My turn isn't up yet." As he reaches for my leggings, he shimmies away from me, his waistband snapping against his abs.

"No fair!"

After dropping my leggings to the floor, he looks down at me but says nothing. Instead, he lowers his mouth to the exact spot he was before and continues worshipping my skin down to my toes. The sensation of his fingers and mouth inching up the inside of my thigh makes my core clench. Sam draws his finger along the lace edge of my thong before hooking the sides and drawing it down my legs. Lifting one thigh against the back cushion, he spreads the other, sliding his arm under my knee. He draws a finger upward along my slit and back down before circling my nub with his thumb. My hips move against him.

A myriad of concerns flood my brain, the most urgent of which is do I need to tell him? Inhaling deeply, I calm my brain and relax against the cushion. I might as well be a virgin considering how long it's been since a man touched me.

"Savannah."

I open my eyes to see his dark eyes gazing down at me.

"Do you want me to stop?"

"No, I need you to go slow."

After an extra moment to gauge my comfort level, he continues drawing circles with his thumb before plunging two fingers inside my core. While twisting and turning, advancing and retreating, Sam causes my muscles to clench and convulse. My belly tightens as my release rapidly approaches. I grind against his hand as I climb, and my orgasm intensifies. Shuddering with pleasure, I clamp my hand around his forearm to ground myself. Slowly, the shaking subsides, and I open my eyes.

"I never came that hard on my own."

A grin briefly appears on his face as he turns. Now we're lying on the couch, my back against the cushions. His arm slides around my waist, holding me tightly.

"How long?"

"Myself… two days."

He raises an eyebrow.

"Honestly? Have you looked in the mirror lately? The memory of your mouth is dangerous. A man… years."

"How is that possible?"

"Never had many opportunities. I worked three jobs for over four years. I didn't really date, and if I did, none really led anywhere when I refused to have sex on a first date."

"Are you a—"

"No, but that was senior year of high school."

He presses his lips to mine. The moment I snuggle closer, a sweet wail comes through the monitor.

"I'm sorry," he whispers against my temple.

"Sam, look at me."

He draws back, concern in his eyes for what I will say next.

"I'm fully aware that I need to share you with Emme. Don't ever apologize for being her father. I'm not going anywhere."

"I don't know what to say." He kisses me again as he rises from the couch, leaving the room.

SAMSON

In the wee hours of the morning, Emme wakes for another feeding. I wasn't asleep. My mind is spinning, preparing to see Maria-Luisa tomorrow. I'm terrified that she knew about Margaux's deal with Marisol. I would never cut her out of Emme's life simply because of Marisol's choices. Honestly, I would love for her to care for her granddaughter like she did for me, Cash, Billie, and Auggie. One baby should be a piece of cake.

The moonlight streaming through the glass illuminates my daughter's face. Not once in my wildest dreams did I see my life taking this turn, but she's angelic and I can't imagine my life without her in it. With a dry diaper, full belly, and tight swaddle, I set her back into her crib like Savannah taught me. At the threshold, I glance at her for a few moments, wondering how it's only been a short time since she became my world.

Sliding back in bed with Savannah, I imagine making this my reality. Having her live with us, especially now that Scarlett has moved out. My head is screaming, hell no, it's too soon. My heart can't imagine sleeping alone ever again.

When I wake again, my bed is empty and cold. My eyes must be deceiving me. The clock indicates it's near seven. A moment of panic slices through me. Is Emme still sleeping? Padding to the kitchen, I don't find Savannah. Then I hear faint talking from the nursery.

"Aren't you a good girl? You slept a bit longer and are eating well."

I lean against the doorframe watching Savannah with my daughter. It's a striking image when the woman you care about has taken to your child. Savannah glances up as I step into the room. Her mouth curves up into a small smile. She lifts Emme to burp her and rises from the chair. A few steps later, she brushes her lips across mine.

"Morning. I could have done that."

"I don't mind. You got up with her at three; plus you were sound asleep. Do you prefer to do it all yourself?" She tries to keep the tone of her question even.

"Yes. No. Can we talk about this over breakfast?"

"Sure." Savannah sets Emme in the swing before joining me in the kitchen. "What can I do?"

"Coffee please," I reply, throwing veggies into the pan with the eggs. I plate the scrambles and set them on the table. Turning back I almost crash into Savannah. I grip her waist to steady myself and her. I kiss her softy before guiding her to the right. I gaze over at Emme before taking a seat at the table.

"I need you to clarify what you meant?"

Setting my fork down, I take her hand in mine. "You're my girlfriend. I don't want you to feel forced to care for Emme like you did for Scarlett."

"Do you think that little of me?" She pulls her hand from mine.

"Of course not!"

"She's part of you. I can't ignore her existence."

"I don't want you to feel obligated to be her mother figure too."

"Don't I get to choose what I want or don't want?"

I start to speak, but my words fail me. I have no answer for her.

"I care about you. I wanted you long before you learned about your daughter. It took us awhile to go on a proper date that wasn't a business event, but still. I don't feel obligated to care for her; I want to. Same as I want to take care of you. Please don't push me away again."

"I care about you too. I'm not ungrateful; however, I didn't plan on Emme. My life plan was strictly conventional. She flipped everything in my life on its head. Can you promise me one thing?"

She tips her head forward slightly before meeting my gaze.

"If you ever feel like I'm taking advantage of you concerning Emerson, I need you to tell me."

"I promise. It won't happen, but I promise."

I cup her face, drawing her lips to mine. Pulling away, I glance over at Emme who is fussing in her swing. Gulping down my cold coffee, I unbuckle her and hold her at the table.

"What time is Maria-Luisa coming over? How do you want to handle it?"

I gather my thoughts before answering her. "She'll be here at nine, so we should get dressed. I want to talk with her about Marisol and the money before I introduce her to Emme. Would you mind keeping her in the nursery while we talk?"

"No, I don't mind. Do you plan to tell her about me?"

"Savannah, the only opinion about you that matters are mine and Emme's. I don't care what Maria-Luisa, Margaux, or anyone else thinks."

She smiles, kisses me lightly, and rises from the table with our dishes in hand. Buckling Emme in her chair, we finish the dishes and hurry to get ready.

Jimmy announces that our guest arrives precisely at nine. I wait for her by the elevator.

"Good morning, Maria-Luisa. How are you?"

She steps into my home, taking in the space. Considering she was my nanny, the luxury of it shouldn't faze her in the slightest. Although I suppose knowing her granddaughter will live here at least for the time being makes her curious.

"Morning, Samson. I'm doing the best I can. I apologize for the awkwardness. I'm not sure how to handle this."

"You're fine. Would you like some coffee?"

"No, thank you."

I lead her to the couch, offering her a seat.

"There isn't an uncomplicated way for me to handle this. Did you know about the money?"

"No." Her answer is emphatic and unwavering. "I learned about the money from Ramon after my Marisol...." Tears fall from her eyes. "I would've told you if I knew sooner."

She has no reason to lie to me. While I could keep Emme away from her if she knew, I wouldn't. Maria-Luisa knows I wouldn't do that. Her, Henry, and Salma raised me better than that.

"I have spoken with Margaux. Eventually she came clean. She isn't welcome here, my office, near me, my daughter, or Savannah."

Maria-Luisa nods, still blotting the tears falling from her eyes.

"Would you like to meet your granddaughter?"

"Yes, very much."

"I'll bring you to her." I guide her to the nursery. Savannah is changing her diaper.

Maria's face lights up as we step into the room. I kiss Savannah's temple and wait for her to finish. I cradle Emme and turn to Maria-Luisa.

"Maria-Luisa, this is my girlfriend, Savannah."

They shake hands.

"Hi. Nice to meet you."

Savannah replies, "You as well."

"This is your granddaughter, Emerson."

She steps closer to me and gently touches Emme's fingers. "Can I hold her?"

"Of course. Have a seat."

She removes her sweater before sitting in the chair. I set Emme in her arms and step back.

"We'll be in the living room."

"Thank you, Samson."

I nod and follow Savannah out of the room. The moment we're alone, I draw her against me, pressing my lips to her head.

Lifting her head, she asks, "How are you?"

"She didn't know about Margaux or that Emme could have been mine. I believe her. She has no reason to lie. Even if she did know, I wouldn't make her pay for Marisol's choices."

"I wouldn't think you could. Keeping Emme from Margaux is one thing, but Maria-Luisa is something else. Do we need to do anything else before leaving?"

"I packed more than enough clothes, even though I'm certain Cash and Noelle have a washing machine. The only other thing is to prepare some bottles for the flight."

I'm looking forward to seeing my family in Maine. Unfortunately, Auggie can't join us because of the late notice. I move to the kitchen and prepare the bottles with water while Savannah fills the formula container for her diaper bag. The rest will go in our luggage. Once we finish, we curl up on the couch to wait for Maria-Luisa. Shortly after we sit, I hear the familiar tune of a Spanish lullaby that she sang to my siblings and me when we were young.

She steps out of the nursery, leaving the door ajar. "Do you have a monitor?" she asks as she approaches.

I feel Savannah tense like we're doing something wrong.

"I'll get it." As Savannah rises from the couch, I grasp her wrist. Catching her gaze I remind her without words that I don't care about Maria-Luisa's opinion. She nods before walking away.

"Samson, thank you for allowing me to spend time with her."

"Of course. Are you still working?"

"No, I only volunteer a few days a week. Can I come back soon?"

"Absolutely. We're going to see Cash and Billie for the weekend. Does Wednesday afternoon work?"

She throws her arms around me and hugs me tight. "Thank you."

Savannah returns with the monitor in her hand.

"It was a pleasure meeting you, Savannah."

"You as well."

"Have a safe trip."

I escort her to the elevator and wait for the doors to close. That went well overall. I knew the woman who effectively raised me would never keep something so monumental quiet, even for her own daughter.

SAVANNAH

The flight to Maine is largely uneventful other than some hilarious moments attempting to secure Emme into the plane seat. The ride to Cash and Noelle's is picturesque. The streets are lined with large, mature trees. Once we get close to the village, the ocean appears to our right.

"It's beautiful here."

"It is." Sam returns his gaze out the window.

I reach over and take his hand in mine. He looks down at our hands but says nothing.

"Where are you?" I hope he'll share his thoughts. Imagining the things that might be going through his head is a minefield.

"Sorry. I'm working through what I need to do for Emerson in the next week or so. I want to get back to the office."

"Anything I can help with?"

"Not really. You have been nothing short of amazing about handling the office. I sincerely appreciate you going beyond what you're required to do."

"It's no problem. Your life is topsy-turvy right now." Doesn't he realize that I want to help him with the office and Emerson? Perhaps he needs more time to see I'm in this with him.

Turning onto a narrow side road, we approach a gorgeous house with a large front porch. Just past the house, I can see the shoreline. Cash, Noelle, and a dog, dutifully sitting by her feet, wait on the front porch. As I tug lightly on Sam's hand, he turns to look at me.

"Maybe you should take the time while we're here to relax a bit too."

"I'll try." He leans forward to kiss me. Unfortunately, the door swings open before he can.

I exhale slowly and follow Sam toward the house. The dog, named Titan, looks like a fluffy German Shephard and walks beside Noelle as we approach.

"Savannah, it's so good to see you again," Noelle says, pulling me into a hug. Her belly brushes mine.

Did we already know she's pregnant? I think to myself. Maybe Sam does. "You too! It feels like forever ago."

"Hi, Savannah," Cash says while gushing over Emerson. He's touching her hair, her nose, and squeezing her toes.

"Do you and Sam have any plans for tonight?" Noelle asks as we move into the house.

"Not that I know of."

"Good, you're coming to girls' night in with me. I'm excited for you to meet everyone."

"Sure." I'm only reluctant because I'm unsure if this trip is for simply visiting or…. "Your home is lovely."

"Thank you. Let's get your stuff to the guest suite." Noelle leads me to a large guest suite with adjoining bathroom and balcony.

"I'll let you get settled. I need to steal my niece away from her father and my husband for a bit." Noelle smiles and leaves the room.

I slide open the balcony door and step outside instead of unpacking. The left side of the property abuts a wooded preserve with hiking trails. Across a small private lane is a beach that only the four houses on the street have access too. It's beautiful.

My only concern until recently was Scarlett. Where I work and live revolved around her. Now I suppose it revolves around Sam. Spending the night at his place was amazing. Not only is the view spectacular, but I got more time with him. Vivid memories of last night crash through my mind. Aside from his stellar kissing, I've never shattered before him, and we didn't even—

"*Cara mia*," Sam calls from inside the bedroom. "There you are." He slides his arms around me from the side, pressing a kiss to my temple.

"What's wrong?"

"Nothing. I feel out of sorts. My intention isn't to make you angry, but I might. What does 'trying' mean to you?"

Releasing me, he scrubs his hand down his face. "I'm still figuring out how to be her father. As you already know, I haven't had a girlfriend in years. Clearly, I'm failing at the boyfriend part."

"Not necessarily. I need to know what my boundaries are because I feel like I'm failing too."

"You aren't. This is solely on me. Before Emme, I had an idea how to handle a new relationship with you. Now, I don't even know where my boundaries are. I refuse to let you resent me because I ask too much of you for her." He guides me into his lap on the patio chair.

"That's where we don't agree. Being with you and Emme isn't the same thing as caring for Scarlett. It's my choice this time. I want you. Emme is part of you."

"Savannah…."

The look in his eyes nearly tears my heart out. He's scared out of his mind at the prospect of fatherhood and a relationship with me despite his insistence to try.

"I want to be your sounding board. To help you figure out what you need for us and for Emme. Will you let me in? If it's too much, I assure you, I will tell you."

"Yes."

Lowering my head, I pull his lower lip between my teeth. A low groan gets caught in his throat as he wraps his hands around my head. Claiming my mouth, his tongue teases and twists, leaving me breathless.

"Bro, where are Emerson's… oops! At least you still have clothes on. I knocked, but you didn't hear me."

I set my forehead to Sam's, catching my breath.

"It's the pink bag with ruffles on the bed. We'll be right down."

With a chuckle, Cash leaves the room.

As I attempt to move, Sam digs his fingers into my hip, holding me against him. "I wasn't done kissing you." He retakes my mouth for a toe-curling, breath-stealing kiss.

Breathless and turned on more than I should be from a kiss, I stand on wobbly legs.

"Does that always happen?" he asks with a smirk on his face.

"Never before you." I brush my lips across his once more and head downstairs.

SAMSON

Cash and I spend the evening on the patio catching up while Noelle and Savannah go to girls' night at Kelly and Ellis's a few doors away. Every so often, I glance to my right where the ladies disappeared to.

"The girls will be fine. Normally, Noelle comes home tipsy and horny. Now, it's only the latter. Sorry for interrupting before."

That borders on a bit too much information, but I'll file away that pregnant women, at least Noelle, are hornier than when she isn't pregnant. "It's fine. That was the tail end of us laying out some boundaries or at least discussing boundaries."

"What's the issue?" Cash asks. My brother, always the problem solver.

"Me, completely me. She has me tied up in knots. Not once did I ever feel this way about a woman, including Meghan."

"Welcome to the club, bro." Cash slaps my shoulder. "Does Savannah know about Meghan?"

"She knows everything from Meghan, her death, Marisol, and even that I slept with her when she separated from Ramon, not once but twice."

"Damn."

I nod. Savannah is more than I deserve, yet I keep pushing her away. "She doesn't even have the slightest bit of disappointment in me about Marisol."

"Yeah, you can't screw this one up, Sam."

"No kidding. Even so, I tried to push her away because of Emme."

"Why would you do a stupid thing like that?"

"Savannah was forced to raise her little sister, Scarlett, after her mother died and her father checked out. I refuse to take advantage of her knowledge and her feelings for me to care for Emme."

"Does she feel that way?"

"Not at all. Hence, the discussing. I went from single bachelor who recently started dating Savannah to single father in the last few weeks. It's a lot."

"If I've learned anything since meeting Noelle, communication, both talking and listening, is key. If Savannah says she doesn't feel as if you're using her for Emme, believe her. For whatever reason, she wants you. There are very few women who see men like us for who we are, not for what we can offer them. Savannah is one of those women. You could be scraping by and she would still want you, like Noelle would want me. You need to hold on to her."

"Thanks, Cash." I'm glad that he can see that Savannah is like Noelle. It makes me feel more secure in my feelings for her. Twisted, a little, but men like us are targets for gold diggers. Hell, Billie was in the same position as far as wealth. She refuses to take advantage of it. It's one significant reason Cash and I haven't dated until recently, probably Auggie too. Although, I see him with his best friend, Caroline, when he realizes how perfect she is for him.

"Anytime." After a few minutes of silence, Cash heads inside to refresh our beers.

While he's inside, I close my eyes and absorb the stillness of this place. There's no traffic, no constant hum of people going about their business. I hear the lapping of waves on the shoreline of their secluded beach, sounds of nature, and every so often a loud burst of laughter from Kelly's house. It's peaceful here, calm and inviting. I see why Cash and Billie love it.

Cash rejoins me on the patio and lights the firepit.

"Maine suits you," I observe. My brother looks calm and settled here, which differs significantly to his demeanor when he lived in the city. Cash was wound tight from the time he got up until he finished boxing with Evan in New York. For a brief time afterward, he was relaxed until the stress of his jobs and life got to him again.

"Surprisingly, it does. At first I was concerned that I would miss the city, but I don't. Not at all. There's no bustle, no hurrying, no photographers. That one is key. I don't even miss the conveniences like takeout at two in the morning or grocery delivery within the hour. Considering a move?"

"It isn't out of the realm of possibility, but there are so many variables. Emme, Savannah, Scarlett, my business to name a few."

"To be fair, there is only one variable you need to consult."

"Savannah."

"The answer is always talking to her. You can decide for yourself, your business, and Emerson. Only she can decide for her." Leave it to my younger brother to set me straight. "What are your plans for tomorrow?"

"Savannah needs to go to So Elegant to look for a dress for the wedding. Otherwise, I'm free."

"Sweet, the guys are going kayaking. You should come."

"I'll talk to Savannah when she gets back. What time?"

"We leave around nine. Do you want to walk the girls back? I'll stay here with Emme."

"Nah, go ahead. I'll stay here and enjoy the serenity a bit longer."

There's a house between here and Kelly's. I gather Cash doesn't know them well enough to walk across the lawn since he goes down to the private road. I close my eyes for a moment before Emme starts crying. Grabbing our empty bottles and the monitor, I step into the house. I set the bottles in the sink before climbing the stairs to my daughter. She has kicked out of the blanket, and she's soaked from head to toe. I set her back down, which increases her wails more.

Expeditiously, I gather a new set of clothes and diapering items before returning to her in the portable crib. The instant her wet pajamas are off her body, the crying ceases.

"Don't you worry, angel. Daddy's got this."

She can't speak yet, but I know she understands. Emme looks up at me as if I hold the answers. To her, I do. Once she's clean and dry, I swaddle her, set her in the middle of the bed surrounded by pillows, strip the crib, and remake it. Gently, I move Emme from the bed back to the crib, hoping not to wake her.

I hear a soft chuckle as I slowly step away from Emme. When I look up, Savannah is standing at the doorway. I put my index finger up to my lips. Reaching for her hand, I lead her back onto the balcony and kiss her thoroughly. She was only gone for a few hours, but honestly, I missed her.

"How was girls' night?" I guide her into my lap again.

She clasps her hands around my neck. "It was fantastic. Your sister is a riot. Kelly is beautiful and fun. Gen wasn't fun at all. She was more interested in watching a Gerard Butler movie than talking with anyone. I met another designer named Poppy who works for Kelly and Billie. She's super cute, tiny, and has a pixie haircut. She seems reserved, though. That could be because she doesn't know everyone well. Are you going kayaking tomorrow?"

While I'm listening to her talk about her get-together, her perfume is messing with my senses. It has since the day we met. Until recently I would never think to ask for more details.

"I was going to ask if you mind keeping Emme."

"No, not at all. Billie will be there too for some auntie time."

"Thank you."

She closes the space between us, sliding her lips across mine before replying, "Of course."

"You smell amazing." I press my mouth to the curve of her neck, nipping lightly, eliciting a soft moan.

"Thank you. I wear Baccarat Rouge 540."

I add that to the list of things I need to remember. I continue kissing, sucking, and nipping along her shoulder, pushing the fabric of her shirt out of my way. The lacy red strap of her bra plunges all the blood in my body southward. She's shifting in my lap the longer my mouth touches her skin.

"Sam, let's go to bed." Her words are sultry and inviting, which pushes my thoughts into territory that scares me. Don't mistake my hesitance for a lack of interest. The mere fact that she may be the *one* makes me consider slowing down a bit. Yet with a mouth as talented as hers, resisting might be futile. Kissing her makes every other woman pale in comparison.

Savannah slides off my lap and takes my hand, leading me back into the guest suite. Once we're inside, she lifts her shirt over her head, revealing an unlined red lace bra. It leaves nothing to my imagination. Her aroused nipples screaming to be tasted. I tug her close, dip my head, and take her nipple between my teeth.

"Sam," she rasps, her head falling back and her fingernails digging into my biceps.

Noted, cara mia. Unclasping her bra, I pull it forward, caressing her breasts while moving further into the room. After her bra slides down her arms, she lifts my shirt over my head. She kisses a path across my chest and down my flank. Lowering my hands, I pop the button of her jeans, sliding my hands along her hips to push them off. I bend before her, tugging the jeans over her bright red polished toes. As I rise, I press open-mouth kisses, alternating from one leg to the other before teasing the hem of the matching red thong with my tongue, alongside her breast, before finishing at her lips.

Savannah drags her fingertips up the front of my thighs before cupping my shaft through my jeans. Her nimble fingers open the clasp of my jeans, and she pushes them to the floor. Stepping out, I walk us to the edge of the bed. As I wrap my arm around her slim waist, a soft cry echoes in the room. I press my lips to her forehead. With monumental reluctance, I lay Savannah on the bed and go tend to my daughter.

After feeding and diapering Emerson, I stalk back to the bed to find Savannah barely covered by the satiny sheets and sound asleep. Rounding the bed, I lift the sheet and savor the view of her round ass before climbing into bed. Draping my arm around her middle, I nestle her against me and let sleep claim me.

SAVANNAH

Thin streams of moonlight filter into the room. Sam's hard, muscled body creates a warm cocoon for me, and I don't want to move, but I need to. Slowly, I slide out of his embrace and search for a shirt. Finding Sam's draped on the chair, I tug it over my head and pad to the en suite bathroom. After a quick search, I locate a condom in the vanity drawer.

As I return to the bedroom, I notice Emerson squirming. Grabbing Sam's watch, I see it's near five and time to eat again. She slept for almost five hours. Unfortunately, I fell asleep last night too—a blunder I plan to rectify as soon as I can.

A few soft whines filter into the air as I prepare her bottle and pull out a fresh diaper. Thankfully, I'm able to start feeding her before Sam wakes. After setting Emerson back into the crib, I lift off his shirt and climb back into bed.

This man is more than I ever hoped for. He's lying on his back with one arm tucked beneath his head. I snuggle close, pressing my mouth to the divot at his hip that makes me crazy. Moving upward, I kiss along his side and up to his pec. I feel the moment he fully wakes. His body tenses before relaxing once he realizes where he is.

"Savannah," he whispers. "What are you doing?"

"Finishing what we started last night." I draw a path with my tongue along his chest and up his neck to his jaw while moving to straddle his hips. I twist my hair and set it on my shoulder while gazing down at him. He's hardening beneath my heated center. The look in his eyes is hard to discern. "Do you want me to stop?"

"No, I'm… never mind."

"Sam, please tell me."

"I care about you, and this moment feels different, bigger than it ever has before."

The implications of his statement aren't lost on me. I also try not to read into them either regarding his past. "I care about you too, or I wouldn't be here."

He hesitates slightly before pulling my lips down to his. Sliding down my body, his hands skim the sides of my breasts, sending bolts of need spiraling through me. Deliberately, I grind against him, savoring the feel of his rock-hard shaft against my sex. Pushing off his chest, I stand on the bed and push my thong downward. At the same time, he shimmies out of his boxer briefs.

Holy hell! I thought he was big when I stroked him yesterday, but seeing him is something else. A sliver of concern slices through me. Even so, my body betrays me with heat and wetness pooling between my thighs. I lower myself back down to the soft sheets as he sits up, wrapping his arms around me.

"Lie back." Sam murmurs.

As I lie back between his legs, Sam's fingers tease my center, drawing up from my bottom to my nub and back down again. Aching need builds even more as he plunges two fingers into my wet center. When he moves, the sensations build at the base of my spine and my lower belly tightens. The moment he adds a third finger, I buck against his skilled hand as my release captures me.

Catching my breath, I push up. Hovering over him, I tear open the packet and slide the condom down his length. He aligns the tip, teasing me.

"Savannah, go slow."

I nod and lower myself, taking an inch of him inside me, even though I want to take him fast and deep. Taking my time, I wait to stretch and accommodate him. Not only has it been an exceedingly long time, but he's large. Pushing closer, I take more of him, allowing my body to adjust. Lowering the rest of the way, I settle against him, his entire shaft buried inside me. Never have I felt this full.

"*Cara mia*, you feel…."

Sam circles his hips as I push down. I meet him thrust for thrust. His fingers dig into the flesh of my hips, marking me and controlling my movements. I notice an odd look on his face. Before I can address it, he wraps his arm around my waist and flips us over. With one hand holding my wrists above my head and the other holding my thigh up, he pushes into me with steady, sensual strokes.

"Oh my…." As with most people, my first time was awkward and not pleasant. Being with Sam is a wholly different level of pleasure. I tighten my inner muscles around him.

"Do that again."

I repeat the movement and note he swells more inside me. Again, I clench around him. That's all it takes; my body shudders and convulses as he explodes in hot bursts. Releasing my thigh and my wrists, he lowers himself on top of me, his face buried in the crook of my neck. Our breathing regulates in its own time.

"That was…." So many words ping around in my head to describe how I feel right now. None seem adequate.

"It was. Did I hurt you?"

The concern in his voice makes my heart squeeze. "No, not at all."

He pushes up and moves off the bed. "I'll be right back." Sam disappears into the bathroom and returns a bit later with a towel in his hand. Gently, he cleans me before setting it on the floor. He pulls me into his arms, and I rest my head on his chest. His heart pounds against my temple.

"Your heart is beating fast. Are you okay?" I tip my head up so I can see his face as he responds.

"I'm beyond okay. Let's get ready and make some breakfast."

I join Sam in the luxurious shower. While we explore one another more, we don't have sex again. I believe Sam's concerned about me since it has been so long.

Once we're ready, the three of us join Noelle and Cash in the kitchen for breakfast.

"Morning," Cash grumbles, staring at the coffee streaming into his cup.

"Morning," Sam and I reply in unison, waiting to make coffee for ourselves.

Noelle is talking to Emerson in hushed tones. She's clearly a morning person.

"How did she do last night?" Noelle asks Sam.

"I fed her at midnight, and Savannah fed her near five."

"That's fairly good. She'll probably need to eat again at the shop."

I nod and hand Sam a cup of coffee. He attempts to give it back, but I insist he take the first one.

Cash starts chuckling. "How long have you two been talking to one another without words?"

I blush and look away as Sam replies, "About six months or so, especially when I need to get off a work call."

Titan lifts his head and barks at Peter and a man I've never met as they crest the front steps. Yet, the man looks vaguely familiar.

"Come in," Cash calls from the kitchen. "Morning, Peter. Ellis."

"Hi, Sam. Savannah. Nice to see you again," Peter says, hugging us both.

"Morning, Ellis. This is my girlfriend, Savannah. Savannah, Ellis. Kelly's husband." Sam introduces me to the guest with Peter.

"Pleasure to meet you, Savannah." *Holy crap!* Ellis Barnett, Hollywood's most sought-after actor and director is Kelly's husband. He's even better looking in person.

"You as well." I manage to contain my inner fangirl.

Sam and Cash are shoveling pastries into their mouths from a box labeled The Perk. If I recall correctly, Peter's adopted sister, Kelsey, owns that coffee shop.

"Are you ready to leave, Sam?" Cash asks.

"Give us a minute and I'll be ready." He takes my hand and leads me back to the bedroom.

"Are you sure about this?" Fear, concern, and another emotion I can't pinpoint dance in his gorgeous eyes. "You haven't left her yet, have you?"

"No, so please don't be offended."

"I'm not. Your overprotective mode is sexy, and to be honest, I thought that before Emerson came into our life." I said *our,* hopefully it doesn't freak him out, especially considering our morning together. "We're going to the shop. I'll be there, along with at least one family member. Emme will be fine. Go, have fun with the guys."

"Thank you, *cara mia.*"

"What does that mean?" I lift my gaze to his face.

His eyes soften before he replies, "It means 'my beloved' in Italian."

"Sam" escapes my lips in a breathy tone a moment before he seals his mouth over mine.

He kisses me deeply before trotting down the stairs. I pack Emme's bag and descend the stairs in time to see all the guys walk out the door except Sam. He whispers something to Emerson before kissing her head. After a wink in my direction, he bounds out the door for his kayaking adventure with the guys.

SAMSON

She said *our*. Our life. Truthfully, I never doubted Savannah's words. She believes me regarding Marisol. I could build a life with her—the life I always pictured but with Emerson too.

"Bro, you good?" Cash asks as I walk past the Rover.

"Yeah."

"I recall that look. I know the moment it happened too," Peter says, and Ellis agrees.

"Me too," Cash interjects.

"What look?" I turn to face my brother, future brother-in-law, and friend.

"The *I found her* look," Peter quips.

"What am I supposed to do about it?"

"Don't screw it up!" Cash shouts, getting into the driver's seat.

The rest of the guys laugh as they pile into the Rover. I let his words marinate for a bit. My relationship experience is limited. I was engaged to Meghan, but it was young love. I loved Marisol but as my friend; it wasn't a romantic type of love. Otherwise, there have been no other women in my life other than a few first dates here and there. My brain is telling me to take it slow with Savannah, but my heart is screaming hold tighter.

Entrenched in my thoughts, I don't notice that Cash has parked and the guys are unloading the kayaks.

"We don't know each other well, but I knew the moment I met Kelly that she was the one for me. Time together only solidifies your feelings. If it feels right to you, don't worry about what anyone else thinks," Ellis shares as he passes my door.

Taking a kayak from Peter, I follow them to the water. I'll simply remind myself that Savannah is perfectly capable and Emerson will be fine. Never once did I think leaving my daughter would be this difficult, and it has nothing to do with trusting Savannah.

Once we shove off, we paddle in silence. The inlet is placid and serene. On either side there are trees or a short shoreline. Nowhere in the city can I find this much solitude, even with the guys along for the trip. There are no other people, at least that I can see.

From childhood I envisioned how my marriage would be. I knew my parents' marriage wouldn't be a shining example. I wonder if they ever even liked one another. Henry and Salma's marriage is what I'm striving for. Savannah and I could have a marriage like that. They met in a small diner where she was the cook and he applied to be her sous chef. From the moment he was hired, they were inseparable. Henry found the posting for the job for my parents. They hired Salma on the spot, but she had one condition, that Henry was offered a job as well. She was a shrewd negotiator, and even when Margaux pressed her, Salma stood her ground. In one of the rare times in her life, Margaux relented and hired them both.

Salma handled all the food preparation, and together she and Henry handled service. Once we were born, Maria-Luisa was hired as our nanny. All three were around for my entire childhood. Learning Emerson is my daughter has also made me consider how I want to raise my children. I assumed I would have a wife before considering how to raise a child. That isn't the case anymore. I want Savannah's input, but I don't want to burden her either.

Maybe that's the problem. *I'm* the problem. Savannah doesn't see Emerson as an issue. She wants both of us. Temporarily content with my recent decisions, I paddle closer to the shore to watch a few deer in the brush.

"You good?" Cash asks as he glides by.

"For now. I need to make some decisions, which will require talking with Savannah."

"Fair enough. Does she make you happy?"

"Happier than I ever thought possible."

"Good, want to race back?"

"You're on!" Before we can take off, Ellis and Peter rejoin us. We line up the points of our kayaks and take off back toward the truck. It's been a long time since I had fun working out. The four of us are paddling furiously to win this race. About three quarters of the way back, Peter falls back into fourth place. Ellis slows next and pulls his phone from his pocket. After glancing at the text, he shouts back to Peter and hustles to catch up to us.

"We need to get to the shop," he yells as he approaches and passes Cash and me. We load the gear and hurry to the shop.

"What is going on, Ellis?" Fear rises in my chest as we rush to our women and my daughter.

"Kelly texted saying they have an unwanted visitor."

Given Kelly had a stalker and the paparazzi still seek her out, it could be anyone. Paparazzi near Billie and Emerson is also an issue in my book. Thankfully, Kelly has personal security at work. Blackthorne Security provides a guard for Kelly at the shop, for movie premieres, and the like.

"Did she say who? Who is with Kelly?" I ask.

"No, she didn't. Christoph is with Kelly." Ellis informs us.

We park behind the store and enter through the rear door. Kelly leaps into Ellis's arms, kissing him hard. We can hear the loud voices in the back room.

"Mother, what are you doing here? You're not welcome." That's Billie's voice. *Wonderful*, Margaux is here.

"Warren left for a trip of unspecified location and duration. Also, I attempted to visit Sam yesterday. The concierge turned me away. I assumed your wedding was this weekend, so I came. This is the only place I know where to find you."

"Why do you think that is? I don't want you here. You're not invited to my wedding. I don't ever want to see you again."

I move closer to Kelly and whisper, "Where are Savannah and Emerson?"

"When she arrived, Savannah ducked into the fitting room."

I nod and consider my options. Peter is hovering near the door ready to support Billie anyway he can. The moment I hear Emerson cry out. I suck in a sharp breath.

"Is my granddaughter here?" Margaux asks Billie.

I move to the threshold of the doorway. Cash and Peter block my entry into the showroom.

"Even if she was, you aren't going to meet her," Billie states empathically. My sister, fierce as always.

"Who is going to stop me?"

"I will." Savannah steps out of the fitting room wearing a fitted, red satin dress that hugs her body perfectly—presumably one that she was trying on for the wedding. She looks beautiful, which is not something I should notice right now, but there it is.

"You? Hardly. You're not good enough to be her nanny, let alone be with my son," Margaux insults Savannah.

Ironic considering she's the nanny's granddaughter too.

"Lucky for me, it doesn't matter what you think."

Savannah standing up to Margaux is sexy as hell. Emerson cries again. She must be wet, hungry, or both.

"Will Samson be paying for that dress?" Margaux insults Savannah again.

"I don't need or want Sam's money. I have my own."

More confirmation that Savannah genuinely wants me, not my money or status—confirmation I don't need.

"I find that hard to believe considering your mother is dead, your father is a drunkard who can't hold down a job, your little sister spends her time at questionable establishments with unsavory people, and you live in a walk-up in The Bronx."

"None of that matters. You won't meet her while she's in my care."

"Of course it matters, dear. You aren't good enough for my son." Margaux takes a step closer to Savannah.

Christoph steps in front of Savannah.

"Ma'am, you need to leave the premises. If you don't, Mrs. Barnett will contact the local police."

I step around Cash and set my gaze on Savannah. She shakes her head tightly before returning her eyes to my mother. Given Christoph's size, Margaux doesn't see me yet. Hell, I would be scared to come across him alone at night.

"Mother, I suggest you heed his warning."

Margaux's eyes dart directly to mine. "Samson, wonderful, you're here. I would like to meet my granddaughter."

"Are you out of your mind? Absolutely not! Was I unclear when I visited you? You attempted to keep my daughter's existence from me. You paid off her mother to protect our family name—a name which, in my opinion, you don't deserve to carry given all the trouble you have stirred up over my lifetime." I step between Christoph and Savannah effectively putting another layer between Margaux and Emerson.

Billie hands me the diaper bag, which I give to Savannah.

"I'm stepping back in there to see if I can calm her down. She's probably wet," Savannah murmurs near my ear.

I nod at her soft words. Her breath on my skin momentarily shifts my focus to illicit places. Regaining my composure, I stand firm, waiting for Margaux's next move.

"How dare you? How dare you disrespect me like that?"

"Disrespect you? I'm not having this conversation again. My sentiments match Billie's. I don't want you near me, my daughter, Savannah, my home, or my business. Is that clear?"

"Fine. At least I still have August on my side." Margaux turns for the door.

Noelle skirts behind her into Cash's arms while I step into the dressing room. Interestingly, Margaux doesn't address Cash and Noelle at all.

Savannah is sitting with Emerson in her arms on the chair against the wall. My daughter is now content with a dry diaper in Savannah's embrace. I fall to my knees on the floor and kiss my tiny angel's head.

"I'm sorry. I didn't know what else—"

I crush my mouth to hers. At first she's stunned but opens for me as I tilt her head to meet mine. Never have I felt like I do right now—exhilarated, happy, and relieved. While I trust Savannah, I don't trust Margaux, not even the slightest bit. After sharing all my feelings in this kiss, I pull back but don't release my hold on her.

"Watching you stand up to Margaux was the sexiest and fiercest thing I've ever seen. Not only did you tell her off unflinchingly, you protected Emerson. I would never ask for anything more than that for my little girl."

"I would never let her near Emerson."

"I know, and I'm grateful. I'm sorry you had to handle Margaux."

A small smile cracks on her face. "I would do anything for both of you."

It's in this moment that I know I've fallen head over heels for Savannah. No other woman has ever seen me so clearly, handled Margaux, and is willing to accept me and my daughter without hesitation. Now what do I do about it?

"That dress… I don't have words to adequately describe how sinful you look."

Her cheeks turn a gorgeous shade of pink. "That's too bad; I wasn't planning on selecting this one."

"Really? I want to see the other one."

"No chance. I want it to be a surprise."

I frown. Savannah is unmoved.

"I'm sure you'll look ravishing in any dress you pick." I press a kiss to her lips and rise from the carpet. Peeking out, I find everyone chatting in the store, but Margaux is gone.

"I locked the door; she won't be coming back," Billie informs me.

I turn back to Savannah. "I'll take her so you can change." I scoop Emerson into my arms and offer Savannah my hand. Once she's standing, I kiss her again before slipping out of the fitting room.

SAVANNAH

Never did I expect Mrs. Morgan to show up at the shop. My only priority was to keep Emerson safe and away from her. Sam has no intention of allowing his mother to see her, and I don't blame him one bit. Her actions require a harsh response.

We're on our way back to Cash and Noelle's to clean up for dinner. Billie and Peter are hosting a small dinner party.

"Hey, how are you?" I whisper to Sam.

He looks at our intertwined fingers, squeezing tightly. "I wasn't expecting Margaux to show up here. It threw me. I'm grateful Kelly still has someone from Blackthorne with her at the shop. Thankfully, Jimmy prevented her entering my home, but I'm beginning to wonder if I need more security or if I need to leave the city altogether."

That statement could have so many implications for me. "Is this something that came up today?" I ask cautiously, wondering if it was always the plan to move out of New York City. Although, there truly isn't anything keeping me there anymore. Scarlett is an adult. She doesn't need me to take care of her anymore, hasn't for the last few years.

"Moving? Yes, for the most part. The thought crossed my mind last night while Cash and I were hanging out. It's peaceful here. Overall, Billie and Cash don't have any run-ins with the paparazzi."

"Oh."

"I haven't made up my mind, sweetheart. However, I plan to speak with Jacob of Blackthorne when we get back to New York. I'm not comfortable leaving Emerson with a nanny without security. It isn't good for her to be trapped inside. I could move to Cash's place. His terrace would afford some time outdoors with complete security. I'm not a fan of you not having security either, if I'm being honest."

"I don't need security, Sam." No one has bothered me, but if I have Emerson with me, it could become an issue.

"I disagree. I'm suggesting we talk with Jacob and go from there. Does that work for you?"

"Okay. To be clear, I'm not agreeing to anything except that for now."

Nodding, he lifts my hand and presses a kiss to it. "Thank you, *cara mia.*"

Every time he calls me that, I fall more. What am I willing to bend on to be with Sam? I've worked my ass off to provide for myself, Scarlett, and pay for her education. There are so many questions, ones we should discuss but probably not now.

After a wonderful dinner at Billie's, we return to Cash's and turn in for the night. He's tucking Emerson into her crib. I grab a blanket from the chair and step outside. Tucking my legs under me, I cover myself with the blanket.

"Can I join you?" Sam asks a few minutes later, standing in the doorway.

Confusion crosses my face. "Why would you think you have to ask?"

"You were distant at dinner. Did I upset you before with my talk about security and possibly moving?"

"No. Yes. Maybe a little." A deep sigh slips past my lips.

"Please tell me. The atmosphere here is significantly different than in the city. I wholly understand why Cash and Billie love it here. I haven't made any decisions. I wouldn't without your input anyway." He sits on the ottoman, his hands surrounding mine.

Surprise courses through me. "Why?"

"I'm crazy about you. I realize we became a couple recently, but it isn't as if I need time to make sure you're not loony. I already know you aren't. We've worked together for a year. I know more about you than most couples who are only this far into their relationship. You're brilliant, diligent, kind, and sexy. Your shoes and pencil skirts drive me to distraction, but after work Savannah is equally, if not more, attractive."

"Puh-lease." There's no chance that is true.

He grins. "Seriously, workday Savannah is a driven, no-nonsense woman with exacting standards for herself, her work, and even her boss. After work Savannah is real; you asleep, snuggled against my chest is perfection, your lips on mine is heavenly, and the woman who protected my daughter today is more than I could ever hope for—for me and for her."

"Sam, what are you saying?"

"I want a future with you. I don't know what it looks like regarding where we live and work, but as long as you're beside me, we can handle anything."

"What does your future look like?"

"I want the fairy tale—a partnership with my wife, a bunch more kids, and a welcoming home."

I raise an eyebrow.

"Where did I lose you? A bunch of kids?"

"Maybe. What does a bunch of kids mean to you?" He could say he wants ten children, and I would consider it.

"Four."

"I want you too. There are a lot of things to figure out. For now, I'll talk to Jacob with you, but I'm not sure it's necessary to spend money for someone to follow me around. Generally, I don't go anywhere alone."

"Thank you. I appreciate you hearing him out at least."

Leaning forward, I cup his face before dragging my tongue along his lips. A low groan seeps from his throat. I circle his lips again before dipping my tongue into his hungry mouth, exploring to my heart's content.

"*Cara mia,* let's go to bed."

Sam slides his arm around my waist, pulling me to my feet, before lifting me in his arms. Once back inside, he locks the balcony door, adds space between us so the blanket drops to the floor. I lift my fingers to the buttons of his Oxford shirt and unclasp them one by one. When a few inches of his hard chest are visible, I drag my tongue downward until I reach his waist. We dance to the bed, stripping the remainder of our clothes as we go. After Sam lays me on the bed, he jumps off and hurries to the door.

"What are you doing?" I lean up on my elbows to watch him. I could watch him for the rest of my days, even when he's being silly.

"I'm not taking any chances with that view." He locks the door and returns to the foot of the bed.

I chuckle softly.

Sam sets his mouth to the top of my foot and worships every inch of my body up to my mouth. It takes restraint not to hurry him up. The sensations running up and down my spine make me shiver.

Pressing my lips to his, I kiss him slowly and deliberately. Reaching for the side table, he opens the drawer.

"Sam, I have an IUD. I want you bare."

As the words fall from my mouth, he returns his gaze to mine as he lengthens against my hip. The heat in his eyes shifts from straight lust to something deeper. I feel it too, the sense that, after our conversations, this is somehow even bigger than this morning.

"Say something," I beg, looking at his now closed eyes.

"No one has ever trusted me with so much," he whispers.

I don't miss the fact that he was safe with Marisol and Emerson is still here, but that doesn't concern me. He's an honorable man.

"I do. I trust you that much." Lifting, I kiss him softly.

His hand slides around my neck, holding me tighter. I feel his chest expand fully before he exhales excruciatingly slowly. Sam's grip loosens as he draws back. Claiming my mouth, he kisses away my newfound concerns about his previous relationships. He's never had unprotected sex with anyone including his fiancée.

I widen my thighs, renewing my invitation. This time, without hesitation, Sam positions the tip of his shaft at my opening. Even that slight graze makes my core tighten with anticipation. Staring into my eyes, he pushes forward languidly, inch by perfect inch until he's fully seated. My eyes flutter closed for the briefest of moments to revel in the decadence of how I feel. They fly open as he pulls almost completely out before plunging deep into my center again.

"Holy hell, that feels—"

"Savannah." My name dripping from his lips sounds like a prayer.

With purpose, Sam moves inside me, sending spikes of increasing pleasure spreading over my entire body. The beginning of my release swirls low in my belly, a knot forming in my lower back. I cling to Sam as he pulses in my wetness. Shudders take over as my orgasm causes my muscles to clench and convulse around his length. The rippling of my sex pushes Sam over the edge as he explodes inside me.

Lowering himself on top of me, he rests his head on my shoulder. If I thought I didn't have words the first time, that pales in comparison to my feelings now.

I close my eyes to regain control of my breathing only to open them with the sun filtering into the room from the balcony door. Sam's body is draped over me, but we're covered. I strain to find a clock, hoping to see what time it is. Not only do I fail in that endeavor, but I wake Sam.

SAMSON

"Good morning, *cara mia*." Pressing a kiss to the elegant slope of her neck, I imagine when I'll get to enjoy this again. I want to wake up with her every day, but it's so soon.

"Is it even morning?"

I smirk against her skin. "It should be. I don't want to wake Emerson."

"She didn't get up last night?"

"No, she slept right through until now. I'm sure it's a fluke and a miracle, but I'll take it," I whisper, snuggling closer to Savannah's lush curves.

"I like waking up with you."

"Me too."

Lifting my head, I seal my lips over hers. As if on cue, Emme starts wailing from the crib. Shaking my head, I roll over to sitting. Savannah sits as well, pulling on my shirt from last night. *Damn!*

"You look hot in my shirt," I murmur before kissing her quickly.

"Thank you. Be careful, I may raid your closet the next time I'm over."

"You can take whatever you want." I grab a diaper while Savannah prepares a double bottle for Emme. It has been six hours since she ate last. Emme's cries decrease once she's dry. I tuck her into the crook of my arm and settle against the headboard. Savannah places a cloth on my shoulder and hands me a bottle before taking a seat facing me.

"What time is our flight?"

I suppress a laugh. "Cash is flying us home, so we can leave whenever we want. Why?"

"Yesterday Billie, Kelly, and Noelle gave me a list of things to see before we leave. It includes a lighthouse, a restaurant with taffy in the window, a coffee shop, and a store with floor-to-ceiling candy. Do we have time to check some of them out?"

"We have as much time as you want, beautiful."

Content with my response, Savannah gathers what she needs for a shower. She leans forward to search for something and bares herself to me.

"Savannah." I choke out while burping Emme. If I weren't holding her or she was still asleep, I would be drawing my hands up the backs of her thighs as fast I could get behind her.

"What?" It takes her a moment to realize that she's naked beneath my shirt. Straightening up, she saunters over and kisses me. "I'll try to behave."

Interesting little twist, Savannah is part vixen. I love it. "No need to behave on my account. You can be as naughty as you want."

After showering and packing for the trip home, we head downstairs for some breakfast. It appears that Cash and Noelle are still sleeping. I leave a note on the table, borrow Cash's keys, and we set out on an adventure. A quick search and we secure directions to the coffee shop the girls recommended and notice it's only a short walk to the Goldenrod Restaurant where the taffy is made.

After securing Emme into her stroller, we step into the Perk.

"Good morning, welcome to the Perk. What can I get for you?"

"My sister recommended the cinnamon swirl latte and a scone to my girlfriend last night."

"Who is your sister?" A look of concern must have crossed my face. "I didn't mean to overstep. I'm the owner, Kelsey Ramirez," the curvy brunette says, extending her hand.

"My apologizes. I'm not used to people not having an agenda outside of kindness. I'm Sam Morgan, and this is my girlfriend, Savannah Clemons. Cash and Billie are my siblings."

"Well, that makes complete sense. You look like Cash, or he looks like you if you're older."

"I'm older. It's a pleasure to meet you, Kelsey." I freeze the moment she looks down at the stroller. I'm ecstatic that Savannah accepts Emerson, but I don't want to explain my shortcomings each time someone meets her.

"Isn't she gorgeous. What is her name?"

"Emerson." I hold my breath, waiting for the next obvious question. When it doesn't come, Kelsey vaults to the top of my list of good people.

"Well, congratulations! What can I get for you, Savannah?"

"I'll have the same latte, but I would prefer a sweet scone instead."

"No problem." Kelsey steps away from the counter to prepare our lattes.

Returning with our spoils, Kelsey rings us out. "Will I see you at the wedding?"

"Yes, we'll be there. It was a pleasure meeting you." I reply.

"You as well. Have a great day," Kelsey says before turning to her next customer. Even though it's a bit chilly, we walk the short distance to the Goldenrod Restaurant, enjoying our breakfast while watching the taffy stretch in the window as well as watching the freshly cut pieces twisted into their wrappers. Billie is right, the latte is delicious.

Rounding the building, Sam points out Billie's condo.

"That view must be spectacular. I dare say it might be better than yours."

"I would agree. My view is great, but the ocean across the street is even better. Want to sit for a few minutes or are you cold?"

"No, let's sit. Emme will be warm enough."

We sit on one of the benches along the sidewalk. It's clearly the off-season here as there are very few tourists milling about.

"This is amazing!" Savannah scoots closer to me.

"It is. The peacefulness of this quaint town was evident when I dropped in on Billie after my trip to Italy last year for the Rossi policy."

"Is that why you were gone an extra day? You came here before coming home."

"Yes, I came to thank Billie for helping Auggie. I was also able to meet Peter."

"I think you left out the grilling part."

Containing my grin is impossible. "Guilty. If I had known that Cash took care of it, I would have been nicer from the start. A big brother has to check things out."

"How is that going to work for Emerson? She's the oldest."

"She's not dating until she's thirty."

Savannah laughs before taking a sip of her latte. Her laugh is soothing and fun. It wraps around me like a warm, cozy blanket. My phone vibrates in my pocket.

Cash: What time do you want to leave?

Me: We're headed to the lighthouse and then back there. Does that work?

Cash: That works. I'll be ready.

"That was Cash. We should head to the lighthouse, but we're going to need to skip the candy store this time."

"Okay. No problem." She rises and tucks the blanket around Emme again before we stroll to the car.

As I drive up the winding road, the houses get more luxurious as we climb. We pass Billie's house along the way.

"If I had realized we were this close last night, I would have suggested it."

"It's fine. I didn't notice either." I respond.

I pull into a spot on the right after curving into the driveway. The Nubble Lighthouse is straight ahead and simply majestic. I hop out and round the truck to open Savannah's door. After securing Emme into her stroller, we walk side by side to the placard on the rock. The waves crash on the jagged rocks below. It's beautiful here. The stately lighthouse is set across a narrow channel from where we're standing.

"Thank you for bringing me here." She slides her arm around my waist as I settle mine on her shoulders.

"Of course. You're welcome. It wasn't far." I'll go wherever I need to for Emme and Savannah. Hopefully, she'll understand that soon.

"I meant here as in this weekend." She looks up at me. The sheer desire in her eyes hits me square in the chest.

I lean down and kiss her softly. "*Cara mia*, I want to clear something up right now. I want you... with me, with us. If it were practical or if I thought for one moment you would be amenable, I would have you move in with me. I realize it doesn't make sense yet, but I have no intention of letting you go now that you're in my life outside of work."

"Sam, I'm speechless."

I turn to face her, drawing my thumb across her lips. She rises on her toes to meet my lips. A few tempting, promising kisses later, I draw back.

"We should go home." Unfortunately, that means I'm sleeping alone tonight.

She nods, grabbing the handle of Emme's stroller.

"Excuse me." A woman with graying hair approaches us, waving.

"Can I help you?"

"My sister and I are here to check off another New England lighthouse from our bucket list. Anyway, when I was taking a photo of this one, I caught the two of you. You're a gorgeous couple."

"Thank you."

"Oh my! How old is she? She's perfect."

"A few weeks," I reply.

"You look fabulous, dear," the woman addresses Savannah.

"She's—"

I cut off Savannah's response by setting my hand on her arm. I don't feel it's necessary to explain, nor do I want to put Savannah on the spot right now.

"Anyway, if you could give me your phone number, I can send the photo to you."

I hesitantly provide my phone number, and she sends the photo. Quickly, I glance down and I'm glad she shared it. It captures the moment my lips touched Savannah's. The image is stunning.

"Thank you. I appreciate this so much. I hope you get to finish your bucket list."

"You're welcome. Have a lovely day." The woman returns to where her sister is looking on. With a wave, they walk toward their car.

"Can I see it?" Savannah asks, and I turn my phone so she can view the image.

"Wow, I've never seen so much emotion in one image before."

"Me either." I kiss her forehead and escort her to the truck. Hours later I'm stepping off the elevator at my penthouse without Savannah beside me. I don't like how I feel, not one bit.

SAVANNAH

Our weekend away was simply magical. Cash and Noelle were gracious, and Billie is funny and friendly. Not even my run-in with Margaux will mess up how I feel about the trip. Now I'm washing laundry alone at my apartment wondering where our boundaries are. He said he wants me to move in with him, and as much as I want to fall asleep with Sam, it's way too soon to even consider giving up my apartment. I send him a text before going to bed.

Me: Good night, Sam.

I climb into my cold bed, set an alarm on my phone, and burrow into the covers, wishing I weren't alone. Once again I'm counting the divots on my ceiling.

Sam: Good night, cara mia. *Why don't you bring the files over near lunch?*

Me: I will.

Even with a shortened timeframe, sleep still eludes me. After sleeping through my morning run, I hurry into the shower and get ready to take on overflowing inboxes and voice mail.

The flashbulbs illuminate as I step out of the building. Ignoring the questions, I walk straight to the car Sam sent for me. I knew better than to argue with him on the flight back to New York. Right now I'm grateful he was adamant. Also, the absence of paparazzi in Maine is even more notable now.

"Good morning, Miss Clemons," the driver greets me at the door.

"Morning." I slide into the back seat and exhale harshly.

"To the office?"

"Yes, thank you." The ride to the office passes quickly and quietly.

Saul, as the name tag indicates, escorts me into the lobby this morning. "Have a great day, Miss Clemons."

"Thank you. You as well."

As the doors open, I step into the office, shrug off my jacket, and tackle my stuffed inbox. The printer spits out page after page of work from inquires, policies, and quote requests. After separating everything into the appropriate files, I fall into Sam's chair and cull through his messages. Now, the printer is humming again. I prepare a fresh cup of coffee and tackle those files. The first time I glance at the clock, it's near eleven. That gives me plenty of time to gather the rest of these, categorize them, and meet Sam and Emme for lunch.

Near noon, I shove the files into my bag and ride down to the lobby. When the doors open, I'm gifted with a spectacular view, Sam and Emme waiting to ride the elevator up.

"Hi." I push out, flustered by their presence.

Sam skims his lips across mine lightly. "Hi, gorgeous. We came to escort you to lunch."

"I thought we were eating at your place."

"We are. I decided to take Emme for a walk." Sam takes the files and stows them under the stroller before offering me his arm.

I loop mine through his, and we walk back to his place. It's not as chilly in the city as it was over the weekend. The crispness of fall is fading away to the drab cold before the snow starts to fall. We walk a block deeper to use the side entrance of Sam's building. "How did she sleep last night?"

"Pretty well, actually. I fed her at eleven, and she slept until five."

"That's great considering her age."

Sam nods. "Do you have appointments tomorrow morning?"

"No, why?"

"I'm meeting with Jacob and Finn, one of his staff members from Blackthorne, at ten to discuss security. I would like you to be there."

"Okay. I'll gather the latest items first thing and then come over."

"Thank you. Do you think that Scarlett would be able to join us as well?"

"I'll ask her." Pulling out my phone, I send a quick text to Scarlett to see if she's available tomorrow morning.

"I know you aren't keen on having someone with you."

"It's more that I don't think it's a necessary expense. Is the press annoying? Sure. Will they harm me? Unlikely."

His demeanor shifts after my last statement. Before he addresses my words, we speak to Jimmy briefly and ride upstairs.

The instant we step into his home, he gathers me into his arms. "That's what you don't understand. First, the press could harm you like they did Billie. You don't have any details, but suffice it to say, it was horrible."

"What happened to Billie?" I ask softly. Billie is vibrant and happy. No one would ever know something awful happened to her.

"After the gala a few years ago, paparazzi stalked her, causing a car accident. She had extensive damage to her face, along with smaller lacerations on her arms. The surgery took hours. It was a close second to the torture of waiting for the paternity results for Emme."

"I'm sorry. I didn't know."

"Also, I know you don't care about my wealth. If I thought you did, you wouldn't be here. I don't care if protecting Emme, you, and Scarlett bankrupts me, I'll do it."

"Sam, that's insane."

"It's not, *cara mia*. As arrogant as this may sound, I don't have to work another day of my life, and it still won't decrease my wealth. My parents created a trust for the four of us at birth. Along with my siblings, I receive a set amount of money each month. There are strings attached to the money, such as gainful employment, never tarnish the Morgan name, and acting with class in public when requested as a family, like the gala. In my opinion, the last part is negotiable at this point considering the status of my parents' marriage and Margaux's latest actions. At age thirty, we can request the corpus be turned over to us for investing on our own."

"Have you and Cash made that request?"

"Yes, but my parents believe that Cash and I rely on our trust payments to survive. That we party and squander our salaries from our jobs. That is wholly inaccurate. In fact, we live off our salaries. We have taken our trust payments, pooled them, and invested wisely for the last ten years. We offered to pool Auggie's when he graduated from culinary school this past spring."

"What about Billie?"

"Billie is a different case. When she moved to Maine after the accident, my parents cut her off completely. Cash and I sent her money each month to make sure she was comfortable. She only used a small portion of the funds and returned the rest when I dropped in on her after my Italy trip. When she stood up to them and refused to marry Thorsten Thomas, they sold her loft and turned her entire trust over to her. She hasn't touched a penny of it. Eventually, she'll find a use for it, but for now it's gaining interest at a decent rate. I believe Cash offered to pool her money as well, but she hasn't responded."

"I had no idea."

"I know. Protecting you is important to me. It'll destroy me if something happens to you because of our relationship. It's one thing that you work for me; it's something else now that were a couple."

The intercom buzzes. "Sir, there is a delivery for you."

"Thank you, Jimmy. Send it up." Sam accepts the bags from Jimmy and he leaves.

"Did you order the entire restaurant?" I ask, stepping out of my shoes.

"No, I skipped breakfast, and apparently that's reflected in our lunch options." A grin splashes across his face.

We dig into the feast that Sam ordered before tackling the stack of files I brought over. Hours later, our review is finished and the leftovers have been eaten for dinner. Emme is stretching on the blanket. Sam settles into the corner of the couch, and I cuddle next to him, setting my head on his chest. His arm holds me close with his hand gripping my waist. I want to stay here. Instead, I need to go home to a quiet, lonely, empty apartment. Should I consider moving in here? *That's crazy!* We've only been dating for barely a month. *Does that really matter though? Ugh!*

"Why did you tense up?"

Crap! I can't hide anything from him—not that I'm trying to.

"I need to go home."

"That can't be it." Clearly, he can read me well.

"Can I be brutally honest?"

"Always."

"Spending the weekend with you was absolutely perfect. Skipping my chat with Margaux would have been ideal, but aside from that…."

"I agree. What does that have to do with right now?"

Inhaling sharply, I admit, "I don't want to go home."

"Then don't go home. Stay."

"I can't, at least not yet, despite wanting to more than I should at this point."

"Will you agree to spend the weekend here?"

"Yes."

"Then, whenever you're ready, we would love for you and Gray to move in with us. Please think about it."

Deep down I know that if Emme wasn't here, he would end up staying at my place because he wouldn't let me ride home alone. Presumably, what my proposed security would do.

Leaning up, I intend to kiss him softly. Within seconds of my lips touching his, I'm flat on my back looking into his dark eyes.

Sam savors my mouth, ensuring I know he meant what he said and cracking my resolve deeper with each sweep of his tongue. After exploring the depths of my mouth, along my jawline, and neck, Sam pulls back. The unspoken words in his eyes are screaming at me. I'm falling hard and fast too.

With a kiss to my forehead, he leans back on his heels, and I swing my legs to the floor. After rising, I touch Emme's cheek before sliding on my shoes.

"I'll be here in the morning. Hopefully, with Scarlett. Good night, Sam."

Closing the gap between us, I kiss him again before stepping into the elevator.

SAMSON

After nine, Savannah and Scarlett step off the elevator. Savannah is dressed for work in an emerald green sheath dress and the heels with the ankle bow I love so much, while Scarlett is wearing a graphic tee, distressed jeans, zippered hoodie, and combat boots. With Emme on my shoulder, I kiss Savannah and welcome Scarlett to my home.

"Would you like some coffee?"

"No, thank you. I'm fine," Scarlett replies, looking around. As I observe Scarlett, I would put her in the not dateable column for someone like me. She sees the luxury and opulence of my home whereas Savannah was more concerned about me when she was here the first time. More succinctly, Savannah sees me whereas Scarlett only sees my wealth.

"Savannah, can I have a word with you in my office?"

She follows me. Once we're alone, I set Emme on her playmat and kiss Savannah like I won't have an opportunity to kiss her for a few hours, which I likely won't.

"Morning to you too." A gorgeous smile graces her face.

"Thank you for coming and dragging Scarlett along."

"You're welcome."

"I'm really glad Scarlett didn't pilfer those shoes when she moved out. They're hot!"

"Interesting. this pair or all of them?"

"All of your shoes make your legs look a mile long, but that pair is my favorite. Are shoes your thing?"

"I don't really splurge on anything specific. I set any extra funds aside for Scarlett's tuition."

"If you could splurge, what would you buy?"

"I've never really thought about it. I have everything I need. I've taught myself not to want extras for Scarlett."

Her responses are in no way helping me learn more about her. So far I know she appreciates flowers, good company, and jazz music. She has no interest in expensive shoes, handbags, or lingerie. I'll have to hope she likes what I choose.

Jimmy announces our guests as we return to the living room.

Jacob and Finn exit the elevator. Jacob embodies what private security looks like—tall, built, and a hardened look that would make anyone pause. Finn is younger, blond, and equally as built as Jacob.

"Thank you for taking this meeting, Jacob."

"You're welcome. Norah will take any excuse to shop, especially in New York City. The dent she'll make in her bank account for shoes and lingerie in the time I'm here meeting with you would blow your mind." Norah and Jacob got married a few months ago. Norah's sister Kelly is married to my brother-in-law, Ellis.

I laugh.

Jacob owns Blackthorne Security. He's highly recommended, having worked with Ellis and Kelly for her stalker and when they went public as a couple. He also assisted Cash and Noelle when they lived in the city. Since their move to York Beach, he handles their property security and special events only.

Savannah is securing Emme in her swing. Jacob sits on the armchair, and Finn takes a seat in the corner of the couch. Scarlett sits next to him with a fair amount of space between them. I take a seat across from Jacob. Savannah sits on the arm of the chair beside me. She declines my offer to take the chair.

"Would you like coffee?" I offer Jacob and Finn after we're all settle in the living room.

"No, thank you. Let's get started. It's my understanding that Savannah works for you at Morgan Insurance and has for a little more than a year. Recently, you started dating and learned that you have a daughter."

"Yes."

"What is the situation with her mother?"

"Marisol is deceased."

Jacob nods curtly. "Are there any other maternal family members that will be near Emerson?"

"Marisol's mother, Maria-Luisa, has and will continue to spend time with Emerson. In fact, I hope Maria-Luisa would be willing to care for her when I return to work."

"Is the situation with your family the same?"

"No, my father, siblings, and their significant others, including Caroline Waterman are welcome here to spend time with Emerson. Margaux is not welcome anywhere near me, Emerson, or Savannah. Frankly, I don't know that she's aware of Scarlett at this point."

"I understand. There are also concerns with the increased press at your home and Savannah's."

"Yes."

"As you're aware, I can't do anything about the press except assist Savannah, Scarlett, and Emerson safe passage through them."

I nod. I'm fully aware of this limitation. The deeper we get into this conversation, the better Maine is looking.

"Scarlett, you recently moved into a new apartment with two friends. Has the press followed you there?"

"No, not that I've seen. I have seen photographers on the edge of campus though." Scarlett is fidgeting with the cuff of her sweater.

Jacob and Finn both nod. I also notice Finn sets his hand on Scarlett's wrist to calm her down. We spend almost an hour going over our regular schedule and plans, like hiring a nanny, my going back to the office, etc.

"In the short-term, I would recommend that someone escort Savannah when she leaves the office, home, or here. Overnight security doesn't seem necessary unless the press escalates. For Scarlett, I recommend the same thing, an escort when she leaves home, campus, or work at the supper club."

I notice that Scarlett begins fidgeting more when Jacob mentions her workplace. Something is off there.

"What is your plan for your daughter?" Jacob asks pointedly.

"She'll be with me the rest of this week. I plan to hire someone for mornings at a minimum. Do you recommend security for Emme or me?"

"It shouldn't be an issue for a same staff member to cover Savannah and your daughter. Once Savannah is at work, based on her schedule, she doesn't leave. After our team brings her to the office, he or she would be able to escort your nanny wherever they need to go with your daughter. If it becomes too difficult, we can add someone specifically for Emerson. As far as you, you aren't the story. Savannah and Emerson are. If you're at work or out with Savannah or Emerson, one of my team would accompany you as they would be assigned to her. I don't think you need your own."

"I understand. What will you need from us?" I thread my fingers with Savannah's.

"I'll need a list of anyone you'll be in contact with regularly. Sam, I don't need you to list your family. I thoroughly check them monthly for Billie and Cash. List any events you plan to attend and any get-togethers that include people other than your siblings, their significant others, or any of the couples in the Maine girl gang. Savannah, I know you're estranged, but the latest address for your father would be appreciated. Scarlett, I need your roommate's names, your boyfriend, and your boss. Does anyone have questions?"

"Is this really necessary?" Scarlett whispers.

"Scar—"

Jacob cuts Savannah off. "Based on my assessment, you probably have about a week, maybe ten days before the press finds your new place. Finn will be as discreet as possible and not interfere with your life. He'll simply escort you where you need to go. It's paramount that you're forthcoming with him about your schedule, and no sneaking off."

I'm glad Jacob sees that Scarlett is hiding something as well. I'll talk to Savannah about it later, but at least Jacob is aware.

"Savannah, you met Christoph over the weekend, right?"

"Yes."

"Perfect, he'll meet you at your apartment to escort you to work in the morning. What time do you need him there?"

"I leave by seven," Savannah replies, tightening her grip on my fingers.

"No problem. Scarlett, what is your schedule for the rest of the day?"

"I have a class at one and then a shift from five to midnight." She's rolling the cuff of her hoodie again.

"Fine, you're free to leave. I need that list of information by the end of tomorrow. Please understand having Finn with you is for your safety and your sister's peace of mind, not a punishment."

Scarlett stands along with Savannah. She escorts her sister to the door with Finn still talking with Jacob. I watch them. Scarlett is clearly not happy about the situation, but whatever Savannah says appeases her, at least for now. The only words I can make out are *thank you* from their conversation near the elevator.

Once Scarlett leaves, Savannah rejoins us in the living room.

"She's hiding something," Jacob states plainly.

"I agree, but I don't know what it is," Savannah replies.

"Finn is older than he looks. It's one of the reasons I chose him. My other available staff members are younger. He'll be able to handle Scarlett and keep her safe. If she's in any precarious situations, Finn will alert me and maintain her safety."

"Thank you, Jacob."

"I appreciate you traveling for this meeting," I add before his departure.

"Of course. I understand your need for discretion and privacy. Please let me know if anything changes."

"I will." I shake his hand, and then Jacob shakes Savannah's. Then she moves to Emme who is squirming and whining in her swing.

The buzz from the intercom announces I have a guest. "Sir, I'm sorry to interrupt but your brother is here."

"Thank you, Jimmy. He can come up." After a short chat with Auggie, Jacob leaves to meet Norah and her copious shopping bags. My brothers and I all look strikingly similar. However, Auggie is a bit thinner than Cash and me considering his limited time to spend at the gym.

"Hey, bro. How are you?"

Auggie agreed to watch Emme for me so I can spend some time with Savannah alone. I sincerely hope she doesn't hate surprises. We're going out for the afternoon so that Auggie can prepare dinner for us.

"I'm well. Where is my niece? I want to get in a little alone time before Caro arrives."

I laugh as Savannah returns to the living room with a freshly diapered Emme.

"Hi, Savannah."

"Hi, Auggie. It's nice to see you again."

Auggie reaches out his arms, takes Emme, and cradles her as if she isn't his first niece.

"She shouldn't need to eat for a few hours. There's a bottle set up on the counter. Diapers are in her room past the office."

"Sam, what's going on?"

"You haven't told her?" Auggie asks with a sly grin on his face.

"Nope, she has no idea."

"Smooth, Sam."

"Savannah, we're going on a day date. Auggie and Caro are going to watch Emme for us."

"That sounds wonderful, but what about work? My boss is very particular about his timelines for completing new business."

"I spoke with him, and he's going to give you extra time for any work that came in since Monday morning."

"That's very generous. So, where are we going?"

"That's a surprise, sweetheart." I kiss my daughter, high-five my brother, and offer her my arm before pressing the down button.

SAVANNAH

Auggie is right. *Smooth, Samson.* Looping my arm in his, we ride downstairs to a waiting car.

"What are you up to?"

"I knew this morning would be difficult for you and Scarlett, so I gave us the afternoon off. Well, you mostly."

"Thank you. I truly wish I knew what she's hiding. Although I don't know if it would be any different if she still lived with me. She's clearly been hiding things for a while."

"I care about what you're saying, but I don't want to talk about Scarlett, Jacob, Finn, Christoph, or anything surrounding this morning until tomorrow."

"Okay," I reply, glancing out the window.

"That won't help you figure out where we're going, *cara mia.*"

Shaking my head, I ask, "Will you give me a hint?"

"Nope, but I'll kiss you to get your mind off your lack of information."

"That might work."

Sam unbuckles my seat belt, tugs me into the middle of the seat, and re-buckles me next to him. He worships my mouth long after we've come to a stop in front of our destination. I'm not surprised; each time Sam touches me, even if it's to take my hand, everything around us ceases to exist. The only reason I'm aware is that our driver knocks on the window to alert us we've arrived.

"I guess we need to get out," he murmurs against my neck.

All I can do is nod. The last thing I want to do right now is move out of his arms. With a deep inhale, I unbuckle and wait for Sam to exit the car. I slide my fingers into his and step onto the curb. He tucks my arm around his, holding it with his opposite hand.

"I'll return at the designated time, sir."

"Thank you." Sam leads me into a nondescript door at the rear of a building.

"Sam, where are we?"

A young woman appears from the right after we enter the building. "Good afternoon, Mr. Morgan. Miss Clemons. If you follow me, your tour window will begin soon. Here's a map in case you need guidance. Your path lays out the most advantageous route to your destination."

Unfortunately, her name tag doesn't offer me any clues. As we round the corner, a wall of windows comes into view. Wherever we are, it's beautiful.

"Thank you," Sam replies without answering my question. Tugging me closer, he pushes open the door.

We're surrounded by lush gardens and striking blooms. It smells wonderful too! I haven't spent much time taking in tourist attractions in this city.

"This is… wow! Where are we?"

"We're at the Brooklyn Botanic Garden."

I pull back on his arm slightly to make him stop walking. After pressing a chaste kiss to his lips, I smile and start walking again.

Sam and I spend the next few hours walking through the immense and gorgeous gardens. There's a Fragrance Garden, which includes a section that allows touching the plants. The Shakespeare Garden features plants mentioned in his works, including daffodils, dwarf irises, squill, and spray asters. Next we stroll through the Water Garden. The area is beautiful.

"Sam, look." I point to our right. There's a small group of butterflies on some asters. We pause to watch them for a few minutes.

Our last stop is the Osborne Garden. The path we followed seems odd until I notice the small tent set up near the side. Of all the different ones we saw today, this one is my favorite. The pergolas are draped with wisteria, although they aren't in bloom right now. The foliage of fall decorates the space with crisp reds, deep oranges, and bright yellow hues.

"Good afternoon, Mr. Morgan. Miss Clemons. I'm Lenora. I'll be here if you need anything else."

Sam thanks her as we step into the small tent. Inside there is a small table set for two with a charcuterie board, a bottle of wine, and two glasses. The upper half of the tent and the ceiling are clear so we can see outside but still have some privacy.

"This is too much, Sam." I don't need all of this. He doesn't need to spend money on me.

"What do you mean?"

"I don't need more than the average boyfriend could make happen."

"The average guy could make this happen with a lot more lead time. The only thing my name got me today was a shortened timeframe. *Cara mia*, I was honest with you when I told you about my wealth. I could never spend it all. Sometimes, like having security and gifts I may purchase, you may feel like it's overboard. The only thing I can promise is to attempt to reel in the costs after you open this." He hands me a small navy bag.

"What's this for?"

"I wanted to get you a gift. It was harder than I thought it was going to be. You're practical, and you haven't given me any clues as to what you might like."

Lifting the crinkly tissue out of the bag, I find a small black box inside. The most beautiful emerald ring nestles in the velvet cushion. A tear falls from my eye. "Did you know?"

"*Cara mia*, please don't cry. Did I know what?" Sam slides the pad of his thumb across the ball of my cheek, wiping my tear away.

"The only gift I ever received from my mother was an emerald ring right before Scarlett was born."

"Why an emerald?"

"It's my birthstone."

"I didn't know, but I'm glad I chose it."

"Why did you choose it?"

"Emeralds are said to be the gemstone of the goddess Venus. She's known as the purveyor of hope and love." He takes the box from my shaking hands. Lifting my hand, he slides it onto my ring finger.

How it fits perfectly is beyond me.

"It's beautiful, Sam. Thank you." Without releasing his hand, I round the table and tug him to his feet. Once he's standing, I kiss him softly, at least that was my intention. Rapidly the tenor of our kiss increases exponentially to the point where I force myself not to unbutton his Oxford, and pull back from his sinful mouth.

"Are you ready for the next part of our date?"

"There's more?"

"Of course. I couldn't possibly take my woman on a date without feeding her a meal. Let's go."

"Your woman?"

"Not a fan of that?"

"Quite the opposite, I'm absolutely comfortable with that."

If I've learned anything today, I won't ask any questions about dates. Sam is a master planner. Everything about our dates have been amazing, especially the ones that were spontaneous like at the Nubble Lighthouse. We walk to the car with our hands linked.

SAMSON

Learning about Savannah is becoming one of my favorite things. She clearly has shifted her opinion on personal security, or at least she's willing to indulge me. I'm grateful she brought Scarlett along to this morning's meeting as well. Thankfully, I can spoil her if I want to, and I plan to. I need to keep learning so I know what to give her—although I'm certain she truly only wants my time.

When we arrive at my home, Auggie is plating something in the kitchen. Caro is setting the table while Emme is snug in her swing.

"Perfect, right on time," Auggie says as we finish shucking our coats and shoes. Before sitting, I walk over the Emme and kiss her head. Savannah and Caro are hugging and chatting beside the table.

"How did it go here?"

"She's an angel. She ate about an hour ago, but she's been awake ever since then." Caro shares the update while filling our wine glasses. Then she leans over the island and grabs two salad plates before setting them at the table.

Once both Savannah and I are sitting, we dig into the first course. I couldn't tell you what we're eating. Caro fills us in as we take our first bite. The salad is parmesan brussels sprouts with pomegranate.

"This is amazing! I know you shared that Auggie went to culinary school, but I've never tasted anything this yummy!" Savannah savors her second bite.

"Thank you!" Auggie shouts from the kitchen.

Both Caro and Savannah laugh. A relaxed and happy Savannah is all I want. I lift her hand to my lips to kiss it.

Instead of letting go, she tugs me closer. "You're pretty good at the whole being my man thing."

"I'm figuring it out as I go."

"I need you to continue communicating with me honestly and we'll be fine. I may not like having Christoph or someone from Blackthorne with me, but I understand why you and Jacob feel it's necessary." Her lips taste like wine when she presses them to mine.

"I can do that."

Caro returns and takes our plates back to the kitchen. I would like Savannah to move in, but I don't want to have that conversation with Auggie and Caro here. I love my brother and Caro, but I would prefer privacy for that as well as her thoughts on moving to Maine. We haven't truly discussed that in depth either.

Emme starts to cry in her swing. Savannah and I both rise from the table, but Auggie swoops in and steals her away. The look on Caro's face is unmistakable. She has serious feelings for Auggie. I saw that look on Noelle's face when Cash was fawning over Emme. I make a note to tell

Auggie to figure out what he wants because Caro wants him. It may be on the same level he wants her.

He returns to the kitchen with his now soothed niece as Caro sets the main course before us.

"Auggie, you have outdone yourself. This looks and smells delicious." I lean down to fully smell the aroma.

"Thanks, that's pan-roasted chicken with a demi-glace paired with twice-roasted squash with parmesan butter and pepitas."

Savannah savoring her first bite and the noises coming from her mouth are too much for me to handle.

"So delicious, Auggie. Thank you."

"You're most welcome. Caro, can you help me with the dessert in the kitchen?" Auggie asks.

"Sure." She follows him into the kitchen.

"What's the deal with Auggie and Caroline? She's beautiful. Does he know she has feelings for him?" Savannah inquires, watching them slyly.

"Yes, she is. I'm sure he isn't aware of her feelings. He has been in love with her since boarding school."

"Might be time for him to consider asking her on a proper date," Savannah suggests, watching them in the kitchen.

I nod and continue inhaling my dinner.

"Sam, what's on your mind?" She sounds concerned.

Hiding my feelings from Savannah is not an option anymore. "It's not something I want to talk about now."

"I understand."

"Sweetheart, it's not bad. I would prefer complete privacy."

She nods and finishes her dinner. Lifting her glass to her lips, she savors the wine Auggie paired with our food.

"What is the one thing you can't live without? Thing, so I can't be the answer." I have no clue what she'll say.

Her cheeks turn bright pink. "Would I be your answer if I asked about a person?"

"It would be a tie."

"I don't collect anything like your albums, which I would love to listen to by the way. There really isn't anything. I love fabulous coffee and wine, but I could live without both if I had to."

She has always put other people ahead of herself. We're similar in that way.

"What about you? Do you collect things other than the albums?"

"No. The albums started when I was in boarding school. Meghan gave me the first one; I have been searching for original vinyl by jazz legends ever since."

Glancing past Savannah, I notice that Emme has fallen asleep. Caro breaks my line of sight, gathering the plates from dinner.

"Are you ready for dessert now?" Caro asks.

"No, thank you. I'm stuffed," Savannah answers.

"I could use some time too. Auggie, if you want to give us instructions so you can head out, that's fine."

"Sure, no problem. Savannah, step into my lair and I'll teach you how to plate it." Savannah enters the kitchen, and Caro takes her place at the table.

"She's amazing, Sam."

"More than I deserve." I turn to see Savannah intently listening to Auggie about our dessert. She does everything diligently.

"I don't know about that. You've taken a few hits lately, but you're triumphing."

"That's kind of you. What about you? When are you going to tell Auggie how you feel?"

"I have no idea what you're talking about," a now flustered Caro replies.

"Caro, I've known you for years. The last time I saw you look at Auggie like that was after the gala. If you have feelings beyond friendship for my brother, you should tell him."

"He doesn't want me. He's made that abundantly clear. I'm concretely in the friend zone."

"You might be surprised if you talk to him."

"Do you know something I don't?" she asks, hoping for more than I should share about Auggie's feelings.

"After seeing Cash fall head over heels for Noelle and how I feel about Savannah, I've seen that look both you and Auggie try to hide. Talk to him. You could be a conversation away from your happily ever after."

"Thanks, Sam. I'll think about it."

Auggie and Savannah join us near the table.

"Ready to go, Caro?" Auggie inquires.

"Sure. It was a pleasure seeing you both again and spending time with Emme."

"You too," Savannah and I reply in unison. We walk Auggie and Caro to the elevator and hug them both.

"Thank you for the amazing dinner."

"Anytime. Hopefully we can get together again soon," Auggie says before the door closes.

"As grateful as I am, I thought they would never leave." I pull Savannah into my arms and kiss her with urgency. Stepping backward, we glide toward the master bedroom. With each step, articles of clothing litter the floor. As much as I want to savor her, I need her tightening around me now.

"Savannah, I can't take this slowly tonight. Being with you all day and not being able to kiss you with abandon has been driving me mad."

"Good, neither can I."

Surprised but elated, I cup her from behind and find her wet and ready for me.

"What were you thinking about?" I want details, all the details. She has never been this wet before.

"You and how many different ways we could be together. Sam, I need you to fill me, now!"

"How adventurous are you?"

"Whatever you're thinking, you would be my first."

"I want to take you from behind. It has been on my mind since you settled Emme on your bed surrounded by pillows."

"I admire your self-restraint."

"Is that a yes?"

"That's a hell yes!"

Savannah's inner vixen is ready tonight. Without further prodding, I widen her stance and bury my shaft into her hot center. She's so tight. Her inner muscles clench around me as I stroke inside her. Reaching around her slim waist, I set my thumb against her clit, rubbing circles.

"Sam, don't stop!" Her words drop as her mounting release steals her focus.

With precision, I thrust harder to chase my own orgasm with her. Her legs shudder and quake. We fall over the edge into pure ecstasy at the same time. As we catch our breath, sweet whines echo through the monitor.

SAVANNAH

It's been a few weeks since our meeting with Jacob. The press coverage hasn't decreased. There's even a ticker along the top of Page Six called The Morgan Marriage Meter. Christoph or Connor have been with me daily. Now, they run with me to allow me to bypass the growing swarm of reporters each morning. Their numbers have been growing the longer Sam and I have been a couple despite a lack of confirmation from either of us. There are more staking out at Sam's as well. So far, they haven't bothered me. They simply hurl questions in my direction—some are offensive regarding the size of Sam's manhood, others innocuous about why he chose me—but generally they allow my security and me to pass through. I've learned to ignore the questions. Finn has been handling Scarlett well. I'm surprised at how well she has adapted to him. Grateful too.

Maria-Luisa has been caring for Emme in the mornings while Sam is at the office. Each afternoon, Sam works from home. For the most part, I join him, but some days like today, that isn't possible, especially considering I have to wrap up these files before spending the weekend at Sam's.

Near six, I call Connor, who is with me for the next two weeks while Christoph works with another client who requested him personally. All of Jacob's staff are highly trained, so it doesn't matter who escorts me where I need to go.

"Ready, Miss Cl—"

I interrupt him with the side-eye. It's professional to call me Miss Clemons, but that isn't me.

"Ready, Savannah?" Connor asks after stepping further into the office.

"Yes, thanks." I grab my tote, empty coffee mug, and overnight bag from the floor. Connor dutifully takes it from me before pressing the down button on the elevator. Generally, there is less press here at the office entrance as compared to my home and Sam's. The numbers are higher this evening.

"Going to your other job?" one reporter asks.

"Does your boyfriend know about your moonlighting?"

What the hell does that mean?

"Does insurance not pay well enough?"

The last one gets to me. I turn to face the petite, blonde reporter whose words affected me.

Gruffly Connor whispers, "Don't," in my ear and all but shoves me into the car. The moment the car doors slam, Connor is on his phone.

"Jake, we might have a problem brewing here." He finishes that call and dials again.

"Finn, call me with a status update at your earliest convenience."

"What makes you think there's a problem?"

"Their questions were different today. Generally they ask about you and Sam or something about your unconfirmed relationship. These were different—more personal, about you alone."

I consider his observations. "Fair enough. I don't have a second job anymore."

"Don't worry, Blaine will find it out."

"Who's Blaine?"

"Blaine works for Jacob. He's a white hat hacker and purveyor of information. He'll figure out what the press is talking about. The best thing for you to do is ignore them."

"That isn't as simple as you think."

"I know it isn't. If I've learned anything in this job, the women who aren't gold diggers, like Kelly, Noelle, and you, have a harder time dealing with the press and personal security."

"I'll take that as a compliment."

"As you should. Eventually, you won't be the story anymore. Once the Barnetts and the Morgans confirmed their relationships, the press coverage decreased significantly overnight. Even more so after they moved, at least for Noelle."

Due to the increased presence at the office, Connor has the driver pull into the underground garage. He escorts me to the elevator and straight to Sam's penthouse. As the doors open, Sam is nowhere to be found.

"I assume you want to talk to Sam."

Connor nods curtly.

"I'll find him. Would you like a drink?"

"No, thank you. I'm fine."

I leave Connor in search of Sam and Emme. After checking his office and the nursery, I walk past Connor toward the master bedroom. Emme is strapped into her chair on the floor of the bathroom wearing a cute pajama set with llamas on it. I smell fresh soap, Sam's soap. It's crisp, soothing, and completely him. He's stepping out of the shower. Odd for this time of day, but I'm thankful for the early glimpse of his expertly toned chest. My eyes follow the droplets of water down his chest as he tucks the towel around his waist.

"Everything okay?" I ask, hoping to focus on something other than my boyfriend's insane body.

"She threw up all over herself and me. Changing my clothes wasn't going to cut it. Is everything okay with you?"

"I'm fine, but Connor wants to talk to you."

"Okay, let me put on some clothes."

I purse my lips and look up at him.

"Don't pout. You can take them off later."

"Deal." I step into his waiting embrace. With great reluctance, I pull back from his hard chest and kiss him chastely. We certainly don't want to make Connor wait longer than necessary. I unbuckle Emme and scoop her into my arms. Returning to the kitchen, I find Connor leaning against the island.

"He'll be right out."

Surprisingly, Connor reaches out for Emme and touches her hand. Connor is a large, fit guy, but seeing his huge hand gently touch Emme's is heartening. I don't know much about him, but he wants to be a father someday.

"Sorry to keep you waiting, Connor. My little angel decided her dinner was best served on me."

"No problem. When we left the office, there were a few odd questions from the reporters today, different questions than usual. I reached out to Jacob to let him know. Blaine is likely already working on it."

"Great, thank you."

"Will you be going out tonight or tomorrow?"

"Tonight, no. For tomorrow, we have no plans now."

"Please contact me if you want to go out."

"Have a good night, Connor."

After the doors close, Sam draws both of us into his arms. "Are you okay?"

"I'm fine. I tune out the actual questions at this point. Connor pointed out they were different."

"Do you remember them?"

I share the questions I recall with Sam and start cooking dinner. Since I have been spending weekends here, we typically stay in on Fridays. Near eleven, Emme falls asleep with Sam on the couch. I settle Emme into her crib, prod Sam to bed, and curl into him to sleep.

SAMSON

In my head, I know it's soon, even though it's been a few weeks since our dinner when I first mentioned needing to discuss some things. My heart says otherwise. After feeding Emme, I make a huge breakfast for Savannah. Blueberry pancakes are my specialty, at least after Auggie's coaching. The fact it's what Maine is known for makes this breakfast even sweeter.

After setting our breakfast on the tray, I move Emme back into the bedroom in her chair and retrieve the tray.

"Wake up, gorgeous. We made you breakfast in bed."

Savannah is beautiful all the time, but freshly waking is my favorite. With crazy hair and a makeup-free face, she's real. I can see myself waking with her for the rest of my life.

"Morning," she mumbles, scooting up against the headboard. Once she's settled, I hand her a cup of coffee. "Thank you. You don't have to go to all this trouble for me."

"It's no trouble at all. Plus, I want to talk with you, and it seems that mornings are the least hectic time around here. I guess we have about three more hours before it gets truly crazy."

"Are you expecting someone today?"

"No, not at all." I hand her a fork before grabbing one for myself and digging into my plate of pancakes and sausage.

"These are delicious! Did you really make these or is Auggie hiding in the kitchen?"

"I'm offended." A grin graces my face. "I admit to asking for help, but I did in fact make this breakfast from scratch by myself." I take a deep breath before speaking again.

Her hand slides over mine. "What are you nervous about?"
I look into her eyes. All I see is concern. That isn't my intention. "So many things." Typically, I know how a conversation will play out or at least have a fairly accurate idea. The pros and cons have filtered through my mind at least ten times before I speak. "Thank you for standing up to Margaux and protecting Emerson. I could never apologize to you enough for her behavior."

"You don't have to. Her choices are hers, not yours. I'm glad I wasn't alone with Emerson. What else?"

I settle my mind once more. There's no reason for me to think that Savannah isn't ready to move in. She has been honest with me from the beginning, especially about Emme.

"Two things. Well, one thing with two parts, I guess."

Again she reaches for my hand. This time she gently pulls me closer, setting her lips on mine. "Breathe, Samson."

I take a few deep breaths. My nerves are off the charts today with this. "I've never had to make decisions this way before. Until you, I weighed each choice and decided. It's foreign to me, so bear with me." I collect my words before speaking. "Aside from Emme, waking up and falling asleep with you and having you here has been a highlight of my days. Will you move in with me, with us?"

"That's what you're nervous to ask me?"

"It's the first question for today."

"What's the second, Sam?"

"Will you answer the first one? They kind of build off one another." I would give almost anything to be able to hear her thoughts right now. Her facial expressions aren't giving me anything to work with. I wouldn't say I'm an expert at reading Savannah, but I'm close.

"Yes, I will."

Our plates clink together as I launch over the tray to kiss her. Shaking my head, I slide off the bed to set the tray on the floor. After determining that Emme is sleeping peacefully, I climb onto the bed, lowering her beneath me. Then I kiss Savannah breathless.

A few rounds of knee-weakening kisses later, she asks against my mouth, "You said there were two questions."

I draw back slightly. "I did, didn't I?"

"You did."

"With everything that has changed in my life over the last few months, I'm seriously considering moving the headquarters of Morgan Insurance out of the city. While I loosely considered having a family, I didn't think it would be this soon or under these circumstances. I don't want Emme to grow up in New York City."

"Oh, where out of the city?"

"To Maine."

If she's shocked by the location, she doesn't show it. "When?" I see the wheels turning in her beautiful brain. Unfortunately, I don't know if it's good or bad for me.

"I want to be ready to stay in Maine by Billie's wedding." That gives us plenty of time to find a home, daycare for Emme, an office, and file all the necessary paperwork to transfer Morgan Insurance to a new state or create a subsidiary.

"Okay." Her words are so innocuous that I can't tell if there is any hint of concern or if she will turn me down flat.

"Savannah, will you move to Maine with us?"

The same look from before is in her eyes. Her brain is processing all the implications of her moving out of the city with me. The time she's taking to consider her answer causes me to panic. Did I misread her? Does she not want something long-term with a new single dad?

"*Cara mia*, please say something? I'm sure you have run down your list at least four times by now."

"It's scary how well you know me already. I have gone over the list at least that many times. I want nothing more than to put myself first. However, I'm concerned about Scarlett."

"What about her specifically?" She's her mother figure. It shouldn't surprise me that my perfect-for-me girlfriend is putting her sister before herself. She does that for everyone. My siblings would say I do the same thing.

"She'll be alone here in the city. I mean, she does have two roommates. I'm sure every parent feels this way at some point. It's as if Scarlett is going to college in another state, except it's me leaving. Please don't mistake me taking a few minutes to process this as disinterest. I want nothing more than to be with you as much as possible."

Her words infuse some air back into my lungs. I was concerned. I lower my mouth to hers to gather my words. "She has Finn with her as well. That won't change when we move."

"I'll set up a time to meet her for coffee or something to talk to her. Are the two offers mutually exclusive?"

Part of me is screaming, hell no! I want her in my bed each morning and night. The other part is screaming, hell yes! I don't want to wake with her for a few months and then move to Maine alone. The selfish part will win. The part that wants to learn as much as I can about this spectacular woman who seems to want the real me. She's my unicorn. The bigger question is will I move to Maine without her.

"Selfishly, no, they aren't."

"When can I move in?" She pulls her lower lip between her teeth in an unconscious movement that makes blood run south. *Damn, that's sexy!*

"How's this afternoon? We could go scoop up Gray and most of your clothes."

"Works for me, as long as Connor is free."

My gorgeous woman agreed to move in with me. Hopefully, when I include her on all the other decisions, she'll shift her thoughts to moving to Maine with me. "Should we celebrate now or later tonight?"

A flicker of her inner vixen flashes in her eyes. "Both." With strength I didn't know she possessed, she flips us both, straddles my hips, and pulls me to sitting. Her hands grip the hem of my T-shirt, yanking it overhead.

"That view will never get old."

"I feel the same way about this one." I draw her shirt upward, kissing each exposed inch of skin.

As I wet her skin with my mouth and tongue, she grinds against my shaft. If I wasn't ready to strip her naked with her simply sitting in my lap, the sensations from her taking what she needs is making me even harder. After throwing her shirt to the floor, I bite her nipple.

Sounds of approval fall from her lips, along with the increased movement of her against me. I continue nipping and sucking her full breasts and belly.

"Sam, I need you now. I want to try to be on top again. Why did you switch us last time?"

She didn't question it then, so I went with it. "Truthfully, I needed to slow my reaction to you. You're so tight, and the deeper you surrounded me, the faster I approached my release. I wanted our first time to last longer than that, so I flipped us over so I could control myself."

A charming blush brightens her face as she slides down my legs, taking my shorts with her. Before climbing back onto the bed, she wiggles out of her thin pajama pants and lace panties.

I meet her lips as she moves over me. Sliding my hand between us, I coast my finger back and forth over her nub. She moans into my mouth as I increase my pace.

"Sam…." She shudders above me. Watching her fly apart is exquisite. She looks like a goddess hovering over me while her body shakes and spirals with pleasure. The moment she regains control of her breathing, she sinks down over me in one motion.

"Sweet mercy, you feel amazing wrapped around me."

Without a word, she slides up and down my shaft all the way to the root every time. My release is already building at the base of my spine. I'm glad I switched our positions before. She clenches her inner muscles around me, sending a wave of pleasure through my entire body. I feel her shudder, and her thighs start to shake. Her hips lower over me faster while she rides out the sensations. She drops to her forearms, changing the angle of her hips. That's all it takes. I empty into her with long, hot bursts, drawing her lush breasts against my chest.

I want this every day. Now I need to support her until she realizes that Scarlett will be fine on her own, especially with Finn shadowing her. A long and sensual shower later, we message Connor and get Emme ready.

SAVANNAH

The ride to my apartment is largely silent. I opt for the back of Sam's Land Rover with Emme so Sam can have the leg room in the front. This beautiful angel has a grip on my pinky finger and refuses to let go. She has as tight a grip on my heart as her daddy.

When we visited Noelle and Cash, it was wonderful to see that side of Sam. Calmer, more relaxed, and dare I say happier. I loved it there too, aside from my run-in with Margaux Morgan. Not having a mother figure present for my most formative years, I truly pity her. She has four of the most amazing children and one adorable granddaughter. If she could let them handle their own lives, everything would work out better for the entire family. All these thoughts lead me to Scarlett. She's a grown woman who doesn't need me to watch over her. Yet I'm still torn about moving to Maine.

"Sam, are we going out tomorrow?"

He turns to look at me over the center console. "I don't think so. Why?"

"I'm going to see if Scarlett can stop by."

"Okay, no problem."

I pull out my phone and text my sister.

Me: Hey there! Are you free tomorrow early afternoon?

Scarlett: Yeah.

Me: Will you come to Sam's?

Scarlett: Sure. Everything okay?

Me: Yes. I haven't seen you in a while.

Scarlett: Sure. I'll be by around one.

Me: See you then. Love you.

Scarlett: Love you too.

We follow Connor up to my floor and wait while he checks out my apartment. After offering him a drink, Sam and I move upstairs to pack my clothes. It doesn't take as long as I thought considering Sam has some nifty tricks for my closet. He took large garbage bags, made a hole for the hangers, and packed my work wardrobe in literally ten minutes.

Emerson is on my bed surrounded by pillows with Gray purring away by her feet. While I pack my dresser, Sam packs all my shoes with more care than necessary.

"Should I give you some time alone with my shoes?" I giggle.

"What?"

"All of those shoes probably cost about as much as one of your suits. You don't need to be that careful with them. Seriously, Scarlett kicks them around when she wears them."

"I happen to love a few pairs of your shoes. I'm simply making sure you have them in your closet at my place."

"My closet?"

"Yes, of course. There are his and hers closets in the master bedroom at my penthouse with a shared dressing room in the middle."

"Oh."

"Tell me, gorgeous."

"I'm…. You're so…. I could ask you for the sun and you would find a way to get it for me."

"I would, but you wouldn't ask because it's not who you are. I know you don't care about my wealth, but I also don't want it to be an issue either."

"It's not an issue, but it's something I need to get used to. I've never had extra money, if you will. Everything was always budgeted for, saved for. There were no extras for me or Scarlett."

"That may be true, but some of the things you consider extra, I consider necessary." He stops working on my shoes and moves next to me, one hand bracketing my waist and the other against my jaw.

"Such as?" I ask pensively. I love my ring, but it's more than I'm accustomed to. I suppose that's how everything will be going forward.

"Date night, gorgeous flowers to make you smile for no reason, couture dresses designed by Billie or Kelly for events along with matching jewelry, to name a few."

None of those seem over the top except the jewelry for one event. "I promise to be more accepting of the things you want to do for me."

"Thank you. I would appreciate a few hints here and there since there's no way I'll get lucky again after choosing your ring so expertly on the first try."

"I'll consider it, but you don't need any help. You did fine on your own."

He lifts my hand, kissing right behind the ring he gave me before pressing his lips to mine. "We should get moving. I'm pretty sure we have some more celebrating to do at home in bed later."

Home hits me. Home to him is where I am. My chest constricts, making it hard to breathe. "Yes, yes we do." I throw the rest of my workout and sleeping clothes into a tote and set it near the door.

"What's left?" Sam asks.

"I need to clean out the fridge, empty Gray's litter box, and gather my books in the living room." Sam lifts two totes and trots down the staircase. I secure Emme in my arms while looping the other arm through one of my bags filled with personal items. Unbeknownst to me, Connor has been making trips to the Rover with my stuff.

"Is there more?" Connor asks, taking the bag off my arm.

"Thank you. There's another bag near the bed." I set Emme on a blanket on the floor by the couch.

"Do you mind if I get it? I'll make another trip outside." For whatever reason, Connor thinks we should leave my apartment sooner rather than later.

"No, first door on the right." Turning my attention to the kitchen, I empty the fridge efficiently and move into the half bath for Gray's litter box. Securing Gray, I wait for Connor to return while Sam changes Emme.

"Sir, we should get out of here. The throng of reporters is growing each minute we're here."

Sam nods. "How much longer do you need, sweetheart?"

"I'm good except for taking the trash out back to the dumpster."

"What's your plan, Connor?" Sam asks. This is Connor's domain. Sam will heed his advice like I will.

"Before I came back up here, I called a unit mate of mine who works for the NYPD. He's on his way. Any chance you have a wig, Savannah?"

"Scarlett does, if it's still here." I hurry upstairs into Scarlett's old room and rummage through her closet. Luckily, the red wig is still there.

Once back downstairs, I overhear Connor on his phone sharing my address.

"Cruz is on his way up. Sir, the best plan is for Savannah to go with him. They're expecting the four of us to leave together. If she can slip out with Cruz, he'll take her to your house."

"Savannah, I'm going to need—"

There's a strong knock on the door. Connor checks the peephole before opening the door just enough for his friend to step in. Cruz and Connor hug, slapping one another on the back.

"Cruz, this is Sam Morgan, Savannah Clemons, and Emerson."

"Pleasure to see you again, Sam."

"Likewise, Cruz. How is your mother?"

"She's well. Thank you. Yours?"

"No comment."

"How do you know one another?" Connor asks.

"It's a long story for a later time. Can we get Savannah and Emerson out of here?" Sam answers.

It's the first time I've heard concern for my safety. It's scary that he's worried but makes me love him even more. *Love him?*

"Savannah, you need to look like you know Cruz well. Like you're going on a date. He'll escort you to his car and drive you home. We'll wait at least ten minutes before following you."

I nod my head in understanding while I smooth the wig.

Sam draws me closer and whispers, "I'll be right behind you. Savannah, I…. Please do what he says."

"I will." Taking a deep inhale, I loop my arm around Cruz and we step out the door.

"Don't worry. Everything will be fine. Simply pretend you like me."

As we approach the foyer door, I lean over and whisper, "I don't dislike you. I don't know you. I trust Connor. If he thinks you're trustworthy, then so do I."

"You're a natural. You don't even realize it." Before I know it, Cruz is opening the passenger door for me. The photographers are none the wiser. We pull away from the curb and ease into traffic.

"What did you mean?" I ask.

"How long have you been dating Sam?"

"Dating, a few months, but he's my boss. I've known him for more than a year."

"What I meant was you seem accustomed to the press."

"No, not even a little. Before we started dating, we were photographed together a few times at business dinners or events, but the press coverage has increased significantly since we started dating and with Emerson's arrival. Sam asked me to have security. I understand his concerns, so I have Connor or Christoph with me when I go out. Well, and you."

"Sam is a good guy and has dealt with some tough issues over the years. And all of Jacob's staff are great."

"How do you know Sam?"

"As he said, it's a long story, and he should tell you."

When we approach Sam's building, the press contingent is small. Even so, I direct Cruz into the garage and up to the lobby.

"Hi, Jimmy. This is—"

He does a double take because of the wig but focuses more on my companion. "Lt. Cruz, good to see you." Jimmy and Cruz shake hands. Apparently, the story is over a long time as well.

"Connor, Sam, and Emerson should be here shortly; there was increased press at my apartment."

"No problem, Miss Clemons."

"Also, my sister and Finn from Blackthorne will be stopping by tomorrow afternoon."

"I'll escort them up."

"Thank you."

Cruz and I ride up to the penthouse. Once inside I offer him a drink and pace the floor, waiting for Sam and Emerson.

SAMSON

My anxiety is through the roof right now. The throng of reporters is significant outside of Savannah's apartment, so much so that Connor is concerned. I'm grateful that Jacob and Connor have deep networks of people they trust for situations like this. Little did I know that Cruz served with Connor and Jacob. It appears he knows Christoph somehow as well.

I overhear Connor on the phone with Jacob. "Jake, when was the last check-in from Finn? I called, but he hasn't returned. Also, any news from Blaine?" Connor listens to Jacob's responses and then hangs up.

"Finn has been checking in with Jacob as required. I suppose calling me as well was too much to ask. Anyway, Jacob will reach out regarding the information that Blaine uncovered later this evening after I inform him you're safely at home."

Cruz: We're safely inside the car.

Me: Roger. We'll leave in ten.

Cruz: Roger.

"That was Cruz. They're safely on their way home," Connor shares before checking all the windows again.

I exhale sharply. Now more than ever, I need to convince her to move with me. My siblings have adjusted fine to life outside of the city. Emerson deserves a peaceful life without prying eyes of paparazzi following her clothing and dating choices. Maybe spending the holidays there will help, especially by including Scarlett too.

"Ready, sir?"

I check Emerson's buckle again, loop my arm around her carrier, and bend to grab Gray. He's crying loudly in the carrier. I gather he isn't likely in there for this long normally.

The flashbulbs are blinding as we step outside. The questions from the reporters come fast and furious.

"Are you aware your girlfriend has odd hours?"

"How many jobs does your girlfriend have?"

"What is her stage name?"

That one really makes my blood boil.

One reporter sticks his microphone in my direction. "Do you condone her new profession?"

Unfortunately, their questions surround me as I secure Emme in the truck. and I fail to close the door completely. With all the questions zinging around in my head all I can manage is "No comment." *What the hell is he talking about?*

"Where are these questions coming from? Savannah is always with me."

"Sir, how much does Scarlett resemble Savannah? Is it possible they mean Scarlett?"

I gather Connor has never seen a photo of Scarlett. "Close enough that they could be mistaken for one another," I grumble, gazing over at Emme who has no clue about the concern and anger coursing through me.

Connor pulls into the garage near the elevator. Expeditiously, we load Savannah's clothing so we can only make one stop in the lobby.

"Hi, Jimmy."

"Good afternoon, sir. Miss Clemons and Lt. Cruz are upstairs. Would you like some assistance with those items?"

"No, thank you, but I'm going to set Emme here for a few minutes."

"Of course, sir." Jimmy smiles at Emme and playfully touches her hands, playing peek-a-boo while Connor and I shift to the upper floors elevator.

After thanking Jimmy, the three of us ride up to my home. The first thing I do is set Gray's carrier on the floor and open the door. Later Savannah and I will point him to his litter box. With assistance from Cruz, we empty her stuff into my place more rapidly. Savannah unbuckles Emme and moves into the nursery to change her. I offer Connor a drink and Cruz a refill. They take seats at the island.

Before I even get to kiss Savannah hello and check on her, my phone is ringing.

"Hello."

"Sam, it's Jacob. I have an update. Is Savannah there with you?"

"Yes, I'll get her." I walk toward Emme's nursery. As I approach, I hear Savannah singing to my daughter. Even if I hadn't fallen already, that would have done it without question. I need to tell her and soon. When I cross the threshold, she faces me with a bright smile and a dry baby in her arms. "It's Jacob. He wants to talk with both of us."

Savannah nods and follows me out of the room. She lays Emme on her playmat in the living room before meeting me in the kitchen.

I set the phone on the counter, activate speakerphone, and draw Savannah against me.

"Good ahead, Jacob, I put the phone on speaker. Also, Connor and Cruz are here."

"Hey, guys."

Both Connor and Cruz mumble responses.

"When the odd questions started happening, Connor reached out to me and I contracted Blaine to dig deeper into Savannah and Scarlett. He has uncovered some concerning things about both of them. Well, mostly Scarlett."

"Go ahead, Sam knows everything there is to know, at least about me," Savannah responds.

"Your father, Arthur R. Clemons, was released from a stint in rehab about two months ago and spent the last few weekends in lockup in New York City drying out. All information points to Scarlett bailing him out of jail on more than one occasion in the recent past. Additionally, he has racked up some serious gambling debts in Atlantic City. Were you aware of this, Savannah?"

"No, the last I knew, Scarlett had no contact with our father like I don't."

"Very well. When Scarlett moved out of your apartment, she moved in with Elizabeth Perth and Isabella Danforth. Both have arrest records that include solicitation and prostitution. Additionally, there are concerns with her place of employment. I never ask how Blaine gets his information, but he's never steered me wrong. The Apple Supper Club appears to be a front for an illegal gambling parlor and strip club that caters to prominent, wealthy men and a few women. Based on Finn's observations, it appears that Scarlett is at least hosting at the underground club, if not worse."

Savannah is vibrating with anger and concern. I slide my arm around her waist and tuck her even closer into my body.

"What do you suggest I do?" Savannah's voice cracks.

I can only imagine how harshly she's judging herself and quite possibly considering moving back to her apartment for Scarlett. I will not let that happen. I don't care if I need to rent another apartment in this building for Scarlett. I refuse to let Savannah take all the blame for this. Scarlett's choices are hers and hers alone.

"When this information came to me, I requested additional coverage for Scarlett. I want someone with her twenty-four seven. There's less room for her to sneak away. Christoph and Maia will be in New York by tomorrow afternoon. Maia will work with you, Savannah, and Christoph and Finn will trade off shifts with Scarlett. As far as what you should do, I recommend you talk to her and strongly urge her to find another job and do it quickly."

"Okay, she's coming over tomorrow for a different reason. I might as well blow up her life completely in one afternoon."

I lower my lips near the shell of Savannah's ear. "I will not let you blame yourself for her choices. You did nothing wrong. We'll figure this out."

She shivers in my arms, although I'm not sure if it was my words or my proximity to one of her sexy spots I love so much.

"Do either of you have any questions?"

"No," we both reply, and Jacob hangs up. Gray is whining somewhere.

"I'm going to find him and set up his litter and food. It was a pleasure meeting you, Cruz. Thank you for your help earlier." Savannah informs us.

"You're welcome."

Savannah faces me and tells me without words that she's worried and needs some time alone. Searching for Gray and unpacking some of her clothes will work fine. I'm in awe of the fact that we understand one another so well so soon. I really need to tell her how I feel, but now certainly isn't the right time and likely not tomorrow either.

SAVANNAH

How did I miss all of this? Until now I had no reason to mistrust Scarlett. Now I have a whole host of reasons. My main concern was school, which now appears to be the least of my problems. Quietly, I move through Sam's home… my home. I hear Gray whining, but I haven't located him yet. Each time I think I'm close, he stops. Content that I need to let him come to me, and I'm sure he's in this guest room, I sit in the middle of the plush area rug with the blue swirl pattern and close my eyes.

A few minutes later, Gray curls up in my lap. His sweet purring calms me even further. After a few solidifying breaths, I scoop Gray into my arms and leave the room to locate his box and litter. After setting everything up, I set Gray into his litter box.

"There you are. Good, you found him. Connor and Cruz left. I gave him the night off so they could go out for a beer. You're stuck here with us tonight."

"No place I would rather be."

Sam folds me into his body. At least wrapped in his arms, Jacob's call isn't the first thing on my mind, although it's a close second. The moment I relax against him, he draws back slightly.

He lifts my eyes to meet his before speaking. "There's nothing that she could do to make me think less of you. You took on more than should have ever been expected of you. So far, other than two questionable choices, Scarlett is doing fine. Let's wait until you talk with her before you make any rash decisions like refusing to unpack for a quick return trip to your apartment."

My eyes widen at his words. "How do you do that?"

"*Cara mia*, I'm crazy about you. I'm not letting you run away from me over this. I want you here with me always."

"I'm crazy about you too." *I'm in love with you, but I scared out of my mind to say it.* Partially, because he's Samson *freaking* Morgan, New York's most eligible bachelor. Everything that comes along with his status is a lot to absorb. I wholly understand why he wants to leave the city. I can't blame him, and I'm closer to saying yes. The bigger part is that I can't handle the devastation of starting over again with everything from my job, my home, and mending my shattered heart if we don't work out. I've never had to rebuild my heart and don't want to start now. Cowardly, I know.

Once the litter box and food are set up, we decide on some takeout for dinner. After eating and cleaning up, we bathe Emme and put her to bed. All my clothing and other personal items are in the bedroom; I plan to unpack all tomorrow morning. Sam and I cuddle in bed, staring at the amazing cityscape outside his window. My head is on his bare chest with one arm curved around his waist. One hand is flat against the small of my back, his fingertips grazing my ass. His other hand and forearm are over mine at his waist. I feel content here in his arms, in his bed. I feel him take a deep breath.

"Did I miss something in Jacob's call?

"No." His response curtly and more gruff than I'm used to.

Leaning back so I can see his reaction, I ask, "What do you need to tell me that has you worked up?"

Surprise crosses his features. "How do you know I'm worked up?"

"Your heart is racing. Please tell me."

"It's not about Jacob's call or Scarlett. The timing isn't great though. I want to book a long weekend in Maine for us to look for a home. Unfortunately, I need to travel to California in two weeks as well. Would you be willing—"

"I'm equally as crazy about Emme as I am about you. I'll take care of her while you meet with the Regents about their new acquisitions. What else?"

"Will you spend the holidays with us?"

"I would be honored. What does that look like for you?"

"This year the plan is for everyone to go to Cash's for Thanksgiving and Lake Tahoe for Christmas."

"Wow, you guys go big."

"It's been a bit different the last two years. Before Billie and Cash moved, we would have Thanksgiving here or at Cash's. Christmas has always been away from the city. What did yours look like?"

"When I was very young, they were joyful but there never were many gifts for me. I understood my parents weren't educated and barely made ends meet. I was lucky to get something I needed like a dress or new shoes.

After my mom died….” I inhale slowly. I don't talk about her often. It's still difficult even after all these years.

“What was her name?”

“Eleanor. Everyone called her Ellie.”

“That's a beautiful name. Please continue when you're ready?”

“Are you sure you want to hear all this?”

“Of course, it's a large part of who you are. How you became the brilliant, feisty, passionate, and undeniably sexy woman you are.”

“Thank you.”

“Every word is unquestionably accurate.” He leans down, pressing a tender, soft kiss to my forehead before sidling closer to me.

Steeling myself, I continue the story. “After my mom died, we didn't really celebrate anything. The major holidays merely marked a day that our father was home and drunk on the couch before lunch instead of by seven in the evening. As an adult, I tried to bring Scarlett around slowly, but she's against celebrations of every kind.”

“I'm sorry. I must warn you though, holidays are a big deal with my siblings. Birthdays and Christmas call for an overabundance of gifts for everyone. So please prepare yourself in advance.”

“I appreciate the warning.” Turning my head, I savor his skin with my mouth.

“Savannah.” My name sounds decadent falling from his lips.

“Samson. You promised me a celebration tonight as well, if I recall correctly.”

"You're right, I did." Within seconds, he's hovering over me on one forearm while freeing my breasts from my silky pjs. My skin grows hotter the longer his gaze is on me. I push his boxer briefs down his legs and toe them off with my feet.

Sam repositions us to our knees facing the magnificent view of the city. His mouth travels along the curve of my neck while his hand slides down my belly to cup my sex. With precision, he hefts my breast in his hand and twists my nipple. A shot of pleasure launches straight to my heated center. As if he knows, he expertly pushes two fingers inside me. Almost instantly my muscles clench around his hand.

"Wow, what's different?" This time feels different than the last time. More fullness.

"You mean this?"

"Oh my God, Sam! Yes, that. What are you doing?"

"I'll never tell, but I'll keep doing it."

"I think you should tell me anyway."

"Why, so when you get sick of me you know what to ask for?"

"Never going to happen," I rasp, riding his fingers until the coil in my belly unravels. "You're everything."

"Only for you. Ready to move?"

I shake my head and lean forward, putting my hands on the luxurious duvet. Glancing over my shoulder, I see Sam. His expression is serious and contemplative.

My core is aching, spread before him, and yet he's deep in thought. I'm not sure if I should be honored or offended. I'm leaning more toward honored. Later I will figure out what he means.

He slides his hands over my body from my ankles to my hips before positioning the tip of his shaft at my folds. As he pushes inside, I take him deep in one blissful stroke.

"Damn! That's...."

Sam withdraws completely before reburying his shaft deep into my core. Sweet mercy! The fullness and depth are so much more in this position. Lowering to my forearms takes it even a bit higher. My belly is tightening again already, and that's before he curls his arm around my hip and pinches my clit. Alternating between pinching and flicking rapidly brings my second release closer and closer.

"*Cara*, let go with me."

Once the words leave his mouth, I tighten my inner muscles and he's exploding into me in long bursts. Whether purposeful or not, Sam thrusts deeper, sending my orgasm spiraling outward and my inner muscles squeezing around him again.

Withdrawing, Sam flips me over and lowers himself on top of me. Rising on my forearms, I meet his mouth, drawing my tongue around the rim of his lips before plunging it deep.

He's hardening against my hip the longer we kiss. I scoot back to add enough space between us before hooking my leg around his back.

"Sam, again."

With a sensual gleam in his eye, Sam pushes inside me again, drawing more pleasure from my body than I've ever felt before. Spent, he rolls us onto our sides.

"How does that keep getting better each time?"

A grin is plastered on his face. "I don't know, but we should keep testing your theory after we get some sleep."

"Deal."

Sam reaches for the blanket on the tufted dressing bench at the foot of his bed and settles it over us.

"Good night, Savannah."

"Good night, Sam."

SAVANNAH

Since I started sleeping with Sam, I wake naked and sore. Deliciously sore. Through the monitor I hear him humming to Emme. It's endearing, as if I needed a reason to love him more. Finding him asleep with Emme on his chest was the clincher for me, at least as it pertains to her.

I pad to the bathroom. As I'm leaving, I catch of glimpse of my face; I'm glowing. I suppose happy looks good on me. A familiar tightening sensation grasps my heart. It happens every so often when I wish my mom were here. Grabbing one of Sam's dress shirts, I head to the kitchen for coffee while buttoning it.

"My shirts look better on you than they do on me."

My skin heats up with his words. "I'm not so sure about that. You look pretty hot yourself."

He slides his arms around my waist before lowering his mouth to mine. I want this. Every. Single. Day.

"What time is Scarlett coming over?"

"One. Should we go over what needs to be said?"

"As far as you moving in here and to Maine with us, you should just tell her. Scarlett needs to see you have your own life. She made choices for hers; you can make choices for yours. Regarding the information from Jacob, I think you need to impress upon her that she needs to find a new job as quickly as possible. I don't think we need to discuss her roommates. Their issues could very well be in the past. Plus, we don't know where or how Blaine acquired that information."

"I agree. Breakfast?"

"Sure." We prepare a huge breakfast, and then I tackle unboxing my clothes into the *hers* master closet. I have never had this much space for myself. There is a specific spot for everything rather than a rod, shelf, and the floor. It's amazing.

Near one, Jimmy announces Scarlett and Finn. Scarlett dressed in tattered jeans, a leather jacket, and boots steps off the elevator with a scowl on her face. *Great!*

"Hi, Scar. Thank you for coming." I hug my sister close. She feels thinner.

"Hey, Savi."

"Finn, nice to see you again."

He simply nods while scanning the room. I suppose it's a habit of his.

"Mr. Morgan, you have two more guests." Jimmy's voice echoes around me.

"Thanks, Jimmy. Please send them up," Sam answers from the living room where he's cradling Emme in one of the chairs.

Scarlett looks around while tapping her toe on the inlaid hardwood floors.

"Would you like something to drink?"

Both say no as the door opens again. Christoph steps inside with a pretty, petite, fit woman, presumably Maia. It'll be interesting having security that blends in better. It's more conceivable that Maia is a friend of mine based on her appearance. I can get behind that. After introductions all around, we sit in the living room. I settle on the arm of the chair where Sam is sitting with Emme.

"Savi, I have a shift later. What do you need to talk about?"

"I thought you took Sundays off for schoolwork."

"I do, but I'm picking up El's shift tonight."

That response makes me more uneasy. At least El works with Scarlett where Jacob has concerns about the underground activities. "I have two things that need to be discussed."

Sam sets his free hand on my hip out of sight of everyone in the room. It's comforting. This conversation is one I don't want to have with my little sister.

"Jacob has provided us with some information pertaining to your workplace. We've learned that there's an underground gambling parlor and strip club." I stare directly into her eyes. She can't hide a lie from me. Cold as ice. That isn't a good sign. "It's my understanding that you're a hostess. If you're working in the underground portion, I need you to start looking for a new job immediately."

"I don't work downstairs, but I'm aware of what goes on down there. It's hard to miss considering how many girls go down there every night and how they leave out the back entrance with prominent men. I'll start looking tomorrow."

"Thank you." I'm not convinced that she's telling the truth about where she works, but she is about looking for a new job. "Due to Jacob's concerns, either Christoph or Finn will be with you twenty-four seven. If you need to move back into my apartment for more space, you're free to do that."

As if he senses I need a segue, Gray saunters into the living room and weaves in and out of Scarlett's legs.

"You moved out?" Scarlett's voice is laced with angst.

"Yesterday. I only took my personal items. It's still furnished. However, this move is only temporary. I'm moving out of the city in the next few months with Sam and Emme."

Sam's hold on my hip tightens. It takes me a moment to realize that I haven't officially told him that I'm going to Maine with him.

"You're going to leave me here alone?"

"This is the second time I've seen you since you moved out. If it's necessary, someone from Blackthorne will be with you. I need to make some choices for myself now that you're on your own. I'm choosing to be with Sam and Emme."

"Just like that, with your boyfriend's money, you stick me with a hot bodyguard or two and leave. Fine!"

"Scarlett Mae, follow me. Now!"

Reluctantly and begrudgingly, Scarlett follows me into the office.

"Don't you dare accuse me of using Sam for his money. That's so far from the truth, and you know it! No offense to anyone from Blackthorne, I only agreed because it's what Sam asked. After yesterday, I'm glad they were there with us."

"What happened yesterday?" Scarlett's voice is low.

I recap the extra reporters from yesterday and the questions they asked that prompted calling Jacob and increasing our security.

Her expression softens a bit.

"Real talk, Scar, which I don't owe you, even though I act like your mom, I'm not. I'm your sister who happens to take care of you. I need my own life. He's the one, Scar."

"Okay."

"If it will be too much for whoever has the night shift to stay at Liza and El's, you should consider moving back to my apartment. Let me know what you decide soon. If you move back, you need to pay some of the bills. Whatever you're paying at Liza and El's is fine."

"Okay."

After her resigned reply, I suggest, "You're welcome wherever I go, but in your own place. Why don't you think about it for the next week or so? Do you care if you finish your degree here in NY or would transferring be an option? Plus, it's beautiful and peaceful. What's even better, you won't need security anymore."

"I can do that."

"Thanks, Scar."

"Happy looks good on you, Savi."

"Thanks." I pull my sister in for a tight hug and lead her back to the living room.

We discuss the changes with Christoph and Finn before they leave for Scarlett's shift. She agreed to call me with her choice late next week. I'm intrigued that Finn opted for the night shift. Although, I see the way she gazes at him and her slip up about his looks earlier. Then we turn our attention to Maia.

"Thank you for coming. I appreciate it. Did Jacob give you information about how it works for Savannah and Emme?" Sam asks.

"Briefly, but I'm fine with hearing your perspective."

"Generally, you'll escort Savannah to the office in the morning and back home as well. Until yesterday, she lived across town. Now it will be the three of us in the morning. I work from home in the afternoons. Occasionally, Savannah stays at the office. Your priorities are Savannah and Emme. As I discussed with Jacob, I'm not the story; they are. Emme's maternal grandmother cares for her in the mornings. If Maria-Luisa wants to go out with Emme, she'll let you know. I'll provide your contact information tomorrow morning."

"Okay. What time do you leave for the office? Will you be going out later today?"

"We leave about eight. No, we're staying in for the rest of the day."

"Thank you, Maia."

As she leaves, Sam brings Emme to her room for a nap. I head into the kitchen and start pulling out ingredients.

When he returns, Sam asks, "What's buzzing around in your head?"

"Huh?"

"What are you doing?"

"Oh, I bake when I'm upset or sorting things out in my head." I preheat the oven and start measuring the necessary ingredients.

"What are you upset about?"

"I'm sorting, not upset." I drop the flour and spices in the bowl and whip them into a batter.

"When did you make up your mind about Maine?"

"Yesterday when I had to leave with Cruz. I don't want that for Emme."

"What about you?"

I hear the concern in his voice like I would choose to move for Emme only. "Sam, I was honest with you. I don't want to have security, but I will if it's necessary. Emme shouldn't need it from birth. It's unfair to her. If leaving the city will remove it as a necessity, then we should move." I scoop the batter into the pan and slide it into the oven.

When I finish closing the door, Sam lifts me into his arms, setting me on the counter.

"Savannah, I lo—"

"Sir, your brother and Miss Waterman are here."

Sam's forehead drops against mine. "Thank you, Jimmy. Please send them up," Sam replies.

I love you, Sam. I have been waiting for the right time to tell you.

SAMSON

Each day she takes up more space in my defrosting heart. She would move out of the city for my daughter. She's more than I could ever hope for, not only for me, but for Emme as well. I love her. I need to tell her.

"Hey, guys. We weren't expecting you. Is everything okay?"

"Hey. Sorry to drop in, but Caro wanted an Emme fix, and we ran into Dad at the patisserie this morning."

We all hug one another. Once she greets everyone, Caro scoops Emme up and plays peek-a-boo with her.

"It's no problem. You're welcome anytime," I add quickly to avoid any miscommunication.

"What smells good, Savannah, because I know Sam didn't bake anything?"

Savannah laughs. I love that sound.

"Gingerbread bars. My choices were limited by the ingredients we have on hand."

"Smells amazing. What do you mean we?" Auggie asks.

Savannah lifts her head toward mine. "I moved in yesterday."

"That's great!"

The timer sounds, and Savannah moves back into the kitchen to check her dessert. Auggie is right. It smells delicious.

After Savannah sets it to cool on the wire rack, Auggie moves closer.

"That looks amazing. I might need to steal the recipe."

"Stop! You're a talented chef. I literally threw together some ingredients to sort through some things in my head."

"I'll be the judge of that when it cools. I bet it's tasty."

"I doubt it." Savannah smiles and wraps her arm around my waist.

"What did Dad say?" I ask. While I'm sure Caro wanted to see Emme, the information about our father is likely more interesting.

"We were already at the restaurant when he arrived with David Cobble."

"Why would Dad meet with the family attorney in a public place?" I wonder aloud.

"Probably to avoid a scene from Margaux. Once we finished, we approached their table in the back of the restaurant. After a short chat, Dad informed me he's filing for divorce in the next few weeks. He warned that we should be extra vigilant regarding Margaux."

Nodding my head, I say, "That makes sense."

"Is your offer with Cash still open?"

It takes me a minute to figure out what he means. He means adding his money to the pooled trust fund. "Yes, of course."

"What do you need from me?" Auggie asks, but his attention is focused on Caro and Emme.

"I'll email you a list of what we need later tonight." I quickly change my mind. "Instead, let's get it now." I kiss Savannah softly and leave with Auggie.

"You have the list printed out?" Auggie asks, gazing out the large window overlooking the city.

"No. You should tell her how you feel."

"Caro doesn't want to date me. She's made that abundantly clear."

"When is the last time the two of you had a genuine conversation about your relationship?"

Auggie drags his hands through his hair. He's in love with her; he just doesn't realize it yet. "About a year ago, we discussed it again. She reminds me repeatedly she isn't interested in ruining our friendship, even if the sex might be magnificent. Her words."

"Until Savannah, I wouldn't claim to know more about love than anyone else. However, it took me too long to ask her to the gala and even longer for an actual date. You need to tell Caro how you really feel. You might be surprised when you get a different answer."

"Do you know something I don't?" he asks as if Caro has confided in me and I broke her trust.

"No, only my observations and some things both of you have said to me in passing. I'm suggesting you consider it. Neither of you have dated anyone else, yet you aren't dating each other."

"Fair enough. I'll think about it. Let's discuss you. Savannah moving in is a big deal. Got anything else planned for her?"

"I was planning on telling everyone soon anyway. We're moving out of the city in the next few months, likely near Billie and Cash."

"Good for you. It'll be better for Emme," Auggie adds.

"True. Savannah only has personal security because I asked her. She's doing it for me. If we leave the city, no one will need it any longer. I want them to have the best life they can. Cash and Billie are much happier. I want that for my family too."

"Good for you."

"Thanks."

"I may need to leave the city too considering I can't build the way I want here."

"That's a big change from your original plans, isn't it?"

"Yes. It may not be feasible. I'm still working out the details."

"Let me know if Cash or I can help in anyway."

"Thanks. Let's check out that dessert your woman made. I need to get my judging hat on."

Laughing, I follow Auggie to the kitchen. Savannah and Caro are giggling like schoolgirls sharing secrets. They probably are.

"Ready to dish out your creation, Savannah?" Auggie asks to stifle their conversation.

"Yes, Chef."

Everyone laughs and grabs a chair at the island. Caro secures Emme into her chair and moves it onto the large island. Savannah plates four squares of her creation. It looks delicious.

I hear her inhale as Auggie lifts the bar to his mouth.

"Savannah, this is fantastic! Soft, great texture, the right amount of ginger and molasses. I absolutely want the recipe."

Her face reddens. "Thank you, Auggie."

"He isn't lying. This is delish. You could easily pass this off as something he made," Caro adds.

"Thank you."

She takes the seat next to me and leans into my side. I press my lips to her temple and pull the rest of the pan closer for a second serving. We spend another hour chatting with Auggie and Caro before they leave.

"Will you come sit with me for a minute before Emme needs to eat again? I want to get your input on something."

Savannah drops the drying towel on the counter and joins me on the couch.

"What does your dream house look like?"

"Wow, going big, huh?"

"I want to know what you must have."

"Sam, I truly don't need anything spectacular. Just what everyone needs: a bedroom, bathroom, kitchen, office, and a decent-size yard. I'm still in awe of *my* closet. The fact that the bedroom has two closets is still insane to me. Why?"

"I want to setup some showings on the weekend. Griffin helped Kelly, Peter, and Cash find their homes. I need to give him a starting point."

"Whatever you limit yourself to will be more than I would have ever dreamed would be where I get to live."

"*Cara mia*, I want you to be happy."

"I am. It won't matter where we live."

I pull her lips to mine and tell her with my lips that I love her even though I haven't been able to say the words yet. Although I'm not overly religious, it's as if a god created my perfect partner without any input from me.

Once we feed Emme and put her to bed, I plan to lavish every inch of Savannah's curves with my mouth until she begs. An hour later, I find Savannah naked in our bed waiting for me. She's perfection, simply perfection.

SAVANNAH

This week has been hectic. Even though our schedule is settled, the fact that Sam wants to leave early on Friday decreases the time we have in the office. Perhaps it's my own concerns, but I feel as if I'm not as diligent as I was before we were dating. Plus, I need to address the payroll error.

"Sam, my direct deposit was wrong this morning."

"No, it wasn't."

"It was too much."

"Savannah, you have been working here for more than a year. Your probationary period is over, so your salary increased. Did you forget?"

"I did forget, but there's still no way that number is correct." I show him the deposit memo for my account.

"Oh. Well, that's a week early."

"Please explain."

"Here, review this and then it'll make sense. I planned to give it to you tomorrow."

The top of the document has the words Partnership Agreement in bold font across the top.

"Are you out of your mind? It's too soon."

"It absolutely is not too soon. The average time for full broker and partnership in a firm this size is two years. You ran this office on your own while I was handling Marisol's accident and learning about Emerson. You earned this."

"I'm floored. Thank you. Can I take you to dinner tonight to celebrate?"

"Part of me wants to say absolutely not, because I'm a traditional kind of guy. However that won't work for an independent woman such as yourself. I would be honored to have dinner with you tonight."

"I'll take care of everything. Now get back to work." I smirk at him before signing the bottom of the agreement.

Hours later, Maia arrives to escort me home. Sam left at one to relieve Maria-Luisa.

"Hi, Maia. I need to pack my bag."

"No problem." Maia takes a seat in the small waiting area of the office.

"All set. Any issues today?" I hope the press contingent is small outside of my home.

"No issues that I'm aware of. Maria-Luisa and I took Emme for a walk around the park for a bit. We came back quickly due to the temperature."

"Good. Are you joining us in Maine, or is Jacob sending someone to meet us there?" I slide into the back seat and Maia joins me.

"I believe Jacob is meeting you there. He needs to do a preliminary security assessment on any house you may choose. I'm pretty sure Sam sent him the options and he eliminated one for security reasons."

"Okay."

Maia escorts me upstairs. "Will you be going out this evening?"

"No, we're staying in. Thank you, Maia. Are you escorting us to the airport?"

"Yes."

Sam breezes into the room with Emme in his arms. He leans down and kisses me softly.

"Hi, babe. What time are we leaving for the airport tomorrow?"

"I hope to leave here by seven. Will that be a problem, Maia?"

"Not at all. I'll be here. Have a nice evening." Maia presses the call button on the elevator.

"You too."

Once she leaves, Sam kisses me more thoroughly. "I thought we were going out, partner?"

"I decided to have dinner here. It'll arrive in about an hour. Did you really want to go out tonight?"

"No. Doesn't matter to me."

Exactly an hour later, our dinner arrives. I take the bags and plate the food as instructed. My plan was to go to Auggie's restaurant tonight, but it's closed for a private party. Technically, it isn't Auggie's restaurant but where he works for now. However, Auggie agreed to send dinner over.

"Isn't that where Auggie works?"

"Yes. He cooked dinner. I wanted to eat there, but there were no open tables. Not even for you. Something about a private party."

"I prefer to be alone with you anyway." Sam raises his glass of red wine in my direction. "To you, my love."

Heat builds in my cheeks. "Thank you."

Per usual, Auggie has outdone himself with his food. I hope he's able to capture his dream of owning his own restaurant. His dishes certainly should be enjoyed by as many people as possible. After eating, we pack our bags and fall into bed early.

We have the cutest alarm clock. Emme has been eating and sleeping well. She eats near one and wakes about five. At five on the nose, Emme's sweet wails wake me from a sound sleep. I roll to sitting and find Sam isn't in bed anymore.

I wrap my robe around me, grab Emme's bottle, and lift her from her crib. With a dry diaper, I return to the living room and feed her. About halfway through her feeding, Sam returns from the gym.

"Sorry. I was trying to get back up here fast enough." He walks over, kissing us both.

"It's fine. She's almost done. I'll dress her and then get ready."

We are making strides culling the time it takes for all of us to get from waking to walking out the door.

The flight to Maine is as smooth as the last time. I'm insanely excited to search for a home with Sam and Emme. Our first stop is the Perk.

"Hi, Savannah. Sam. Nice to see you again."

"You too, Kelsey."

"Would you like to stick with your order from your last visit?" Kelsey is an amazing businesswoman. She recalls our order. Another reason smaller towns are amazing.

"I would. Sam?"

"I'm sorry, what?"

"Would you like the same as last time?" I set my hand on his forearm, drawing his attention back to the room.

"Yes. Thank you."

Kelsey hurries away to make our coffees.

"Where did you go?"

"I was checking out our surroundings. It's only the three of us here, at least until the showings."

"Isn't the whole purpose of moving so we don't need Blackthorne with us?"

"Yes. I'm used to one of them being here with the two of you. I'm adjusting."

Kelsey returns with our coffee and pastries.

"Thank you, Kelsey."

"You're welcome. Have a wonderful day."

We exit the store, cross the street, and sit on a bench facing the ocean.

"What time are we meeting Griffin?" I scoot closer to Sam on the bench. It's a tad colder than I expected.

"We have about thirty minutes before we need to drive to the first property."

I return my gaze to the ocean and Kelsey's tasty scone. Her shop will be dangerous for my waistline.

SAMSON

"Sam?"

I turn to my left and don't see the person calling me. As I look right, I see Billie walking toward us.

"Hey, Billie." Rising, I wrap my tiny sister into a huge hug. Then she hugs Savannah.

"Hi, guys! I wasn't expecting you until late afternoon." Billie lowers the hood of Emme's stroller and stares at her niece.

"Griffin was able to get us some appointments during the day, so we came earlier. We have three today and one tomorrow morning."

"Griff is great! Well, Kelly and Peter rave about him. Even though he helped Peter find our house, I've never met him. Good luck. I have to open the store. I'll see you later. Whenever you're done, Peter is working from home today."

Billie rushes off to So Elegant, and we head to the car. Jacob is waiting with another man who I assume is Griffin on the porch of the first house. Since she agreed to move, I've tried to get her to tell me what she wants, but I failed. Ideally I'll be able to tell from her reactions which house she prefers.

"Good morning, Jacob." I extend my hand to him.

"Sam. Savannah. Nice to see you again. This is Griffin. I've worked with him before with your brother and the Barnetts. I believe he assisted Peter with your sister's house as well."

"Pleasure to meet you both." Griffin shakes our hands and leads us inside. The first house is large, too large for the three of us, but would be perfect later. It has five bedrooms with a formal dining room and an office with a private entrance from outside. Although it's on the water, it's the farthest away from my siblings.

Before I even ask, I can tell from her reaction that Savannah doesn't love it. I inform Griffin that we're ready to leave, and we return to the car.

"*Cara mia*, tell me what you like and don't like about this one."

"There is nothing wrong with it. It doesn't feel like the one. Does that make sense?"

"Surprisingly, yes. I feel the same way." I follow Griffin to the second house for today.

The second house is closer to what we're looking for: five bedrooms with two master suites. The overall house is more modern and won't require a complete remodel before we move in.

"It's closer, but it isn't the one," Savannah whispers in my ear as we check out the yard. So far, Emme has been content in her stroller with her favorite bunny that Caro gave her.

"I agree. On to the next."

She giggles, kisses my cheek, and loops her free arm through mine.

Once we start up the driveway of the third house, I know Jacob will nix it. Despite boasting five acres of land, the rectangular property borders two busy roads. Even with that knowledge, we inspect the interior of the house. If Jacob doesn't cross this one off the list, I will. It would require a complete renovation inside and out. The owners clearly used outdated photos to list this property.

Back outside, we bid Griffin farewell until early tomorrow morning.

"Would you like to join us for an early dinner at Cash's?" I invite Jacob.

"I would love to. Would you mind if Norah joins us as well?"

"She's more than welcome to join us."

"Let me make sure she doesn't have plans." Jacob steps away to call his wife.

"How are you doing, sweetheart?" I surround Savannah with my arms.

"I'm wonderful. Even though Jacob's here, I don't feel like he's acting like security." I nod as she continues. "It's more relaxed here. I'm ready to stay here today, but I know that isn't reasonable. We have so many details to iron out."

Leaning in, I kiss her softly. "I agree completely. The next few months will not only be busy with all the decisions we need to make but with the holidays too. We've got this."

"Yes, we do."

Jacob returns after his call. "Norah is at Kelly's catching up. She's going to meet me at Cash's."

"Perfect."

Later that evening, after a wonderful meal with my siblings and their better halves, Jacob, Norah, Kelly, and Ellis, we crash for the evening in the guest suite at Billie's. Savannah rocks in a chair while feeding Emme her last bottle of the day. The look on her face shows her deep in thought.

Savannah joins me on the sofa after settling Emme in the portable crib.

"What's going through your gorgeous mind?" Something has been on her mind all day aside from looking for our home.

"How do you…? Never mind. I'm ready to build our life here. Please don't mistake my next statement for hesitation, it isn't. I'm worried about Scarlett. She hasn't made her decision yet. I feel like I could be abandoning her in the big city."

"Of course you feel that way. She's your sister, but you have been her main caregiver for much of her life. I'm sure Scarlett will make the best choice for herself. You have to trust you gave her all the tools."

"How do you always know the right thing to say?"

I shrug, kiss her pouty lips, and draw her close. Near two in the morning, I scoop Savannah up and lay her in the bed before sliding in behind her.

Distant ocean sounds waft into the room. The crash of the waves is soothing first thing in the morning. Reaching for my watch on the side table, I note it's near six. Sliding from beneath the sheets, I glance at Emerson still slumbering peacefully. Turning back to face the bed, my heart tightens in my chest.

Despite everything surrounding us, from Emerson's arrival, the paparazzi, her sister's job, she sticks by me. Her faith in me from the beginning is awe-inspiring. I need to tell her I've fallen for her so deeply my heart aches. The trick is going to be convincing her that she deserves everything I have, even though she doesn't agree.

Tiptoeing past my daughter, I use the bathroom and then prepare for her to wake. Once I snap closed the container with her formula, soft wails escape from her little mouth. Despite my best efforts, Savannah stirs while I change Emme.

"Do you want some help?"

"I've got it, gorgeous. Take the shower first. We need to leave in about an hour so we can stop at the Perk for lattes before meeting Griffin."

She smiles. Her smile makes everything seem brighter. I don't resist the urge to pull her in for a kiss as she attempts to shimmy past me. After a thorough good morning kiss, I swat her ass and gently nudge her toward the bathroom.

Regardless of our progress getting ready in a timely manner, this morning we fail. Thankfully Jacob grabbed our coffee from the Perk before meeting us at the last house for this trip.

We climb the hill toward the Nubble Lighthouse. Surprisingly, Griffin found a property that meets Savannah's yard requirement and my water view request. After we accept our coffees from Jacob, Griffin allows us to view the home alone as it's a new construction. The landscaping requires minimal maintenance. I follow Savannah with Emme in my arms through the carved wooden door.

The living room is large and has a wall of built-ins, including a window seat with a view of the lighthouse as well as a granite fireplace. The kitchen features a waterfall Carrera tile island and double stove.

Savannah would fail miserably playing poker. Approval is written all over her face, and she hasn't left the main floor. She wanders up the wide, inlaid hardwood stairs and peers into each of the four bedrooms. I quietly follow her through the house.

The last room she enters is the master suite. The master bathroom and master closet cause Savannah's jaw to hit the floor. The shower puts mine to shame. It has dual showerheads and jets along two walls. The soaking tub with ocean view might have sealed the deal until she walks into the closet. The setup is like mine in New York, except it's even larger. I was wrong. The clincher isn't either of those things; it's the private master balcony.

"*Cara mia*, what do you think?"

When she turns toward my voice, I feel it deep in my bones. This one is perfect. She'll be happy here and, honestly, that's all that matters. While I possess exorbitant wealth, life provided me with enough strife to know it isn't important. Emerson, Savannah, any future children we have, and my loved ones are important.

"I have no words."

"Savannah, will you move into this home with us?" I draw her against me with Emme between us.

She presses a kiss to Emme's head, then looks up at me before whispering, "Yes."

As I lean down to meet her lips, someone clears their throat behind me.

"Sir, sorry for the interruption, but we have an issue with Scarlett." Jacob informs me.

Every time. Every time I make progress with Savannah, someone puts a wrench in it. "We'll be right down."

"Sam—"

"No." The force of my reply is harsh but necessary.

Shock graces her gorgeous face.

"You aren't going to change your mind. I love you. I need you with me, with us. No matter what happens when we hear Jacob out, that isn't going to change."

"You love me too?"

"Too?"

"I love both of you, and I've been waiting for the right time to say it."

I've been searching for the right time for a few weeks. I suppose blurting it out with no preparation works too. I cup her face with my free hand and draw her lips to mine. All too soon, I pull away knowing we have another issue to deal with. Taking her hand, I lead her downstairs.

I direct my gaze to Jacob. "Any security issues here?"

"No."

I request that Griffin prepare a full price cash offer for occupancy as soon as possible and thank him for his time. Once he pulls away, Jacob shares the information about Scarlett.

SAVANNAH

"What has she done now?" My tone is exactly exasperated enough. For the first time in my life, I'm happy. I've found an amazing man who fills my heart. He has the cutest little girl who has wiggled her way into my heart as well.

"Last night there was a raid at the supper club. They brought everyone in for questioning, including Scarlett. Thankfully, Christoph was there instead of Finn, and Cruz had her released before she was booked."

"I assume Christoph knows Cruz as well," Sam inquires.

Jacob nods.

"Where is she now?" My grip on Sam's hand is as tight as a vise, and my blood pressure is through the roof. I want to scream.

"I had Christoph take her to your penthouse."

"What else?" That can't be it. There has to be more because nothing about this has been simple.

"Unfortunately, there were headlines. Among them was *Sam Morgan and the Prostitute*. The good news is it's untrue. The bad news is they used Savannah's photo not Scarlett's."

"What can be done? Do I need to contact a lawyer?"

Sam tightens his grip on my hip, lessening the tapping of my foot, a movement I wasn't even conscious of.

"I have Blaine looking for information pertaining to where the photo came from. You likely can request retraction, especially considering it's Savannah in the photo. You should put out a press release through an attorney."

"Thank you for your time, Jacob. We'll head back to New York as soon as Cash can make it happen. Please tell Christoph, Finn, and Cruz to use our home as necessary. I'll contact Jimmy and speak with him directly as well."

"You're welcome. Please contact me regarding the alarm system for this property before you move in."

After thanking Jacob again, we return to Billie's and head to the airport to return home much earlier than planned.

Having a boyfriend whose brother owns an airline is convenient right now. A little under four hours later, and much to my displeasure, we arrive home in New York.

"Scarlett?" I call out while toeing off my sneakers.

Christoph rounds the island to greet me. "She's in the guest room past Emme's nursery."

"Thank you for your help, Christoph."

"Of course, Savannah. Good luck. She's a tough cookie."

"Glad to hear I taught her something."

Christoph laughs.

I smirk and walk down the hall. After a strong knock that she doesn't answer, I twist the knob and slowly open the door. She's facing the gorgeous city skyline with a book in her lap and AirPods in her ears. At least she's studying. I tap her on the shoulder and step back.

"Hi, Scar. How are you?"

"This is all your fault!"

"Excuse me?"

"If you didn't shack up with that uber-rich hottie boss of yours, none of this would be happening."

"Don't you dare put this on me. You chose your workplace. You chose to work in the underground club. You lied to my face. You're lucky Lt. Cruz recognized Christoph or you would be in jail right now!"

"For what? I didn't do anything wrong."

"You did. You worked as a hostess in an underground gambling parlor and strip club. It doesn't matter that you didn't strip or leave with one of the customers, Scar. You work there, and I'm sure they would find something to charge you with."

"What are you so angry about? It isn't as if your life is getting turned upside down."

"Seriously, Scar? It's my photo on the front page of the New York Times under a headline using the word prostitute. Not yours."

She opens her mouth to speak twice, but her words fail her. "Your picture?"

"Yes."

"Oh." Scarlett is silent for a few beats before asking, "Now what?"

"Sam is working on it with an attorney. At the risk of angering you more, I need you to stay here for a bit. Do you need anything from your apartment or mine?"

"Christoph said he would escort me later if that was acceptable to you and Sam."

I make a mental note to thank Christoph for preparing her to stay here for the night at least. "Okay. What is your schedule like in the next few weeks for school?"

Scarlett sets out her school schedule. Since we're closing in on Thanksgiving, she only has a week or so of class left, then exams.

I consider my next statement carefully. "Sam and I are going to Maine for the holiday. I would like you to come with us. You can see the area. Maybe it will help you make a more informed decision about leaving the city."

"I will come with you but not to help with my decision. I made it a few hours ago, but I wanted to tell you in person."

I brace myself for Scarlett's next statement. I'm torn between being her sister and her mother figure. Raising Scarlett is one of the most difficult things I have endured to date. Part of me wants her to feel comfortable to stay in the city and live her life. A smaller part wants her to need to be near me at the same time. "What did you decide?"

"I want to move with you. Comparing where we lived when we were young and the years we've spent here, I don't want to stay here. I'm sorry for the trouble I've caused over the last few weeks. I made so much more money in tips in the underground portion, even though I wasn't selling my body like Liza. Being carted to the police department was a huge wakeup call. Will you help me find a school in Maine? I might need Sam's help since I'm sure the deadlines have passed for the spring semester."

"Absolutely. Based on where you choose to go to school, we'll look for an apartment for you. I'm proud of you, Scar."

"Thanks. Did you find a house?"

"We did. I can tell you all about it later. Now I need to talk with Christoph and Sam. Do you want to get your stuff today?"

Scarlett nods and rises from her chair before hugging me tight. "I'm sorry I didn't listen sooner, Savi. I know it wasn't easy being my sister and my mom."

"Thanks, Scar. Love you."

"Love you too." She settles back into the chair as I leave the room.

Approaching the kitchen, I see it's teeming with people. Sam, Christoph, Finn, and Maia occupy the stools. Caro is feeding Emme in the living room. Sam looks in my direction, even though he's on the phone. I continue into the bedroom and close myself into the dressing room for a moment of peace. I burrow into the cozy chair in the corner.

For the first time in my life things are going well. Sam and I are moving to Maine with Emme. Scarlett has come to her senses, at least regarding her employment and remaining in the city. That isn't fair. If she wanted to stay here, I would have handled it. I'm grateful she doesn't.

"Savannah?" Sam calls from somewhere in our bedroom.

"In here."

"*Cara mia*, please tell me." The anguish in his voice is almost too much to handle. I'm sure he's terrified I'll run from him. He kneels in front of me.

"I'm taking a few minutes. Scarlett threw me a curveball on top of dealing with my photo in the paper and everything else that is going on."

"Was it a good curve or a bad curve?"

"Good, actually. She decided to transfer after this semester. She may need your help to do it though."

Sam slides his hands along my hips, pulling me to the edge of the chair in his arms.

"I'm not going to run. Being with you is a lot to handle here in the city. In Maine though, it was more than I ever hoped I would find for myself. You and Emme are more than I ever thought possible."

Sam crushes his lips to mine. Before we're able to take it any deeper, Jimmy announces more guests.

"We're not done talking." Sam states.

I slide my fingers into his and follow him to the main living area. I'm surprised to see who our newest guest is.

SAMSON

"Father. This is a nice surprise."

He looks different, calmer, and less stressed. Perhaps distancing himself from Margaux is good for his overall health.

"Sam. Savannah."

We both shake his extended hand.

"I came to offer my support and contacts to assist with the recent headlines. I also wanted to see my granddaughter."

Caro brings Emme over to my father.

"Caroline, it's nice to see you again so soon."

"You too, Mr. Morgan."

My father carefully takes Emme into his arms. The pit in my stomach is an odd feeling. The last time he was here, he only touched her tiny hands. Caro didn't give him much choice this time. In the recent past, my father has been doing and saying the right things. I hope it continues.

Scarlett joins us from the guest room.

"Hi, I'm Caroline. A friend of Auggie's, Sam's brother." Caro waves from her position next to my father. I appreciate her staying nearby. It doesn't look like I don't trust him.

"This is my father, Warren Morgan."

"Pleasure to meet you, Mr. Morgan."

"You as well. I can see how the paper messed up. You two look strikingly similar."

Scarlett nods and continues into the kitchen. As I turn to whisper to Savannah, I notice that Finn and Cruz watch her intently. Can't say I blame them. Scarlett is a younger version of Savannah. Part of me wonders if there is something going on between Finn and Scarlett. Although, didn't Jacob say he is older?

Pushing those thoughts aside for now, I whisper, "Let's talk about everything so they can get Scarlett's stuff and we can handle dinner."

Savannah nods her head in agreement, and we join the others in the kitchen. We spend the next hour plus hashing out the details of our plan and the necessary changes, at least in the short-term. Late afternoon, the team from Blackthorne and Lt. Cruz leave for the evening, only after assurances that the four of us remain home tonight. Finn agreed to escort Scarlett tomorrow to her apartment to pack her clothes and other personal items.

"Would you like to join us for dinner?" I turn toward my father soon after everyone leaves. If he's taken aback by the invitation, it doesn't show on his face.

"No, thank you. I have plans already. Please let me know if there is any further assistance I can offer."

I nod sharply. Lately my father continues to surprise me, not only with divorcing Margaux but trying to rebuild his relationship with my siblings and my daughter. "You're welcome. Thank you for coming."

Savannah places an order for an obscene amount of Chinese food before changing her clothes. We settle around the ottoman and gorge once it arrives. After talking through the timeline again in a bit more detail, Scarlett turns in for the night. She's decided to move back into Savannah's apartment until the end of the semester after collecting her things from Liza and El's tomorrow. Finn or Christoph will continue to escort her when she leaves the apartment. In turn, Savannah agreed to let her stay there rent free. It doesn't make sense for Scarlett to get another job in the city at this point. Financially, it doesn't matter; Savannah was already footing the rent anyway.

I tuck Emme into her crib and join Savannah in our bedroom.

"Ready to finish our conversation from earlier?" I sit across from her on the opposite end of the couch, beckoning her into my arms.

Crawling on the tufted cushions, she settles against me. "What else do we need to talk about?"

"The office, our house, moving, Scarlett, and I think that's all."

She laughs. "No big deal. Only a few huge things to discuss."

"For the office, we need to start a subsidiary in Maine and finalize any licenses we need. Griffin emailed earlier and said we can take title in the next few weeks. How do you feel about only working out of the house?"

"I don't have an issue with it, except what are your plans for Emme?"

"How well do you know Noelle?"

"Not well other than to say her and Cash are perfect for one another."

I laugh. "Noelle is mostly responsible for my brother's transformation to relaxed and happy. She owns a daycare and runs a consulting business for children with developmental disabilities. She has a spot available in her infant room for Emme."

"Wow! That's amazing. Noelle is a boss babe and has a space for Emme. Then I suppose we need two desks or a large workspace for both of us in the office. I can handle the formation and other licensing issues at the office on Monday."

"That leads to the house. Is there any furniture from your apartment or here that you want to move there?"

"No, there's nothing I want from my apartment. Are you keeping this place?"

"Cash and I are discussing which property to keep and which to sell. While I love it here, Cash's terrace beats my tiny balcony hands down. We were considering selling one and putting both names on the one we keep."

"That makes sense. As much as I love it here, the idea of holding onto it for the memories is silly. Cash's terrace is spectacular. That's really the only difference."

"You and Noelle are going to be besties in no time. Her response to keeping Cash's place was similar. It's the only reason he hasn't sold it already."

"I like her even more now. We need to shop for furniture for the entire house, except for Emme, right?"

"We do."

"I can create a list and we can search for what we want?"

"Okay. One more topic—Scarlett."

Savannah takes a deep breath and crawls deeper into my arms. I'm sure, if it were possible, she would burrow beneath my skin.

"*Cara mia*, everything will be fine. I'm grateful that Cruz stepped in. The photo and a retraction are set to print in the Sunday morning edition. There's nothing that she can do to change how I feel about you. As I said before, she truly has only made one iffy choice. She no longer works there, and she's agreed to leave the city. Overall, that's the best you could hope for."

"I appreciate you handling the photo and the newspaper. I'm ready to leave and start our life in Maine. After your trip, we'll be together for the foreseeable future, and I'm looking forward to that."

"I'm not going to view the Regent's acquisitions."

Savannah pushes off my chest with both hands to look me square in the eyes. Her hands remain flat against me. "What? When did you decide to cancel the trip? Why?"

"I canceled the trip last week. I don't need to fly around the world to successfully insure these pieces of priceless art. While it was over-the-top amazing to see *Le Givre* up close and in person, I don't need to do it. The reputation I've built over the last decade speaks for itself. I'm choosing my family over my business, and I don't feel even the slightest twinge in my chest about it." Her gorgeous face exudes shock. I've rendered her speechless. "I love you, Savannah. I'm not taking any chances with you or Emerson."

She fists my shirt, pulling me up to her. "I love you." Her mouth crashes against mine. After the initial contact, she loosens her grip on my shirt and the intensity of her kiss shifts from hard to sensual.

"Savannah—the door—need—lock—" I push out between presses of her soft lips on mine. Realizing she isn't fully hearing me, I band my hands around her waist and set her feet on the floor. Rising, I press my mouth to hers, dance her over to the door, turn the lock, and slowly strip the clothes from her lush body.

SAVANNAH

Waking naked with Sam will never get old. Even though it's dreary outside, I know it's morning. I hear Sam talking to Emme through the monitor while feeding her. He says the sweetest things, and the lullaby that Maria-Luisa sang to him as a child he is passing down to Emme.

After pulling on some clothes and Sam's robe, I scrounge for some coffee. With two cups in hand, I lean against the doorframe of Emme's nursery.

"Morning, Savi." Scarlett shuffles behind me.

"Morning, Scar. I can help you with the coffee maker in a minute."

"Okay." She closes the door to the bathroom.

Stepping into the nursey, I kiss Sam on the forehead and set the coffee on the dressing table. "Morning. Are we going anywhere today?"

"Morning. I have nothing planned. What are you thinking?"

"I like having no plans with you. Scar is going with Finn at eleven. Then it'll only be the three of us."

"We should get a head start on the furniture shopping. Griffin's latest email indicates we could close early next month."

"Sounds good. I'll get started on some breakfast." Reentering the kitchen, I assist Scarlett with her first cup of coffee.

"I think I need one of these coffee makers. Savi, this is amazing!"

"It is. I'm ruined for coffee at this point. I ordered that machine for the office too."

"I would say you're ruined for more than just coffee. When did you get that ring? It's gorgeous. I've never seen you like this before, Savi."

"Thanks. Sam gave it to me a few weeks ago. I've never felt this way before. I spent most of my younger dating time going to school and caring for you. That's simply a fact. The dates I did go on before Sam were dull and boring. My first date with Sam wasn't over the top either, and yet he stood out. True, the security is something I'm used to now, but the rest not even a little bit. We both have lived without extras our entire lives. I'm working on handling the difference between what extras means to me and what it means to Sam. That doesn't even account for the fact that you could buy a pair of high heels for upward of three thousand dollars. We have always checked the price, saved, and budgeted for things. It's crazy that Sam has never done that in his entire life."

"Does he have a single brother?"

I laugh. "Arguably, Auggie is single, but I believe he already gave his heart away."

"That's unfortunate. Finn will be here at eleven, so what can I do to help with breakfast?" We make a huge breakfast complete with omelets, sausage, and toast. Over our meal, we discuss the details for the holiday in Maine in a few days. We plan to leave early on Wednesday morning. Once we clear the dishes, Scarlett heads to her room to pack and get ready to leave.

With profuse thanks and promises to stay on the right path, Scarlett leaves with Finn. A deep cleansing breath later, I strip off my clothes and step into the already steamy enclosure.

"I love it when you're naked and waiting for me." I slide my hands up the front of Sam's thighs to see him jump.

"Who says I was waiting for you?" A grin plays across his gorgeous face.

"If you weren't, then out. I need the hot water." Giggling, I playfully shove Sam out from under the scalding spray.

"No chance, *cara mia*. I was here first." He pushes me against the cool wall before turning on every jet in the luxurious shower. With elegant precision, he worships every inch of me from head to toe, driving me to the edge of bliss but refusing to allow me to fall over.

"Sam," I rasp out between purposeful swipes of his talented tongue. "I need you to fill me now."

He ignores my pleas and pushes his fingers inside my center, releasing the coil that tightened at the base of my spine. I dig my fingers into Sam's shoulders, shuddering against his mouth. Sam makes me wait even longer, kissing his way along my side, teasing the underside of my breasts before licking his way to my lips.

"Savannah."

I want us for the rest of my life. Never before has my name sounded so decadent, so full of promises for a future.

Bracing one arm on the wall and one around my waist, Sam hoists me into his arms. Setting my hands on his shoulders, I take him deep in one downward thrust. We plunge into the depths of orgasmic bliss all too soon. After regaining our breath, we clean up and step out into the bathroom.

Our afternoon fills with image after image of furniture and a lively discussion about color palettes and design choices. Thankfully we successfully chose the living room, master bedroom, and office furniture. The guest bedrooms and dining room can wait for another day. At some point during the first half of Sunday Night Football, I fall asleep on the couch.

The next morning, the office printer spits out page after page of paperwork for the new subsidiary of Morgan Insurance. Maria-Luisa arrived early this morning to spend time with Emme. Sam and I took the extra time to scurry to the office. I'll be here late today and tomorrow to pull off these filings before the holiday.

"Savannah, do you have anything for me to sign before I relieve Maria-Luisa?"

"I'll be right there." After gathering the files, I join Sam in his office. We fly through him signing the documents while I stand near his desk. "Are you going to tell Maria-Luisa about the move today?"

"Yes. I'm not looking forward to it though. It's best for Emerson to leave the city. She will understand. I will be very clear that she's welcome to visit anytime."

"That is how it should be. Emerson deserves to know everyone who loves her. I'll get these filed and be home as soon as I can with the new inquiries from this afternoon for signature."

The afternoon and the next day pass in a flurry of work and activity for the holiday, including packing. I'm excited to see Sam's family but more so to take in the calm of my soon-to-be new hometown.

SAMSON

Our first stop upon landing is the Perk. We left early this morning. So early that Scarlett didn't eat breakfast. When we step into the bakery, the space is crawling with police officers. My quick count nets six: four in uniform and two in business casual dress. The two out of uniform are behind the counter talking with Kelsey.

"Oh. I'm so sorry." I hear a deep voice from behind me. A uniformed officer frozen in his spot having spilled coffee on Scarlett's arm and down her thigh to the top of her boots. So embarrassed, he fails to share his name with her. On the other hand, he could simply be mesmerized by her.

"It's fine. I'm fine. Only a little coffee."

Turning, I find one of the other officers handing Scarlett some napkins. Surprisingly, Scarlett handles the spill well, very well. A well-dressed, dark-haired man who also has a badge moves to assist Scarlett as well.

"Hi. Please accept my apologies for Officer Smithson. He doesn't function well before his morning coffee. I'm William. My wife owns this bakery."

"Scarlett. Thank you. Truly, I'm fine. Have a nice day."

When we finally reach the counter, a perky girl whose name tag reads Becca takes our order. While we wait, Kelsey, her husband William, and the second casually dressed officer join us.

Kelsey speaks first. "I'm so sorry about your clothes. Will is right. Smithson doesn't function well without his morning latte. Please excuse my manners. Grant, this is Billie's older brother Sam, Savannah, Emerson, and—"

"Scarlett. Based on your features, I'm guessing you two are sisters," William adds.

"Hi. Grant Washington. Peter is my brother-in-law. Pleasure to meet you." We're interrupted by a call over the radios from the uniformed officers who are nearby.

"Hopefully I'll see you at dinner tomorrow," Grant adds before rushing out the door.

William kisses Kelsey, and they exchange a few words without speaking. He hurries out the door. "Always," she says as the bell over the door chimes.

Becca appears with our order. Scarlett cheerily accepts it despite the fact she smells like cinnamon.

"Will you be there tomorrow?" I ask Kelsey.

"We plan to stop by near the end of the day. We're having brunch with his mom, sister, and her wife first. If by chance we don't see you, I'm sure Savannah and Scarlett will join us for a girls' night in at some point after the big move. Have a wonderful holiday." Kelsey walks back behind the counter and waves.

"Wow! Savi, you weren't kidding. Everyone is friendly around here," Scarlett blurts out as we leave the bakery, turning toward the shoreline.

"No, I wasn't. It's quite refreshing."

We take a seat on one of the benches and discuss the rest of our day despite the windy conditions.

"Is there anything specific you want to see, Scarlett?"

"I'm not in any rush. I already chose to move here. So far everything indicates I made the right choice for me, like you two."

I can only imagine that her detainment from the supper club had something to do with her need to leave the city.

"What about you, *cara?*" I interrupt her gazing at the ocean, the calm literally washing over her.

"I was thinking we should walk the Marginal Way and then head to Cash's and get settled."

"That sounds like a great plan. Scarlett?"

"Huh? Sure. That works." I notice that her gaze is far past me toward the playground. It isn't until I see the officers from earlier that I realize what grabs her attention.

The Marginal Way is a short walk along the ocean. The views are spectacular, and there are plenty of benches to take it all in. I'm pleasantly surprised by Scarlett's reaction. Maybe, she'll love it here. We meander through Perkins Cove before driving to Cash's.

Like our last visit, Noelle is waiting for us on the porch with Titan. Cash must be working at Pemberton. That dog is amazing. I probably should consider getting one for Savannah and Emerson.

"It's so great to see you so soon! You must be Scarlett."

"Hi," Scarlett replies guardedly.

Picking up on her unease, she says, "Sorry, I'm Noelle, Sam's sister-in-law."

"Pleasure to meet you."

We follow Noelle into the house. She shows us to our rooms and lets us settle in.

"Scar, you good?" Savannah pauses by our suite.

"Yeah."

I can tell from the expression on Savannah's face, something is up. With a practiced ease, I assemble Emme's portable crib. I change her and set her in her crib. She's due to eat in a little while. But first I draw Savannah into my arms.

"*Cara*, what's wrong?"

"Nothing's wrong. I'm a tad worried about Scarlett, but she isn't ready to talk yet. When's she's ready, she'll tell me."

After sliding my thumb across the bow of her lips, I kiss away all her angst. I feel the moment she gives in. Her completely relaxed in my arms is where she belongs. The closer we get to leaving the city, the less tense I become as well. There's no amount I won't pay for Blackthorne to protect my family, but I would prefer not to need them at all. Once we're here for good, that will be the case.

Pulling back, Savannah looks up at me, her blue eyes soft and bright. "What's on tap for tonight?"

"They're having a small get-together at Kelly and Ellis's, but we don't have to go. Tomorrow we're eating at Billie's at one. Then we have almost three whole days to relax."

She smiles. I know that sly smile. She wants something.

"What are you adding to our to-do list, sweetheart?"

"How do you do that?"

"I pay attention. Plus, you have a tell."

"I do not!"

"You do. Your secret is safe with me." I kiss her softly.

"Fine, I want to make sure we get to Yummies this time."

"I can make that happen." When my lips press against hers, I relax too and decide to enjoy this holiday with my family.

The girls decide to stay in tonight, and Scarlett turns in early, saying she has some schoolwork to do. Savannah doesn't question her, so neither do I. We curl up on the balcony under a blanket before dancing our way to the bed, tangling up the sheets as quietly as possible. There's no place I would rather be.

The bond I share with my siblings has only gotten stronger the older we get and the viler Margaux's actions are. We arrive at Cash's near eleven to help prepare our meal. The aromas filling his home are glorious. Turkey with all the trimmings line the granite island. A long table along the wall in the dining room holds more desserts and pastries than we could possibly consume, but I'm sure my family is up to the challenge.

Savannah is animatedly talking to Maggie and Kelly near the French doors with Scarlett listening in. Her mood has lightened a bit since yesterday. Scarlett is coming around. She may have made her choice without visiting here first, but the area and the people are winning her over handily.

While none of us are overly religious, we have a moment of silence before our meal to consider what we're most grateful for. There is nothing to consider for me: Emerson and Savannah. I'll do everything in my power to make sure they are blissfully happy. The sooner we're here for good, the better.

After a wonderful meal filled with laughter and a few childhood mischief stories, we clean the dishes before lounging for some football. Like Savannah, Scarlett loves football and she's challenging Cash on his view about the Detroit Lions and their ability to win today's game. It's amusing to listen to. However, my focus is on my gorgeous woman cradling my daughter in her arms while she sleeps. There's no other woman on this planet who would accept both of us without reservation. Only Savannah. I'm grateful her resume graced my desk and I didn't take the cowardly way out and not hire her.

During halftime of the first game, the party truly gets underway. William, Kelsey, and their son Benjamin join the group, along with more delicious confections from the Perk. Kelly's newest designer, Poppy, and her contractor, Scott, join us as well. If I recall, Scott is somehow related to Maggie's nephew James, but I'm not quite sure how. Poppy is a petite woman with a pixie haircut. She seems reserved and has been hanging with Scott on the edges of the group since they arrived.

Slowly the party guests start to dwindle in number, and Emerson is almost ready for bed. She has been a trooper through all the football cheering, joyous laughter, and sibling ribbing happening today, not to mention the passing around of her like she was a football herself.

Rising from my seat, I scoop Emerson from Noelle's arms and climb the stairs. I hear Savannah talking with her sister in the next room.

SAVANNAH

Every time I visit here, I love it more. I can only hope that Scarlett feels the same. When I notice she isn't with the guests any longer, I track her down in the guest suite.

"What's on your mind, Scar?"

"Your friends are amazing. This holiday is one of the best I've ever had."

"But?"

"It's a small but. Your friends are… well… old."

I feign anger and then start laughing.

"Scar, I'm sure there are people your age here, especially once classes start in the spring. You'll meet plenty of people your age. This trip was for you to see if you could be happy living here. Plus, I think Kelsey's staff are college students, Becca and a guy, but I don't remember his name. I can ask her for you."

"Thanks. I'm not going to change my mind. Being hauled in for questioning, and probable arrest without Sam's intervention if you will, was enough for me to want out of New York. I'll adjust here like I did there."

"I love you, Scar."

"Love you too."

As I start to leave, Scarlett asks, "Do you have earplugs?"

"No, why?"

"The AirPods didn't drown out you two last night."

I'm sure my face is beet red.

Laughter bursts out of Scarlett's mouth. "You should see your face, Savi. That look is priceless. Seriously, I was just messing with you."

I chuck a throw pillow at her and leave amidst her laughter. As I step into our suite, Sam holds his finger to his lips. Emme went down easily tonight. I'm sure it's tough being the center of everyone's baby attention since Benjamin slept through their visit tonight. Soon Noelle and Cash's twins will join our growing family. Reaching for my hand, he leads me back outside despite the colder temperature tonight. I settle into his lap as he throws the soft, thick blanket around both of us.

"Everything good with Scarlett?"

"It will be eventually. She's concerned because all the people she's met so far are our age. I'm going to talk with Kelsey tomorrow about her staff. I'm fairly sure they're Scar's age. She assured me she's moving. I believe her. We'll solidify her opinion before we leave on Sunday."

"Have I told you how much I love you today?"

"Maybe, but I would be willing to hear it again and again, especially if it includes your hands gliding along my bare skin."

"I can arrange that." Sam presses his lips to my neck.

"One teeny tiny request."

"What might that be?"

"Let's go inside."

A chuckle escapes his mouth as he stands from the chair with me in his arms. Leaning forward, I open the door and close it behind us. Sam lowers me to the soft duvet and starts removing his clothes while I strip down to my maroon, lace panties.

"Is that new?"

"No."

"Good." Sam literally tears the lace from my body before taking me to even higher heights of pleasure than he ever has before.

The next few days in Maine are relaxed and laid back. I imagine that once we move and are working here, the pace would remain the same. Not only does Sam fulfill his promise to take us to Yummies, but we also share the Nubble, York Village, and a local breakfast spot called Rick's with Scarlett. I can see her coming around.

All too soon, we land in New York. Finn meets us at the airport to escort Scarlett to my apartment—her apartment I guess. The only good news is that, within weeks, we'll be Maine residents.

We have handled most requirements to leave the city. We have a home that's almost ours, furniture is ordered, a daycare for Emme, and necessary office equipment ready for delivery. We're simply waiting on the business license approval. There shouldn't be any issues; we simply need to wait the prescribed time.

Back at the office over the next two weeks, I busy myself boxing and preparing the office for the move. Most of our policies are stored electronically, however the office administrative documents from when Sam first started his business are paper. He made the shift to paperless about four years ago.

"Savannah, could you come here?" Sam calls through the intercom.

"Yes. Give me a few minutes to finish this box." I stack the files and slide them into the box before hoisting it up on the table. When I turn the corner, I'm floored. The office lights are dim. There is a huge bouquet of flowers in Sam's arms, along with two small, wrapped boxes, and something smells delicious. He rearranged his office to make room for a small table with covered plates.

"Sam, what have you done?"

"Emerson is spending the rest of the day with Maria-Luisa. We're having a date."

Since I was in the file room, I hadn't noticed the time or that Sam should have gone home about an hour ago.

"We don't have time for that, Sam."

"There's always time, *cara mia*."

I know better than to argue with him. I take the flowers from his outstretched hand. They are spectacular. The bouquet contains colorful blooms of purple roses, ranunculus, seasonal mums, thistle, safari sunset, and salal.

"There is always time to put a smile like that one on your gorgeous face. Plus, you agreed to be more accepting. The flowers are only the beginning for today."

"I'm trying. I didn't make a big deal about the price of the house or the furniture. Trust me, I wanted too, but I don't need—"

He silences me with a toe-curling, knee-buckling kiss to top every other one he's ever given me. Attempting to resist him is futile. I melt into his embrace until he draws back, leaving me breathless and wanting more.

"Gifts aren't something you need. It's something the giver—me, in case if you weren't sure—wants to give. I have significantly decreased the number of gifts I would normally give based on what you've told me. You have been warned about Christmas, so please prepare yourself. I won't hold back then for you or Emerson."

"Sam. There's no chance I can convince you that the house is enough for Christmas?" My tone is breathy and resigned.

"No, no chance at all."

"Did Auggie cook?"

"No, but Mama and Papa Romano are a close second."

I sit in the chair Sam has pulled out for me and lean back as he lays a napkin in my lap. He fills our glasses with red wine, and we feast on the delicious food. Never once have Sam and I run out of things to talk about during our dates. We may not have made it a rule, but we avoid talking about work when we aren't in the office or working at home during the day. In the evening, all work talk ceases. I'm glad because initially I was concerned.

"What else do you have up your sleeve, Mr. Morgan?"

"For the next portion of our date, we need to change. I already took care of your clothes for our date. It's in the bathroom."

With a small smile, I lean forward and brush my lips across his. "I'll be back in a bit." When I step into the bathroom, there is a garment bag with a So Elegant label, a wrapped box on the floor that looks like shoes, and another box on the vanity. My chest tightens. Never have I ever thought a man like him would want someone like me. I'm not putting myself down. I worked very hard to earn my education and raise Scarlett the best I could. Truly I'm not who I thought Sam would be interested in.

Slowly, I unzip the bag with tears pricking my eyes. Inside is a deep aubergine, silk dress that no doubt will slide over my curves. The collared neck allows for the back to plunge exceptionally low, not to mention the slit that is dangerously high. Pulling out my phone, I text Kelly and Billie at the same time.

Me: Which one of you is responsible for this gorgeous dress?

Billie: I was in on the planning, but it's Kelly's design.

Kelly: The design was all me. Well, I designed it to meet Sam's requests.

Me: Which were?

Kelly: Body hugging silk like the blue dress from the gala and as much exposed back as possible.

Me: It's gorgeous. Thank you.

Billie: Have a great time!

Kelly: Have fun tonight.

I shouldn't be shocked, but that's only the beginning. The box on the floor contains a pair of nude Louboutins with sparkles called Follies Strauss. I can only imagine how much these cost. Was Sam done? No, not even close. The final box contains a complete set of lingerie from La Perla. I have no other way to describe it but a trousseau including a robe, panties, bra, chemise, and silk pajamas. I have no words. Knowing I'm likely short on time, I pull on the silkiest lace panties I've ever felt, shimmy into the dress, and slip on the shoes. After fixing my hair, I pull open the door to find Sam waiting for me.

He changed too. Now he's dressed in a custom suit, and his signature scent surrounds me.

"*Cara mia*, you look—"

I press my finger to his lips, effectively cutting him off. "I could say the same for you." Despite my warring feelings, I slide my fingers into his waiting hand. I didn't miss the other packages sitting on his desk. "Sam—"

"Please don't say it's too much. I want to pamper you and give you gifts. Trust me when I say I reined myself in."

"This is reined in?" I inhale deeply and exhale very slowly. He's in an entirely different stratosphere than me. I'm not used to it. Would all of this be acceptable if it were from different retailers? Would I be okay with it then? I probably would. "Fine."

Shock registers across his features. "That's it. You aren't going to put up a fight?"

"No. I'm honoring my word by accepting what you want to do for me. Truthfully, all of this is very thoughtful and took some serious legwork and planning. Even though Billie can design something quickly, it still needed to be made. I appreciate it. I need to deal with the fact that you spending ten times as much on a pair of shoes isn't extravagant. Plus, they are spectacular."

"Thank you because there's one more gift and where we're actually going."

Wrapping our still clasped hands around my back while setting the other over his heart, I reply, "You're welcome. I've never been here before. Setting aside your wealth, I've never been at this point. No man has ever taken the time to learn about me, to spend time with me. You're everything I never knew I needed. I love you."

"I'm grateful every single day for every man who was foolish enough not to see how amazing you are. After Meghan, I stopped looking for a partner. I wasn't ready. Then you rocked me to the core at the gala and continue to do it daily. I'm grateful you fought for us after learning about Emerson. A lesser woman would have run away. I love you, Savannah." He seals his words with a kiss, sending heat over my entire body with his mouth.

The sincerity and passion behind his kiss makes me want to forgo whatever he has planned and take him on his desk. However, I'm sure his date was carefully orchestrated.

"Where are we going?" I whisper.

"Shall we find out?"

"Don't you already know?"

He laughs a deep, hearty laugh that makes me fall even harder.

"Yes. I planned this date myself."

"You're very good at date planning."

"Why, thank you." Grabbing my coat, he helps me pull it on.

"Are we going to be outside?"

"I'm not sharing any details; plus I don't want to share how ravishing you look in that dress."

"Had to get that compliment out, huh?"

"Hell yes! A tiny part of me wants to forgo our date and strip that dress off your gorgeous curves right now."

I feel my skin heat from his words.

"Savannah, please share what dirty thoughts are in your head right now."

"I thought the same thing after our kiss but decided you took the time to plan our date, we should go on it."

"Thank you, sweetheart. Here's the last gift for tonight. While I picked it, I did ask Billie to confirm it was the right choice for long-term use based on your concerns."

Color me intrigued. I appreciate the extra effort. Nestled inside the small box is a pair of diamond earrings. It looks like a pair of studs with a removable jacket with a pear-shaped diamond at the bottom.

"Oh, Sam. These are stunning." My hands are shaking just holding them. He's smart enough to insure all these pieces, right? Of course he is. Regaining my composure, my hands shake less as I insert the earrings.

After gathering my flowers, the packages, and our clothes from the workday, we ride downstairs. Christoph is waiting in the lobby as we exit the elevator.

SAMSON

"Good evening, sir. Miss Clemons." Christoph takes the bags from my hands.

"Good evening," we reply in unison before sliding into the waiting car. The ride to our destination isn't exceptionally long. The traffic however adds at least thirty minutes to our ride.

As we come to a stop outside the building, Christoph steps out of the car before me. After buttoning my jacket, I reach for Savannah's hand. I'm rethinking having Billie make that slit higher than she wanted to. The sheer amount of exposed skin of Savannah's toned thighs dirties my thoughts even more.

"Did Scarlett help you?" Savannah asks once she recognizes where we are.

"No. I did this research all on my own."

A small smile breaks on Christoph's face.

"How? I never told you I've never been here."

"I may have snooped in your pile of books while you were otherwise busy. I noticed that you have a list of priceless art you want to see in person, or at least works by specific artists. Two of those artists can be viewed here at MoMA." I've stunned Savannah speechless. It's one thing to do it with my lips. It's something else to do it with actions. "Shall we check out *Boy in the Red Vest* by Paul Cézanne and *Starry Night* by Vincent Van Gogh?"

"Absolutely."

We're greeted at the entrance by a docent named J.J. who happens to be Jimmy's son, but his name isn't James. Jimmy was very excited to be included in planning this date even the slightest bit. I'll be sure to give him an update when I see him next.

Hand in hand we wander through the galleries. I'm not in any rush; neither is Savannah. It was a wise choice to eat first. Now we can stay here as long as she pleases. Savannah gazes up at the Van Gogh for quite some time before walking through the remainder of the gallery. I'm not sure why, but she studied the Cézanne even longer. For every work she has a comment or tidbit of knowledge that she shares. For the *Boy in the Red Vest*, she's utterly mesmerized.

There's one more small portion of tonight's date left—dessert. After viewing much of the museum, J.J. leads us into a room near a window overlooking the city. With Auggie's help, James set up a dessert tasting for Savannah and me.

"There's no way for me to thank you for tonight," she whispers near the shell of my ear while I pull out her chair.

"None are necessary." I reveal two decadent-looking chocolate creations in front of us. We each take a few satisfying bites of Auggie's dessert. After savoring most of the chocolate goodness, I take her hand in mine. "Why are you interested in priceless works of art?"

"Never in my wildest dreams did I ever think I would make it out of our tiny, little cape let alone to the Big Apple. When my mom died, I knew I had to do whatever was necessary for Scarlett. I selected business as a major because I felt like it has the most opportunities for me to support us. My love of art came from her. Well, that's mostly true. She had a poster of *L'Etoile* by Edgar Degas on the back of her bedroom door. I dreamed of seeing that painting in real life but knew I could never make it happen. I didn't know what it was called until I went to college. Professor Amelia Dorsey featured Degas in her class. Not only was the poster featured but so many other amazing impressionists works from Cézanne, Monet, Matisse, and Van Gogh. I decided that day to make art history my minor."

"*Cara,* why didn't you ever share that before?" I love how her skin turns pink when I call her that. Not only did her mother impact her regarding raising Scarlett, but also her appreciation for priceless art. It's as if I put out the request at the perfect time and Savannah was set in my path.

"You never asked. I didn't think it was important for my job."

"It isn't. It's important because it helps me understand you more fully." Each day I learn a new layer of the spectacular woman that is Savannah Clemons. A woman I want for the rest of my life.

"It never came up until now."

"I would have invited you on my trip had I known sooner."

"It's fine. It was before."

"Before what?" I have no idea where she's going with this.

"Before you and I became an us." Slowly her eyes lift to me.

Rising to my feet, I draw Savannah against me. It's as if time slows down whenever she's in my arms. Softly I press my mouth to hers. The tenor builds quickly so much so Savannah sets her hand on my chest, adding space between us. Her lips are swollen from mine, and her skin is flushed.

"Do you have any idea how much those words mean to me?" I'm floored by this gorgeous woman even more today than yesterday. She's overcome so much. Working to care for Scarlett and herself. Sacrificing her own needs for Scarlett how a mother would, not a sister. Unicorn doesn't even come close to the rarity that is this woman. My woman. My future.

"I do. They mean just as much to me."

I bring my mouth near her ear to the sweet spot that makes her melt in my arms. "I want to peel that silky dress from your curves and make love to you. Let's go home." As I pull away, I feel her shiver from my breath and my words. Intertwining my fingers with her, I lead her to our waiting car.

Upon arriving home, we bid Christoph good night and ride to the penthouse. We slip off our shoes once we're inside. Maria-Luisa is reading in the living room.

"How was your evening out?" she asks.

"We had a wonderful time. Thank you for staying."

Maria-Luisa nods. I get the feeling she has more to say, but Emme starts to cry from her nursery.

"I'll go. Thank you again for staying with her." Savannah grasps her dress and walks to Emme. I watch her walk away.

"Samson."

I return my gaze to my former nanny and the grandmother of my daughter.

"Never once did you look at Meghan or Marisol like that. Love like that is hard to find. It's rare. Henry and Salma provided you with an excellent example of making a marriage work. Use that knowledge and hold onto her. You'll be happy for many years to come. I can feel it."

I'm dumbfounded. At one time I thought she would want Marisol and me to last as a couple. She was never more than my friend. Savannah is everything.

"I don't know what to say other than thank you. I'm sure that is hard for you to admit. Plus, she's here and Marisol isn't."

"You and Marisol were never meant to be anything more than friends. Your friendship gave me a beautiful granddaughter. I'll miss her when you leave."

"You're welcome to visit as often as you wish. Please do so."

"Thank you, Samson. I realize I'm not your mother, but I'm proud of the man you've become. Despite your opulent upbringing, your life wasn't without difficulty."

I hug Maria-Luisa tightly. "Good night. I'll see you on Monday morning."

Once the doors close behind her, I pad quietly toward Emme's room. Savannah is placing her in the crib. When she's finished, I reach for her hand, threading our fingers together. Resisting the temptation of her exposed back is no longer necessary. I splay my hand onto her skin, enjoying her muscles tightening under my palm. I draw circles on her skin as we enter our bedroom.

Our bedroom… that should make me shudder. In fact, it's the opposite. Sharing my home with Savannah seems like it has always been this way. I never want to go back to a day without her. Savannah is gazing at the skyline. Stepping right behind her, I skim my hands over her hips, clasping them around her waist. Her head falls back against my chest. Never did I envision this dress when I asked for it. Kelly outdid herself. Not only is her back almost entirely exposed, but the silk over her curves is so luxurious. Before she has a chance to speak, I brush my lips over her exposed shoulder. Without releasing her, I continue placing a trail of open-mouth kisses across her back. I try to unfasten the neck of her dress with my teeth but fail. Dragging my hands upward over the curve of her breasts, I feel her body react to my touch. Her nipples pebble as I slide my hands higher. I unclasp the collar and let it dip forward.

"Sam." Her voice sounds sultry and raspy.

I nudge her forward, pressing her against the window. Grasping the zipper, I lower it, exposing her perfect heart-shaped ass and the blue lace panties I gave her tonight. I had an image in my head when I ordered them, but that pales in comparison to the real thing.

"Savannah, turn around."

I expect her to turn around with her arm holding her dress up. Instead my sexy siren sets her hands on my chest, allowing the silk to fall to the floor at her feet. Her fingers deftly move down my shirt, shoving it off my arms within moments of stepping out of her dress.

"You are…."

My pants and boxer brief join the pile on the floor. Bracketing her hips, I take steps backward toward our bed. I turn us and hook my fingers under the sides of her panties, peeling them down her toned legs, and climb over her. I lower my tongue to her chest, licking up over her chin before kissing her soft lips.

"I need you," she whimpers against my mouth.

"Now?"

"Right now."

I'm sure the ache she feels is equal to mine. I curl my arm under her left knee, opening her to me before burying myself in her core. With sensual strokes, I drive into her. I'll never tire of the sensation of her wrapped around me. Each time I withdraw, I feel bereft until she surrounds me again. Looking down at her, I realize this time is different. The look in her eyes is pure love for me the man, not the eligible bachelor. Savannah has quietly captured my heart and soul, and I refuse to let her go.

Her muscles clench and her thighs quake as she nears her release. Pushing herself up on her forearms, she presses her lips to mine.

"Let go with me."

No sooner than the words escape her lips, I watch her fly over the edge of pure ecstasy. She's exquisite when she's vulnerable for me. The look of pleasure sends me careening into my release, exploding inside her in hot bursts. I milk this as long as I can, making sure we wring every single ounce of spiraling pleasure from our lovemaking.

Absolutely spent, I uncurl my arm and lower over her, setting my lips to the hollow of her collarbone. Hours later, I wake with Savannah nestled against me and Emme cooing through the monitor.

SAVANNAH

We spend our weekend traipsing through the city with Maia in tow. Aside from shopping for gifts, we gaze upon the window displays, including Macy's and the magnificent tree at Rockefeller Center. Considering the sheer number of bags we're carrying, Christmas is huge for the Morgan family. Despite the beauty of this city, I won't miss it.

Usually, I dress up when I'm in the office. However, the beginning of the week flies by with packing the files and preparing them for transport to the house, so I opt for pants instead of a skirt. Sam joins me in the file room after ten on Thursday.

"Maria-Luisa called. She's concerned that Emme's running a fever. I got an appointment in an hour to have her checked out. I'll be back as soon as I can."

"No problem. I should be able to finish packing the files today." I move next to him near the door.

"I love you. See you later." Sam leans in, kissing me softly.

"I love you."

I return to the files and wrap up near noon. I plop into Sam's chair to print the new business. The printer is humming when I hear the elevator door open. Peering out of his office, I find two large, menacing men I've never seen before.

"Can I help you?" Hiding the fear in my voice is harder than I anticipate.

"We need to speak with Savannah Clemons."

My mind is spinning. Who are these men? How do they know my name? How did they get past building security downstairs? Panic courses through my veins. My heart is pounding in my chest. There is no point in lying. I'm sure they know who I am. "I'm Savannah. Did we have an appointment today?" I'm trying to keep this as professional as possible. However, clients don't come to the office.

"Your father sent us. He needs your assistance."

"I haven't spoken to my father in years and have no interest in helping him."

The two men advance. One in front of me and one circles behind me, close enough that I can feel their breath.

"Miss Clemons, we can do this the easy way where you follow us downstairs to our waiting car or we can go after your boyfriend's daughter at the doctor's office instead."

The sheer terror that they know where Emerson is shakes me to my core. I don't see another option except to comply. I would never purposefully put Emerson in harm's way. If I comply, what are the chances they won't physically harm me? I have no idea, but it's keeping me from screaming and attempting to run past them. My mind is zipping through ways I can get out of this. "I need to write a message to cancel my lunch meeting with my friend Maia. I can drop it off at the front desk as we walk out."

"Fine, but I want to read it."

I retreat into Sam's office, take a deep breath, and scribble a note to Maia.

Maia,

Sorry Our Salads will have to wait another day. workload has Taken me by surprise today.

Savi

I seriously hope these two aren't very bright. If they are, I risked physical harm to myself, Emerson, or both of us. The taller man scans the message and hands it back to me. So far so good. I grab my coat but leave my purse. Fortunately, my phone is in my pocket.

As we approach the front desk, I hand security the note. Matt has worked here since before I started and is aware of the security issues surrounding me. "Please give this to my friend Maia when she arrives for our lunch." I stare at him as long and as hard as I can, hoping to convey that something is wrong.

"Of course, Miss Clemons."

If I'm lucky and I sincerely hope I am, he'll call Sam. Apparently, I wait too long as the shorter guy pushes me forward less than gently. They open the rear door of the town car and shove me inside. Once I settle into my seat, I notice a disheveled man already inside. It isn't until he uses my childhood nickname that I recognize him as my father. Not only are his clothes a mess but his left eye is swollen shut.

"Squirt, I'm so sorry. I tried to keep you and your sister out of this."

"What have you done?"

"They assured me they wouldn't hurt you or Scarlett."

"I'm sure they did. Apparently, my daughter isn't out of bounds. How much do you owe?"

"A lot," my father mumbles.

That's the only logical explanation; I've been kidnapped for my father's debt. Instead of wallowing in my predicament, I watch out the window, trying to gauge where we're going.

SAMSON

Hurrying home, I meet Maria-Luisa and Maia at the door. My beautiful angel is screaming and clearly uncomfortable despite the dose of ibuprofen she has already had.

"Sam, I'm sorry to disturb your workday—"

"Nonsense. Thank you for the call. We should get going."

Once we arrive, Emme is taken straight back to an exam room. I can only guess it's due to her age considering this is our first ever sick visit to the pediatrician.

The doctor enters the small exam room. She's petite with dark hair and red-rimmed glasses. After asking some questions, which thankfully Maria-Luisa provided me with answers, she examines Emme. She determines that Emerson has an ear infection and orders some antibiotics for the next two weeks.

"Have a nice holiday, Mr. Morgan. Emerson will be fine."

I thank her and step back into the lobby. Maia's complexion is ashen.

"What happened? Is she okay?" Panic and anger course through me. I'll never forgive myself if something happens to Savannah because of me.

"We need to get back to the house as soon as possible." Maia ushers the three of us to the car.

When my phone rings, I hand Emme to Maria-Luisa.

"Sam. It's Jacob."

"What is going on?" I'm sure my tone isn't courteous or professional in any way, but I don't care. She's half of my world, and I don't want to find out what it's like without her. Maria-Luisa secures Emme in the car, and we pull away from the doctor's office.

"Savannah was taken from the office. Two men entered the premises and escorted her from the building. However, she was bold enough to get a message to Matt at the front desk. He called me as soon as she exited the building. Matt indicates that Savannah wasn't injured in any way when she left. Whatever they said to her shook her enough that they didn't need force. I'm working with Blaine behind the scenes for information. Lt. Cruz is obtaining the video from the bank across the street."

"What do I do now?"

"Go home and wait for them to call. The only motive I see is money. You should reach out to your carrier and put them on notice. Like your brothers, I assume you have a policy for Savannah, even though she isn't your wife yet."

Yet. I'm begging to make sure that yet becomes a *when* at this point. The level of fear and anguish is unbearable. This is my fault. "Yes, I got a policy for her when she started working for me and increased the coverage when she…."

"Sam, you have done everything right. I need you to be as clearheaded as possible. I realize what I'm asking of you. If Norah were taken, I would be like a caged animal. Please keep the phone line open and stay as calm as possible. Christoph went to meet Finn. They will escort Scarlett to your place and remain with her."

"I understand." After ending the call, we exit the car and ride to the lobby.

"Jimmy, there's a security issue with Savannah. Please allow only those on the list up, an agent from Sterling Insurance, and anyone with Lt. Cruz."

"Yes, Mr. Morgan."

Upon arriving at home, I walk directly to my office safe and pull out the insurance documentation. I place a call to my agent. After a brief call, he assures me he'll arrive as soon as possible.

"Hey, brother. What's up?" Cash answers the video call from my laptop immediately. I'm grateful he's at the office.

"Savannah." I can't even get the words out. The woman I love with my entire heart, more than I've ever loved anyone before, has been taken. Cash must think I've lost my damn mind.

"Sam, what happened?"

"Savannah was taken from the office." I pace back and forth behind my chair, dragging my hands through my hair. My chest hurts more than ever before. I should have demanded security for her at all times. This is on me.

"What do you need?"

I should have made her come with me. The files aren't important. I didn't even fight her on it. I'm lost in my head and the blame game.

"Sam."

"Samson."

"Samson Warren Morgan, fucking answer me!"

I don't even know how many times Cash called my name before swearing at me to get my attention.

"I'm sorry. I can't even process all this right now. I'm madly in love with her."

"Does she know?"

"Yes. I think so." Inhaling deeply and exhaling sharply, I say, "I need to know how much money I can get my hands on in the next four to six hours. Cash, use my money first, not yours or the pooled funds."

"You worry about what Jacob and Sterling say. I'll worry about the money."

"Thank you. Text me, and then I'll call you here. Jacob said to stay off my phone." I settle myself as much as possible before leaving my office. As I enter the living room, Scarlett, Finn, and Christoph step off the elevator.

"What's going on, Sam?" Scarlett asks.

I glance up at Christoph, and he curtly shakes his head, indicating he hasn't told Scarlett yet.

"You should have a seat."

Reluctantly, she sits on one of the stools near the island.

"Savannah was taken from the office about an hour ago."

Scarlett jumps off the stool, shoves me, and starts shouting at the top of her lungs. She continues shoving me until I grab her forearms. "This is all your fault! You did this! You, your insane bank account, and status in this city. I can't, I just can't. If something happens to her, so help me I'll—"

"Scarlett, there is nothing I won't do to bring your sister home."

At those words, Scarlett twists out of my hold and steps back. I can't read the look on her face. The elevator opens again. Cruz, along with two other officers, join us as Maria-Luisa brings Emerson back into the main living area to prepare her bottle.

"Cruz, do you have an update?"

"Nothing much yet. We grabbed the license plate from the security camera at the bank across the street. So far there have been no hits on the identities of the men. But we were able to see that there was another man in the car. We haven't identified him yet though. The picture was grainy, and he appears to have been beaten."

The door keeps opening into my home, and the agent from Sterling arrives.

"Sam." Steve Sterling extends his hand to me. "Can I have a word in private?"

I extend my arm toward my office and walk away.

"Steve, thank you for coming. What do you need from me?"

"Since we recently updated this policy, I assume you recall how this works. Have you received a demand yet?"

"Yes, I recall. No, but I don't see any reason to take Savannah other than money. I want to be prepared. Cash is looking into how much capital I can raise in the next few hours."

"Good. That was my next suggestion. When they call, make sure you ask to speak with Savannah after they make their demand."

I sign some paperwork that Steve provides, and we leave my office. My phone rings, but unfortunately it is Jacob.

"Go ahead, Jacob."

"What is the status there?"

"Scarlett and your team are here. Cruz and two other NYPD officers, Steven Sterling from the insurance company, as well as myself, Emerson, and Maria-Luisa."

"Blaine was able to determine that Arthur Clemons is the catalyst for the kidnapping. He apparently owes more than four million dollars to various loan sharks who work the Atlantic City casino crowd. We also have identified the men who took Savannah as Joe Briggs and Carl Maxwell. Both men work for Mikhail Drake. Carl is his right-hand man. Blaine is still digging as to why they sought out Mr. Clemons."

"Thanks. Please keep me informed." After ending the call, I return to the main living area.

The kitchen is packed, and Scarlett is pacing the length of the couch with Finn keenly watching her. Perhaps he's concerned she will shove me again. I can take whatever she needs to dish out. Even though this is on Mr. Clemons, I'm at fault too.

"Scarlett, can I have a word?"

She stops pacing and joins me near the hallway.

"When is the last time you spoke with your father?"

"It's been awhile. Why?"

"Don't lie, Scarlett. We know you bailed him out last month after his relapse." My tone precisely matches my demeanor right now.

"This is about—"

The shrill ring of my phone quiets everyone in the room.

SAVANNAH

Following our route to the best of my ability, I believe we're in The Bronx somewhere. Unfortunately, I didn't catch any street signs or other distinguishing markers to help Jacob and Cruz. Joe and Carl, at least I think that's their names, hustle my father and me into an unfurnished, ground-level apartment and have us sit against the kitchen island on the floor. So far they haven't hurt me, but given the condition of my father's face, it isn't outside the realm of possibility.

"Both of you need to keep your mouths shut during this call or there will be dire consequences." Carl points back and forth between us before dialing the phone. He sets a device near the phone probably to disguise his voice.

I can't imagine what good that does considering my father and I have seen them and heard their voices.

"I would like to speak with Sam Morgan."

It must be on speaker because I can hear Sam's responses.

"This is Sam Morgan."

"My boss wants five million dollars in exchange for your girlfriend by six this evening. If you fail to deliver the cash, you will never see her again."

The heaviness settles in. As I expected, neither Carl nor Joe is in charge here. They are middlemen, henchmen, the dirty work guys—take your pick of descriptor. Either way, that likely doesn't bode well for us.

"I'll get you what you want. I need to speak with her first." The terror in his voice palpable. It's my fault it's there. Well, my father's fault but mine to bear all the same.

Carl yanks me up by my upper arm near the island.

"Sam."

"Did they hurt you?" The sound of his voice breaks my heart.

"No, I'm fine, but I need you to check on Gray at my apartment."

"I'm so sorry. I should have—"

"Stop, check on Gray for me. I love you." I try to hide the cracking in my voice but fail. Please understand what I'm trying to tell you.

Carl shoves me back down beside my father. "That's enough. We'll call with further instructions for the exchange." He ends the call and squats in front of my father and me. "Your boyfriend better come through. I would hate to harm that delicious body of yours." Carl drags his finger across my cheek and down my arm.

It takes everything in me not to address his disgusting innuendo or shrink back from his touch. "Can I use the bathroom please?" I don't really need to use the bathroom, but I'm hoping there's a window or at least I'm able to get up off the floor.

Joe simply points down the hall. Rising slowly, I gaze out the windows, attempting to gather more information. If I can, I'll text Sam. Whoever my father owes doesn't employ the brightest muscle. They didn't even check me for a phone or any type of weapon. However, I won't let myself believe they won't hurt me if Sam can't come through. Keeping my mind calm and tamping down my desire to throttle my father is enough to keep me busy right now. When everything was starting to look up for me. When I could finally think about myself first instead of Scarlett.

As quietly as possible, I search the contents of the small bathroom. To my surprise, it's fairly clean and even has toilet paper and hand soap. I don't find anything useful, and the frosted window prevents me from seeing outside. Since I'm here, I use the facilities and wash up. After failing to glean any information about our location and Joe banging on the door to hurry me up, I retreat beside my father without texting Sam.

When I take a seat next to my father, he starts to speak. "I'm sorry, squirt. This is all on me. I tried to get myself together and stay dry after rehab, but I failed not once but twice."

The sincerity in his voice gives me pause. "The only reason I'm here is because the man I love has money. I'll never be able to pay him back, assuming he's successful in saving us."

"If he even asks for it, he isn't good enough for you."

"Stop talking about Sam like you know him. You don't. You have no right to question my choices. I haven't seen you in years, and yet here I am pulled back into your mess for one reason. Sam has money. I earn a very good salary, but not enough to come up with that kind of cash. Certainly not by the end of today." More so now that I made partner, which I still can't believe. Either way, I don't have that kind of money. I won't have a choice but to pay Sam back. I can't let him save my father from his stupidity.

"You're right."

I'm floored. Did he really say that? "Excuse me?"

"Losing your mother was one of the most difficult things that ever happened to me. While I was there with you and your sister, I wasn't present. Not even close. It took me years and a substantial number of hours in therapy to realize losing you and Scarlett was something I might be able to repair to some degree. Rehab was the first step. I failed—twice. This certainly doesn't help matters."

"Why now?"

"I know I screwed up—"

"Pipe down! I don't need to hear your family drama. If your boyfriend pays up, you can talk all you want over dinner," Joe admonishes us from his post near the door.

Carl is whispering to someone on his phone behind us in the kitchen. I strain my ears to pick up any information I can. I refuse to be a sitting duck any longer than necessary.

"—he sounded sincere." Muffled words, then, "He will pay it." Then I hear "—drop location" before Carl ends the call.

He said drop to his boss but exchange to Sam. That can't be good. I have no idea what time it is at this point or how long we've been here. If I had to guess, it's been at least two hours considering I'm starving and only had a light breakfast and skipped lunch.

"Let's go, princess. Time to call your boyfriend again." Carl reaches down to pull me to my feet.

"I'll stand on my own." I twist to keep his hand from grasping my arm again. As much as I love this super soft sweater, I'm burning it after today.

Carl dials Sam's phone again.

SAMSON

After finishing my discussion with Scarlett, I contact Cash again and verify the funds will be ready for transfer in less than an hour. I rarely wish for time to hurry, but today I am. I need to pay off these goons so I can get Savannah back. I knew before this whole ordeal that she's it for me, but I don't feel like I've conveyed that to her adequately.

After the call, I began to wrack my brain, trying to figure out what she means about taking care of Gray. Gray is here at my home in Manhattan. Her apartment is in The Bronx. The realization slaps me in the face.

"Cruz! She's in The Bronx." I shout as loudly as I can. That's the only thing that makes sense. Every head in the kitchen snaps in my direction, including Scarlett's.

"Slow down. What do you mean?" Cruz has his hand on my shoulder.

"On the phone, Savannah said to check on Gray at her apartment. Gray is here, so she must be referring to her apartment in The Bronx."

Cruz pulls out his phone and shares that potentially helpful information with his team. "Did she say anything else?"

"Nothing that will help you."

Understanding crosses Cruz's face. Either he has a woman in his life or had one and it didn't work out. He clearly understands what it means to be head over heels for someone.

I update Steve Sterling, sign some more paperwork, and he returns to his office. Generally, the way these policies work, I'll have to pay with my own funds and then be reimbursed by the insurance company. I don't care if I ever get the money back. I need Savannah. It hurts to breathe without her beside me. I don't deserve her unwavering faith or her unflinching love and acceptance of Emerson.

I walk back to my office, leaving everyone in the main area. There is a soft knock on my office door.

"I'm sorry, Sam. I should've known this was somehow our fault not yours."

"I appreciate your apology, Scarlett, but it isn't necessary. I'm at fault some as well. If I were poor, these guys wouldn't have taken Savannah to settle your dad's debt."

"While that may be true, I shouldn't have shouted at you or shoved you. Thank you for loving her. It isn't something I have ever experienced before seeing you two together."

"You're welcome."

She leaves as quietly as she appeared. I have only seen the type of love she's describing between a few couples, including my brother and Noelle. I'm grateful to have found Savannah. I stare out the window at the cityscape. I'm ready to leave it all behind for a serene, safer life away from here.

Christoph appears at the threshold of my office next.

"I'm going to send Finn and Maia to toward The Bronx so they're closer when we locate Savannah. as long as you're okay with Scarlett here with only me."

"That's fine. Considering the circumstances, I'm sure you can convince Scarlett to stay put without my assistance."

A small smile curls at the edges of his mouth. "Thank you."

Dragging my hand down my face, I leave the office as my phone rings. Glancing at the screen, I note it isn't Jacob and quiet everyone.

"Hello."

The same disguised voice comes through the phone. "Meet me at Gapstow Bridge at six sharp. I'll provide wiring instructions. Once the wire is confirmed, I'll release your girlfriend. No cops."

"Let me talk to her." I hear some shuffling and muffled words.

"Sam. I'm fin—"

"She's fine. See you at six."

Well, that didn't help as much as I would have liked. He keeps saying release your girlfriend, nothing about Mr. Clemons.

"Cruz, a word?"

He follows me back into my office.

"The caller keeps saying he'll release Savannah but nothing about her father. Is that unusual?"

"Each case is different. He could only be saying that because your main concern is Savannah not her father. What is the plan?"

"I'm going to Gapstow Bridge before six. I'll have Cash ready to send the wire once I receive the instructions."

"You aren't going alone. I'll be there as well."

"He said no cops."

"I would suggest Christoph then. I'll be nearby. I can leave one of my fellow officers here with Emerson, Scarlett, and Maria-Luisa."

"Whatever you think is best. I'm barely holding it together right now."

"Sam, given our history, I know this isn't about the money. Does she know how you feel?"

"She does."

Cruz nods and leaves to coordinate with Christoph and the other personnel. Pacing behind my chair, I video call Cash again.

"Hey. You look like hell."

I scowl at him. "Thanks."

"Have you spoken to her?"

"Yes, she says she's fine and gave us a tip where she's located. Cruz is looking into it. I need to meet them at Gapstow at six. Can you support five million via wire transfer?"

"Yes. I'll wait for your call and send the wire as soon as I have all the information."

"Thanks."

The sheer terror of this day is almost too much for me. I can only imagine how Savannah is feeling right now. As I leave my office, a flurry of activity begins.

Cruz snaps his fingers to get my attention. I overhear his side of the conversation with the person on the phone.

"I'll send an unmarked to assist. Do not engage until they arrive. You need local law enforcement before you act. They should be there within the next few minutes." He ends the call and updates me. "Finn and Maia took a drive through The Bronx toward Scarlett's apartment based on the information from Savannah. Finn may have recognized one of the suspects smoking outside an apartment building and called me. I suggest they maintain visual until closer to the time for the exchange. I believe they will leave Savannah and her father and show up at the meet without them."

I nod, processing what Cruz shared with me. I need to calm myself. I have a little less than an hour before I need to leave. Needing space, I stalk to my bedroom and pace in front of the large windows.

"Yeah, Sam." Cash answers my call immediately.

"I need someone to talk to me. Tell me she'll be okay. I can't do this without her."

"I have never been in this exact position, bro. However, the pit in your stomach, the knots of fear, I have felt those when I was away and the photogs accosted Noelle. I felt powerless like you do now. You have surrounded yourself with the best. They will get her back."

"I'm terrified. Despite the short timeframe of our relationship, I know she's it for me. My forever."

"I know. I know exactly when I knew Noelle was it for me. You'll be out of this mess in less than two hours and out of the city in a little more than a week for Christmas. You might consider locking Savannah in your home though."

I laugh softly. "She won't stand for that." My feisty woman will hate it. Either way, she isn't going anywhere alone. I don't care what kind of fuss she puts up. She'll have security unless she's in this house until we leave the city.

"Maybe not, but you should at least try."

"Maybe. Thanks, Cash."

"Of course. I'll be here when you need me to send the money."

"Thanks." I drag in a harsh breath and release it slowly. I repeat this a few times before a soft knock pulls me out of my head.

"Son, is there anything I can do?"

"Dad, thank you for coming. Who called you?"

"No one. I came to visit Emerson, and the throng of people in your home informed me there was an issue. Although it does appear that your brother Cash contacted Caro and Auggie. Have you spoken to—"

"Sam." Cruz steps to the threshold of the master bedroom. "It's for you."

SAVANNAH

Joe is getting more anxious as each minute passes. He came inside from having a cigarette.

"Do you know what time it is?"

My father looks at his watch.

I notice it's the same watch from when I was a child. It looks worn and tattered, but he wears it nonetheless. "It's a quarter past five. Don't do anything crazy, squirt."

Hearing my childhood nickname softens me to him a bit. "I won't. I'm wondering why Joe is getting anxious. I guess it's close to the time for the exchange."

"Maybe. No matter what, please know I'm deeply sorry for all of this. I have been trying for the past few years to tackle my addiction so I could repair my relationship with you and Scarlett."

"I appreciate it. Let's focus on getting out of here first." I can only imagine the anguish Sam is putting himself through thinking this is his fault. It's my fault, completely mine.

My father nods as Joe pushes off the doorframe. Carl and Joe approach us and zip tie our wrists behind our backs and our ankles. This time there was no innuendo from Joe.

"Stay put. We're going to see if your boyfriend follows through."

They're going to leave us here. I'm confident Sam would never agree to that. He would insist on an exchange. They aren't following the rules. Neither will I. Once I'm fairly certain I've wanted long enough. I slip off my heels, flex, and point my foot until I can shimmy out of the ankle restraints.

"Where did you learn that?" my father inquires with shock lacing his voice.

"Nowhere. I got lucky with the first thing I tried." I scramble to my feet and attempt to break out of the wrist restraints. I raise my arms as high as I can and lower them quickly while pushing outward with my wrists. After two attempts, I break free.

While I was working on my wrists, my father has successfully broken the ties on his ankles. In an effort to assist him, I tighten the ties on his wrists as he attempts to break them same way I did.

I pull my phone from my pocket and dial Sam. It takes me a moment to place the voice answering his phone. "Cruz, it's Savannah. I need Sam."

"Are you okay?"

"For the most part."

"Where are you?"

"I don't know yet. We freed ourselves. Cruz, please, I need Sam." The sheer need in my voice is impossible to miss.

I hear shuffling and Cruz shout, "Sam."

"Hello."

"Sam."

"*Cara*, are you hurt?"

The relief I hear is almost as thick as the relief I feel, even though I'm still not in his arms. The sound of his voice decreases my anxiety even though I'm far from out of this mess. "No, I'm fine. We just freed ourselves, but I don't know where I am yet."

"Hold on."

I hear Sam talking to Cruz. "Can you track her phone or trace this call somehow?" Then his voice comes back on the line. "Baby, I need to go to the meet. I don't want to tip them off. Please do whatever Cruz's team tells you."

"I will. Sam, be caref—"

"I love you, *cara mia.*"

"I love you, Samson."

With the phone still to my ear, I walk around the empty apartment, carefully checking out the windows to figure out our location. My father does the same.

A minute later, I hear, "Savannah, this is Detective Rich Berry."

"Hi."

"Lt. Cruz has requested a trace on this call, but any information you can figure out would be helpful."

"I checked a few windows. They're small, basement size. We're in a lower-level apartment. I don't recall any street names."

"It's no problem. Keep talking with me. Are you injured?"

"Nothing of consequence, my father will need some medical attention though. His eye is swollen shut. I'm not a doctor, but it looks pretty bad."

"Savannah, is there a bathroom or lockable door on the same level of the apartment where you are?"

"Yes, the bathroom locks."

"Good, go into the bathroom with your father and lock the door. Our team has traced this call. Finn and Maia are nearby. I don't want to tip our hand if someone is still watching the apartment. Pick a word or phrase so you know it's Maia and Finn."

"So Elegant."

"Okay, go and lock the door."

I nod, even though Detective Berry can't see me. If he thought my choice was odd, he didn't say as much. "Dad, let's go. They were able to trace the call." I lead my father into the bathroom and lock us in.

"Squirt, I'll make this right. I may not be able to pay your boyfriend back, but I would like to be in your life."

"You need to go back to rehab and stay sober this time. I need you to be sober. Scarlett needs you to be sober. Most importantly, you need to be sober for you." After what feels like an eternity and a series of loud bangs and a loud thud, I hear my name.

"Savannah, it's Maia."

"What is the word I gave to Detective Berry?" I ask even though I'm certain it's Maia.

"So Elegant," Maia replies.

I exhale sharply and slowly open the door of the bathroom. Finn and Maia are outside the door.

"Hi, Maia. Finn. I'm really glad to see you. My dad needs some medical attention."

"Mr. Clemons, right this way. Let's get you checked out." Finn leads my father out the door.

"Savannah, our instructions are to take you home to wait for Sam, Cruz, and Christoph to return."

Renewed fear rushes through me. While they didn't hurt me, they beat up my father. I stare at Maia. Unfortunately for me, she doesn't flinch. I'm not going to get my way right now no matter how exceptional my negotiating skills may be. Resigned I'll have to wait longer, I follow Maia out of the apartment toward the waiting car. There's a very small police presence and an ambulance. I can only identify two possibly unmarked vehicles.

"Maia, I need to talk to my father."

I walk over to the ambulance and watch the EMTs check out my father.

"Savannah, I'm so sorry."

I raise my hand to silence him. I can't deal with him right now. I need to get to Sam and Emerson. "After you get checked out and are able to leave the hospital, we should talk."

My father nods, and the EMT closes the rear door of the ambulance.

"Are you good?" Maia asks as we walk away.

"Not even a little. Since you refuse to take me to Sam, can you at least update me?"

"I'm sorry, Savannah."

"Don't be. You're doing your job. I didn't think for one moment I would get my way. Nor would I expect you to heed my request. It's to ground myself more. I won't be even on the path to good until I literally hold Emerson and feel Sam's hand in mine."

Maia nods as we reach the car, and Finn slides into the driver's seat.

After settling into the car, Maia updates me on the plan, telling me that Sam was set to meet with Carl and Joe at six. Causally, I glance at the dashboard clock and note it's just after six.

Under an hour later, Finn pulls into the garage at our home. Despite all the people and questions, I brush past them and stalk to Emerson's nursery. The pounding in my chest decreases when Maria-Luisa steps to the side to show me she's okay.

"Savannah, I'm glad you're okay." She throws her arm around me while keeping one hand on Emerson's belly at the changing table.

"Thank you. How is she doing?"

"Better. The medication will take care of it."

"Good. May I?"

"Of course."

I lift Emerson into my arms and hold her close over my heart. I may not have given birth to this angel, but she's mine just the same.

"While this may seem out of line or at least awkward, Samson loves you with all his heart. Take care of him and Emerson for me."

Never once did I think I would find someone as amazing as Sam to share my life. Now I have Sam, Emerson, his amazing siblings, and their significant others.

"I will."

Maria-Luisa leaves us in the nursery. I lower myself into the rocking chair in the corner and tighten my hold on Emerson. Never once was she in danger today, even though Carl and Joe threatened as much. It still tore my heart out that my father could mess with my family.

"Savi." Scarlett appears in the doorway.

"Hi, Scar."

"Do you mind?"

"No, I'm sorry for not stopping. They threatened Emerson. I had to touch her for myself."

"How badly hurt is Dad?"

"How do you know that?"

"I overheard Lt. Cruz and Detective Berry requesting an ambulance. I was so scared; I didn't know if it was you or him."

"His eye is swollen shut. Other than that, I don't know much more. They took him to the hospital. I asked him to reach out when he's released."

"I'm glad you're okay, Savi."

"Me too, Scar. Me too."

Scarlett leaves the nursery. I set my head against the back of the chair and close my eyes.

SAMSON

The mere thought of losing Savannah nearly guts me. Along with Cruz and Christoph, I make my way to Central Park. We arrive right before six.

Cruz stops walking about three hundred yards from the bridge and sets his hand on my forearm.

"Don't offer any extra information. Get the wiring instructions and send the money. I don't know who will show up on Drake's behalf. Mikhail Drake's is the most successful loan shark on the east coast with significant reach which has increased exponentially in the recent past. He has acquired the debts of at least two of his closest competitors. From the intel we received from Jacob, Mr. Clemons owed five different lower-level sharks, and Drake bought all of the debt."

I acknowledge his words. Christoph and I continue closer to the bridge. Cruz and I worked together on a few high-end art thefts about five years ago. We were able to establish that the household staff from each theft worked for the same service company. We also worked tirelessly when Billie was injured to find those responsible. We failed only because the driver wasn't really involved with the paparazzi. Cruz is good people. I'll do whatever he says to get back to Savannah faster.

"Mr. Morgan. I'm surprised you're here personally." Cruz identified this guy as Carl Maxwell in the photos before we left. He's the right hand of Mikhail Drake, a guy I don't want to cross. Two other henchmen stand beside him.

"What are the wiring instructions?" I need to get the money sent. "Where are Savannah and Mr. Clemons?"

"All information in due time, Mr. Morgan." Carl reaches out with a small sheet of paper.

Immediately, I dial Cash and relay the numbers. Once he confirms, I hang up. "The wire has been sent. Where is Savannah?" All I know for certain is she's physically unharmed and Maia and Finn are looking for her.

"Once I confirm, I'll give you the address."

Christoph leans down and whispers, "Savannah and her father are safe."

I nod and return my attention to Carl and his cohort. "Where is Savannah?" I'm going to pay the debt knowing she's safe in the hopes that Drake will leave Mr. Clemons alone.

As the words leave my mouth, Carl's phone rings. He answers, saying, "I understand, sir." He turns his attention to me again. "You can find your girlfriend in the ground apartment at 184 E 138th in The Bronx.

"How do I know you aren't lying?"

"You don't, but I have no use for her anyway. Her father was the problem. I'm only the middleman. She was the only way to get to your money. You should know, your girlfriend gave up herself for your daughter."

I pause to process his last statement.

"Sam, let's go." Christoph shoves me away from Carl and his buddies. It takes all my resolve not to break off into a sprint across the park. Walking as fast as possible, we rejoin Cruz and continue briskly to his car.

Once inside the car, I exhale harshly. She gave up herself for Emerson. I never questioned Savannah's commitment, only mine. Truly and madly she loves both of us, and I couldn't possibly be more thankful. So lost in my thoughts, Christoph has to tap me on the shoulder to get out of the car.

"She's in the nursery with Emerson." Christoph informs me. He must have spoken to Maia.

I fidget the entire ride upstairs. I burst through the elevator doors and all but sprint to my world. When I step inside the nursery, Savannah is rocking in the chair with Emerson in her arms. The heaviness in my chest immediately dissipates. Despite the anguish of the day, they are both safe. I fall to my knees at her feet and slide my hands to her hips. All the remaining emotions spill from my eyes, soaking her pants.

When I look up again, tears have fallen down Savannah's cheeks and my angel is blissfully sleeping. Rising to my feet, I scoop up Emerson and place her in her crib.

I draw Savannah into me, lifting her eyes to mine. "I have no words for your insane bravery and selflessness. Putting Emerson first is more than I could have ever hoped for her and for me."

"I love you both completely. There is no limit to what I will do for the both of you." Lowering my lips to her, I claim Savannah as mine for the rest of my life. As soon as possible, I'm going to marry this phenomenal woman and build a life with her.

SAVANNAH

After promising one another a long discussion about the events of the day, we tiptoe out of the nursery and deal with our houseful of people. At some point after I returned, Scarlett ordered enough pizza and wings to feed everyone.

Christoph, Maia, and Finn leave soon after eating but request that the four of us stay put for at least twelve hours for them to get some sleep. Cruz, Sam, and I, along with Jacob on speakerphone, hash out a few details before Cruz leaves for the evening. I agree to have someone with me everywhere I go until we move.

Within three days, Sam has finished packing the office, his penthouse, and obtaining the certificate of occupancy for our new home. During those same days, my father checked himself into rehab again. For his sake, I hope the third time is the charm. We flew to our new hometown from the city first thing this morning with both of our cars on the plane as cargo I'm following Sam who is driving the Rover from the airport to our home. The movers arrive soon after us. A few hours later, they set the last box in the garage.

"Let's order some takeout, and then we can set up Emme's room," I suggest as Sam enters the kitchen.

"No need. Dinner is on its way, along with a small army of helpers."

About fifteen minutes later, a steady stream of family and friends cross the threshold of our new home.

"This is gorgeous. You have a yard and a view," Billie raves, gazing out the French doors on the back of the house.

"Thanks."

Kelly and Ellis brought in the food, followed by William carrying boxes of deliciousness from the Perk.

About three hours later, we've finished eating and assembled Emerson's furniture and a temporary bed for Sam and me. While Sam can work miracles for most things, speeding up the furniture delivery wasn't possible. I don't care.

After refusing help for the boxes labeled holiday decorations, we pack Scarlett's belongings in the Rover and drive to her new place. She is going to live in the same complex as Billie's condo near Short Sands Beach while she attends college. Her plan is to find a job at the beginning of the year. I'm really proud of her for opting to leave the city. Once she's settled into the condo, we agree to meet tomorrow to take her car shopping.

After a short and chilly walk across the beach, we climb the hill toward our home. Once we're sure that everyone has left, Sam and I set to wrapping the copious number of gifts for Christmas in a few days. Due to our recent ordeal and expeditious move to Maine, the Morgan family Christmas will be at Billie's this year instead of Tahoe.

Today is my first Morgan family Christmas. I'm so excited. My early childhood holidays weren't packed with gifts, but they were filled with joy. The delicious smells already swirling around Billie's home are tantalizing. Even though we've been here before, the water view is spectacular. I hope Auggie slept a little last night. He arrived late from New York with Caro. It's before eleven when we arrive. Caro is smiling at Auggie while they work in the kitchen. Their feelings swirl all around them, but they refuse to see it. Eventually someone will break and the truth will be told. Honestly, I think they're perfect for one another.

"You're here!" Billie hurries to greet us and scoops Emme away from Sam.

"Hi to you too, Billie." Sam feigns dejection.

"Sorry, big brother, but my niece is far prettier and more fun than you. Aren't you, Emme?" She can't answer, but Billie is having fun anyway.

"So what did you open already, Savannah?" Auggie asks from the kitchen.

"Our stockings and a few larger items for Emerson." Those present exchange a look that can only be interpreted as mischievous.

"What have you done, Samson?"

"I have no idea what you're talking about, *cara?*"

"What do they know that I don't?" My raised eyebrow is an indication that I'm not buying his answer.

"You'll see in due time. I warned you, and you promised to be accepting. You can't take it back now."

I have no clue what else he could possibly get as a gift. Not only did he buy a house, but furnished it, purchased another SUV for me, and moved Morgan Insurance to another state. Knowing that no matter what I say or do, the outcome won't change, I join Auggie and Caro in the kitchen.

Over the next few hours, I assist Auggie. Mostly we watch him work his magic with the food and wash the dishes around him. Billie is swooning over Emerson while Peter is building a warm fire. Cash and Noelle arrive with some treats from the Perk.

"Isn't Kelsey joining us later?" Of all the people other than Sam's family that I've met here in Maine, Kelsey is my favorite, and it has nothing to do with her delicious treats.

"She is, but she asked us to bring some of the goodies first thing," Cash replies, setting the boxes on the sideboard in the dining room. Once he frees himself from the boxes, Noelle and Cash make the rounds hugging and greeting everyone. Noelle promptly steals Emme.

"Peter, where are your sisters celebrating this year?" I ask as we get closer to dinner.

"My dad, Gen, and Joseph went to Colorado with Kelly and Ellis. Maggie is in New York with Grant's family. Norah decided to celebrate with Jacob's family this year. We had a sibling dinner last weekend to celebrate together."

"I think the Ramirezes and Scarlett are the only remaining people to arrive. I don't expect William and Kelsey until after dinner. They're opening gifts with his family first."

"Thanks."

Soon thereafter, Auggie starts requesting actual help from Caro and me. Scarlett breezes in right before we sit down to eat.

"Hi, everyone."

After a resounding welcome and numerous trips to the dining room, we take our seats and enjoy a scrumptious holiday meal. Auggie is truly a magician with food. The turkey is perfect, the ham dripping with glaze, the rolls are warm and flaky. The side dish, which looks like sweet potatoes, is to die for. I can only imagine what desserts he'll pull from the oven.

After our delicious meal, the guys, except Auggie, handle the dishes while I assist Billie and Noelle setting up the gift exchange. Caro is feeding Emme over near the fireplace. I'm in shock over the sheer number of packages surrounding Billie and Peter's gorgeous tree. It's possible that they equal the number Scarlett and I got over our entire lifetimes.

The family members each have one gift, and everyone opens at the same time. We would be here until next week if we took turns. Sam and I bought Scarlett items for school, a gift card for the campus bookstore for her textbooks, as well as some clothes for the new semester. My gifts from each family member seem to have a theme. Billie and Peter gave me a winter coat with matching hat and gloves. Noelle and Cash gave me boots. I have winter clothes. Maybe they don't think I have enough to live in Maine instead of New York. There are two more gifts for me, but only one for everyone else.

Opening the box from Sam, I see the distinct logo of LaPerla. "Sam, I am not opening this with all these people around."

"Why not?" His tone is serious.

I open my mouth to respond and everyone starts laughing.

"Is this some first-holiday hazing?"

"Maybe a little." Billie smirks, taking the box from me and setting it atop the pile of everything else.

The next gift is big. I have no clue what it is. Everyone is waiting with bated breath for me to open it. When I open it, I find a new set of luggage. Confused doesn't begin to cover how I feel right now.

"Sam?"

"Open it, *cara.*"

Unzipping the luggage, I find a book about impressionist artists with a bookmark. Tears start to fall down my cheeks as I realize what this means.

"Sam. This is…." As I start to speak, I realize that his entire family is looking on.

"It's not. I'm taking you to see *L'Etoile* in person, along with most of the other works on your list tomorrow."

Scarlett shifts closer to me and whispers, "You deserve this trip and so much more, Savi."

Clearly she was in on this little secret with Sam and his siblings. I reach my hand out to Sam and lead him to the back porch.

"*Cara,* why are you upset?"

"I'm not upset. I'm shocked. I shouldn't be, and you told me to prepare myself, but… nothing that I thought up would come close to this gift. Being in the same room as any of those works of art was *never* something I thought would ever happen for me. Thank you for making one of my childhood dreams come true."

"I'll do anything for you. I love you, *cara mia.*"

"I love you."

Following Sam, we rejoin the family and talk about our upcoming trip to Paris in less than a day. Shortly after, William, Kelsey, and their son join us. Cash and Scarlett are bickering about the football game again. She's holding her own, and I think Cash is surprised.

Auggie, Kelsey, and I set the table with plates and silverware for dessert. Hours later, after lively conversations, we head home to pack for our trip.

SAMSON

Savannah's reaction to my gift was not what I expected. I tried to prepare her, but I truly stunned her, not only with my gift but the thought behind it. Billie and Peter agreed to stay at our new home and care for Emme while I take Savannah to Paris. So far our flight has been calm. Savannah is sound asleep next to me. Hours later and little sleep for me, we land and ride to our hotel.

I chose a hotel close to the Eiffel Tower and the Musée d'Orsay because that's where most of the paintings she wants to see are housed. Savannah hasn't said much since we entered the opulent lobby.

"Good afternoon, Mr. Morgan. Miss Clemons. Your suite is ready. Jean will take your luggage for you," the desk clerk states, handing me our room keys.

Like at my penthouse, Savannah's gaze is out the window as soon as we enter our suite. It makes me wonder if she'll miss the city.

"What shall we do first?" I slide my hands over the curve of her hips, setting my chin on her shoulder.

"I wouldn't even know where to start. You have been here before, what do you suggest?"

"I don't want to rush you at any of the larger museums. Let's start with some of the exhibits in the smaller ones."

"Sounds good."

"Savannah, please tell me."

"I'm still in shock that I'm standing here right now. I'm also trying to take it all in."

"Let's go explore and see other things. This view will be more spectacular tonight."

After grabbing our coats, we pass through the lobby and stroll down the street toward the Arc De Triomphe. We take the obligatory photos and continue to the Luxembourg Gardens. Despite the cold temperatures, the garden is still beautiful, and the Medici Fountain is a marvel. The longer we're here, the livelier Savannah becomes. I'm confident she isn't angry with me. She simply never fathomed fulfilling this dream. She may not realize it yet, but I want to know the rest so I can make those come true too. We wind down our first day with the Atelier des Lumiéres display before a delicious dinner overlooking the Seine.

After a full night's sleep and a hearty breakfast, we set our agenda for today. As much as I want to rush to the Musée d'Orsay so she can see the paintings of her childhood dreams, I want her to experience as much of Paris as possible. As we arrive at today's first stop, sheer joy and surprise cross my beautiful girlfriend's face. Today we're learning to make macarons. Thankfully, our instructor was available to assist me. What enthralls Savannah literally confused me to no end. Luckily, my woman is willing to share her decadent creations with me. Next we stroll through the market and along the streets, stopping along the way to eat crêpes. We wrap up our day at the Eiffel Tower with a ride to the summit to see the City of Lights in all its shimmering glory.

Staring out at the gorgeous city, I draw Savannah into me, her body molds against mine. Her signature scent surrounds me.

"What are you thinking, *cara mia?*" My voice so low only she can hear me.

"This is beyond words. Thank you."

"You're welcome. Tomorrow will beat today, I promise."

"We're going tomorrow." Sheer giddiness materializes in her eyes. I've never met anyone like her, so unassuming and grateful for even the smallest gesture of love and kindness. Little does she know that she gave me the most significant one ever possible by accepting my daughter.

"Yes. We have the entire day for you to explore the museum. We can spend as many of the remaining days of our trip there if you wish."

"We should hurry to sleep then." A small, sly smile graces her face. Sleep is the last thing on her mind right now.

"As you wish." I press my lips to her temple before offering her my arm.

Looping her arm in mine, we hurry back to our room and dance to the huge bed overlooking the city.

When I wake the next morning, Savannah's side of the bed is already cool. Turning over, I find her sitting with coffee in hand by the French doors in our room. Her feet are tucked under her, her wet hair falling down her back in my favorite silky robe.

"I can feel you staring at me, Samson."

Rising to my feet, I move behind her without of word. "You're beautiful, of course I'm staring." I plan to do it for the rest of my life. Even her reflection shows her cheeks pinking up from my compliment. "Do you want to order breakfast or eat downstairs?"

She turns to face me. Without question, her cheeks are redder than usual. "Let's eat downstairs. If we eat here, we'll never get to the museum."

Can't say she's wrong. Before showering, I steal a sip of her coffee. Unfortunately, when I finish in the bathroom, Savannah is dressed and ready to go. Either she's hungry or excited.

"A tad excited, *cara?*"

"No, I'm over the moon excited." She steps into my open arms and kisses me fervently.

"I'll be ready as fast as I can."

Instead of walking, we take a cab to the museum. Savannah is literally the second patron through the front door, her fingers intertwined with mine.

"Where do you want to start?" I wonder if she will go straight for her mother's favorite or save it for last.

"I want to save *L'Etoile* for last."

"Lead the way." I didn't get into insuring priceless pieces of art for any reason other than I preferred it over ordinary insurance. It's simply more interesting. Savannah has a deep-rooted love for impressionist artwork started by her mother but fostered by her professor. Watching her face light up as she wanders through these galleries is extraordinary.

As she approaches the Degas, her steps slow. The sheer awe in her eyes is more than I've ever seen before. Her hand reaches for mine as she stands before the priceless masterpiece. Sliding my fingers between hers, I stand beside her, marveling at her more than the painting.

"Sam, it's breathtaking."

"It is."

We stand before the painting she's dreamed about seeing from an early age. I'm confident she could recreate from memory. "What are you thinking right now, sweetheart?"

"I feel oddly calm and I wish my mom was here."

I inhale sharply and turn her gaze to me. "Savannah, most people think my life has been as smooth as a freshly paved road. They would be wrong. While my family's wealth made some things much easier, others were harder. I have been taken with you since the moment you stepped into my office. Since then I have learned so much more, and that impression pales to what I see now. You willingly accept me and every single fault I possess. You stand beside me every single day and help me raise Emerson—an honor I'm not sure I deserve." I lower down onto my knee and pull a ring out of my pocket.

Her hands cover her mouth, and a single tear slides down her cheek. A small crowd has stopped to watch us. There are hushed whispers and bated breaths. I couldn't control this part of my plan.

"Savannah, will you spend the rest of your life with me?"

She exhales sharply before whispering, "I have one condition."

I raise an eyebrow. "What might that be?" She could ask for the North Star and I would find a way to get it for her.

"I want to adopt Emerson."

I'm dumbstruck. As if she knew the one thing I want more than her—to officially be a family.

"Aside from you saying yes, nothing would make me happier. Savannah, will you marry me and officially adopt Emerson?"

"Yes."

Rising, I slide a pear-shaped diamond with a split eternity band onto her finger and kiss my fiancée breathless. The onlookers ooh and aww, clap, and wish us well before continuing their tour of the museum.

"Can we stand here a little longer?"

"Of course, Future Mrs. Morgan." I lift her hand to my lips and kiss it before tucking her against me.

We take a cold but leisurely stroll back to our hotel and spend the evening and the next day in bed celebrating.

EPILOGUE

SAVANNAH

It has been three months since Sam proposed. Within days of our return, Sam started the adoption process for Emerson. Soon I'll be able to say my daughter and not have to explain the entire story of Emerson's life—a story that Sam doesn't like to relive each time we're out as a family. I'm rushing through my work to get to the shop to pick up my dress for Billie's wedding.

Tomorrow she's marrying Peter at the ViewPoint Hotel. Tonight, we're meeting everyone for the rehearsal dinner.

"Are you finished yet?" Sam sticks his head into our office with a babbling beauty with dark hair and hazel eyes on his hip.

"You're back already?"

"Noelle had Emme ready when I arrived. I think she wanted some extra girl time at the shop before the rehearsal. Whatever work you have left can wait until Monday. You should get going."

"Are you going to be like this when it's our turn to get married?"

"I'm sure it'll be worse."

I smirk, close my laptop, kiss Sam thoroughly, and rush out the door. Parking in the lot behind the shop, I round the building. I can hear the roar of my friends before I even get in the door.

"Yes! Finally, my future sister-in-law is here!" Billie is off the charts excited. I can't blame her.

I'm sure my levels would be just as high if I were marrying Sam tomorrow. The entire girl gang is here, plus a few women I don't know. Right away Scarlett squeezes me tight.

"Hi, sis." The move here has been great for her. School is going well, and she started working for Kelsey right after the new year. I'm enormously proud of her. I hug everyone, including Maggie, Norah, and Caro. I'm glad she was able to accompany Auggie. A glass of champagne slides into my hand, and I take a seat next to Kelsey.

"Quick introductions. Del, this is Sam's fiancée, Savannah. Savannah, my bestie and half sister, Della. This is her mom, Camille. I think you know everyone else."

"Pleasure to meet you both." As I lift my glass to my lips, Kelly motions me into the office.

"Hey. Good to see you. Do you want to try this on again?"

"No, I'm sure it's perfect." I take the garment bag with me back to the consultation area. This time I take a seat next to Caro. She's beautiful with long, dark hair and a gorgeous hourglass figure.

"Hey there! I'm surprised you aren't with Auggie working on last-minute food details."

"Hey. I was there, but he sent me here so he could finish on his own. Sometimes I don't understand that man. He may be my best friend, but he's a big pain in my ass."

"Most men are."

"Ha, says the girl with the perfect fiancé."

"No way, honey. Sam isn't perfect; no one is. His imperfections simply work well with mine." I watch Caro process my words. Maybe these two will come clean about their feelings soon.

"Time's up, ladies," Peter announces, followed by a host of obscenely handsome men. He slides his arms around Billie and kisses her softly.

After everything she has been through, I'm truly happy for them. Each man pairs off with one of the ladies here, except for Scarlett and Caro. Until now I've never seen Della's husband, Brant. He fits right in with the others from looks to his devotion to his wife.

We ride to the rehearsal and dutifully follow the planner's instructions about where to stand and how fast or slow to walk. Soon thereafter, Auggie executes a perfect dinner service. Billie and Peter opted for comfort foods for their rehearsal. Auggie's spin on macaroni and cheese is simply perfect, and the pulled pork sandwiches are delicious even if a touch messy. I notice him hovering near the kitchen door during most of the rehearsal dinner with a beer in his hand.

Della, Billie's matron of honor, gives a short, sweet speech, including anecdotes about designing their wedding dresses when they were seven.

Tommy, Peter's college roommate and best man, shares a few inappropriate stories about Peter before we end the night.

We're almost the last to leave. Caro is waiting on Auggie to verify that the kitchen is spotless.

"Hey, I can take care of him. You can head home. We'll see you tomorrow." She peers into the kitchen.

"Are you sure?" Sam asks with a slight note of concern in his voice.

"Yes. I'll make sure he gets to Cash's safely. I haven't had anything to drink, and I still have his keys from earlier when I drove him here."

"Let us know if you need assistance. We live nearby."

Caro nods. "Don't worry. We'll be fine."

With that statement, I head home with Sam to prepare for Billie's wedding day.

CAROLINE

The Morgans have been part of my extended family for most of my life. Auggie has been my best friend since boarding school. He's finishing up the rehearsal dinner cleanup for his sister's wedding tomorrow.

"Hey there! Almost ready?" I lean against the kitchen door.

Even tired and at the end of a dinner service, he's affable and better looking than most men.

"Yeah, I need to recheck a few spots, and then I'll be set to drive home." He wavers a bit, his balance off.

Rarely does Auggie drink too much. The meal he prepared was off-the-charts delicious like all the others. I've never eaten a bad meal he's prepared. "No worries. I'll drive when you're ready."

Auggie shakes his head and makes one more sweep around the kitchen. "Let's go. Billie is getting married tomorrow."

"I'm excited for her. Aren't you?"

He hasn't mentioned any issues with Peter. "Of course. Peter is great." His words come out a bit overexaggerated when he describes his future brother-in-law.

"How much have you had to drink?" I'm slightly more concerned now since I've only seen him overindulge twice. The first time was at a winter formal in boarding school when Jenny Fordham stood him up and the second was after Billie's accident.

"Two beers, but that isn't the problem. I didn't eat enough during service."

Now that makes more sense. I loop my arm around his waist and escort him to the car. Leaning him against the rear door, I open the passenger door and help him settle in.

"You smell tempting, Caro. Always have," Auggie mutters softly after I secure the seat belt.

My heart seizes in my throat. He's drunk. He doesn't mean that. Does he? I have wanted to take my friendship with Auggie to the next level for the last few years. The most recent time we discussed it was almost two years ago after the gala for the arts. I don't want to ruin our friendship for anything less than everything. His position is that he isn't ready to focus on anything other than opening his dream restaurant. Tonight his words strike a nerve. *Always have.*

Rounding the car, I inhale deeply to calm my heart rate. The ride to Cash's is silent in words but not actions. Auggie takes my hand in his and draws circles with his thumb across the top of my hand. That feels.... *Stop, he's your best friend. He's had too much to drink.*

After shushing Auggie, I help him upstairs to his guest suite. Unfortunately, he can't put himself to bed. I step into his room and guide him to sit on the edge of the bed. He immediately grips my hips. His hands are... perfection. Shaking my thoughts away, I focus on at least removing his shoes and shirt. Crouching before him, I untie his shoes. As I rise, he takes my hands in his.

"Thank you, Caro. I know better than to not eat before dinner service and especially before drinking even one beer, let alone two."

"You're welcome." I pull my hands out of his and unbutton his shirt. He always wears an undershirt when he's cooking. Apparently, tonight is the exception to this rule. As I move down the column, inches of Auggie's hard, toned chest and abs are on display before me. I haven't seen Auggie shirtless in at least five years. *Wow!* My scrawny, lanky best friend has been replaced with a fit man with ridges and that V-cut at his hips. "Scoot up and I'll cover you." My voice is raspy and needy if I'm being honest with myself.

Auggie slides to the top of the bed and slides beneath the covers. As I adjust them, he pulls me into his arms. He brushes his lips across mine before kissing me. In all the years we've been friends, nothing romantic or sexual has ever happened between us. The soft press of his lips on mine is heavenly. His kiss coupled with how my hand felt in his on the ride over here, I'm in trouble.

"Stay with me until I fall asleep like we used to," he mutters.

He knows I can't resist that. I step out of my heels, tuck them under the nearby chair, and join him on the bed.

"Thank you, Caro."

"You're welcome." I turn to face him so I'll know when he falls asleep.

He pulls me closer, burying his head into the crook of my neck. I attempt to ignore the rush of feelings he's causing. Being here in his arms is beyond everything my imagination conjured up. The heat emanating off him warms me. My brain is warring with my heart right now. The temptation before me is too much. It takes significant inner discipline not to set my hands on his bare torso.

I stare out the window to stay awake, forcing myself to push away thoughts that don't reflect our relationship. We're just friends. I'm not sure how much time passes, but I notice he's sleeping. Slowly and with precise, careful movements, I slither out from his hold and tiptoe to my shoes.

"Good night, *cuore mio*. I love you. Always have. Always will," Auggie murmurs as I near the door.

He feels the same way I do?

What do we do now?

Thank you so much for reading *Until I Kissed You*!

I hope you love Sam and Savannah. Find out what happens with his brother August and childhood bestie, Caroline. Will all the Morgan brothers find forever?

Pre-Order *Always Have, Always Will* now so you don't miss it!

A new series featuring Blackthorne Security will be released soon. Pre-order *Protecting My Forever*. Is Connor the next to fall?

You don't have to wait for Auggie and Caroline's story. Start the York Beach Series with Genevieve and Joseph's love story *A New Beginning with You*

Did you love *Until I Kissed You?*

Thank you for taking the time to read it. I hope you loved it!
If you liked this book or another one of my books, please consider
posting a review. A short line or two will be perfect!
I appreciate your support.

COMING SOON

Three stories are coming soon!

THE MORGAN BROTHERS
Always Have, Always Will

BLACKTHORNE SECURITY
Protecting My Forever

YORK BEACH NOVELS
THE CAPPELLIS
Chasing Forever

MY BOOKS

YORK BEACH SERIES:

A New Beginning with You

Taking A Chance on Me

Just One More

Kiss You Like You're Mine

Only with Him

My Once in a Lifetime

THE MORGAN BROTHERS

One Unforgettable Favor

Until I Kissed You